MURDER IN THE WINE COUNTRY

MURDER IN THE WINE COUNTRY

A HEALDSBURG HOMICIDE

VALERIE HANSEN

KONSTELLATION
PRESS

Editor: Lisa Wolff

Cover design, map and author photo: Kim Keeline

ISBN: 978-0-9991989-9-5

For Larry, forever

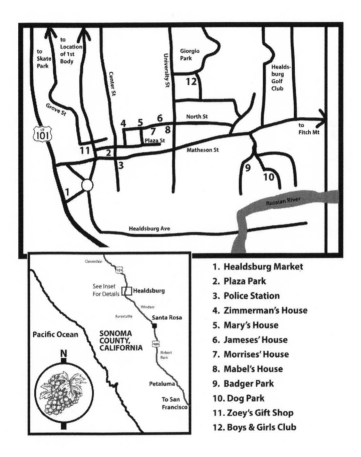

1. **Healdsburg Market**
2. **Plaza Park**
3. **Police Station**
4. **Zimmerman's House**
5. **Mary's House**
6. **Jameses' House**
7. **Morrises' House**
8. **Mabel's House**
9. **Badger Park**
10. **Dog Park**
11. **Zoey's Gift Shop**
12. **Boys & Girls Club**

PROLOGUE

1969

Colleen slowly pulled the razor blade along the inside of her thigh, watching the little red beads form. It had been several months since she'd last cut, and although her therapist asked her to call before she acted out, today was an emergency. She couldn't resist.

She'd confess at her next appointment—for now, she had to do this. Colleen's breathing slowed and she could feel her muscles relaxing. She made two more cuts in the same area, releasing her pent up feelings.

It was that new kid. She'd heard an audible trill of excitement in first period when the English teacher introduced him. His Australian accent alone was enough to make every stupid girl in class bonkers without adding the blond hair, blue eyes and flawless, tanned skin. She was probably the only girl in the whole school that didn't have an instantaneous crush. She tried to keep her head down and hoped he wouldn't notice her face.

But when the bell rang and everyone scrambled to collect their backpacks and slog to the next period, she overheard him ask the circling girls, "Who's the Bride of Frankenstein?" Feeling her face turn red with anger and mortification, she rushed to Spanish so she wouldn't have to hear their answers. Colleen sat in class fuming, not participating in the oral drills. The teacher broke into her thoughts, asking if she was okay, drawing more unwanted attention. It was all she could do to stay in her seat through her last class of the day.

Colleen grew sleepy, looking down at the three parallel, red lines and the rivulet of blood running down onto the towel protecting her bedspread. She carefully blotted her thigh with the edge of the towel and applied a large bandage. Languidly, she rose from the bed and grabbed a package of cinnamon rolls out of her backpack. She tore the package open and pulled out one of the treats. She took a bite, feeling the sweet icing and cinnamon filling melt in her mouth.

Holding the rest of the package in one hand, she plopped back on the bed, picked up her ragged copy of *The Moon Spinners*.

The taunting and laughter from school couldn't follow her into the novel.

1

The woman lay on her back, arms above her head, partially concealed by a large shrub and the raised bed of the railroad tracks. Long, black hair fanned out below her shoulders. Her eyes and mouth were open in surprise. Officer Sam Fry pointed out faint drag marks in the thin leaf mold leading from the parking lot to the body. Detective Greg Davidson stood behind him, looking over his shoulder.

A line of bruising circled the victim's neck, marring otherwise flawless olive skin. She wore a close-fitting dress, dark red, reaching mid-thigh, and black heels with ankle straps. Greg could see she'd been beautiful, before death drained the color from her face and the expression from her eyes. The photographer and sketch artist fanned out, starting to work. Greg noted her fingertips looked roughed up, the painted nails broken.

KTVU's mobile broadcasting van had beat him to the scene and was already raising its antenna when Greg pulled into the parking lot at 1013 that morning. The cameraman was setting up his equipment and a short woman with long, blond hair stood checking her makeup in a small mirror. The chief of police, Liam Friedman, would have to deal with her and all the other reporters' questions later.

The old winery, recessed behind the businesses fronting Healdsburg Avenue, had been deteriorating and buried, like Sleeping Beauty's castle, in a rat's nest of vegetation for decades. Reinforced and cleaned, the brick walls with their arched windows and new roof cupola stood proud once again, housing an architectural firm and interior decorating business.

Half the small Healdsburg police force was already in the parking lot. Two officers, trained as evidence technicians, pulled on light blue coveralls and booties. Sergeant Blake Maddox sat in a patrol car, just outside the crime scene tape, showing two boys, crammed together in the passenger seat, how to turn the emergency lights and siren on and off.

Red and blue lights were flashing on the other emergency vehicles. Liam leaned on the hood of his car, speaking into his cell phone. This being Saturday, he was dressed casually in jeans, his bald head covered with a baseball cap.

Greg slowly heaved his lanky body out of his vehicle and walked over to join Liam.

"The two boys with Blake found the gal." Liam nodded toward Blake's car.

Greg winced inwardly, slipping a pair of booties over his shoes, concerned for the preteen kids who were unlucky enough to stumble on the victim.

"They're pretty shaken," Liam said. "Blake's trying to distract them until their parents arrive. Fry and Garcia are in the building, interviewing the few people working today. The coroner and DA are on their way from Santa Rosa."

As more patrol officers arrived, Liam directed them around to Grove and Grant Streets to seal off any access points from the bike path. One officer kept an eye on the TV and newspaper reporters while a second escorted a slow trickle of employees out of the building to their cars.

"Mom! We're over here!" One of the boys sitting with Blake burst out of the vehicle and scampered toward a woman who stood at the edge of the barrier looking around frantically. She hugged him tightly for a few moments. When the boy pulled away, Greg saw the glint of tears on his freckled face. Greg watched Blake make his way over more slowly and speak to the mother before she wrapped an arm around her son and led him toward her car. Even in his early thirties and wearing his uniform, Blake looked like the kid's older brother, with his round face and tousled hair. The other boy's father arrived soon after.

As soon as he was free, Blake joined Greg and Liam. He pointed toward a slope about fifty feet behind the building. "The kids were playing around the creek when they came across the body. They say they didn't see anyone else nearby."

Foss Creek ran in a gully, alongside the tracks.

"They called 9-1-1 on one of their cell phones at 0905," Blake continued. "The dispatcher advised them to walk to the tire store and wait for us there. She remained on the phone with them until Fry and Garcia showed up. The EMTs arrived right afterward. They pronounced her at 0926. No one else has been down yet."

The coroner drove into the parking lot just as Officers Sam Fry and Ángela Garcia came out of the building.

"There were a few people working in the architectural firm today," Ángela reported. "They were here last night until 2100 and came back in about 0800 this morning—but they didn't hear or see anything suspicious, and none of them recognized the victim from the description we gave them."

As soon as the DA arrived, Liam asked Sam to lead her, the coroner, the evidence techs, Greg, and Blake to the body. They walked single-file across an outdoor patio and along the edge of a dirt path running between the office building and the railroad tracks, careful to step only where Sam had stepped.

The forensic photographer and sketch artist moved closer to the body. Everyone else kept their distance. After pointing out the drag tracks, Sam headed back to the parking lot.

Greg took a careful look around. "We're at least a hundred yards from the street." He pulled out his cell phone and checked a moon chart. "Even with a three-quarter moon last night, there probably wasn't much light getting through these trees. If the perpetrators pulled all the way to the back of the parking lot, and kept their lights off, they wouldn't have been seen."

Janet Flores, the DA, nodded.

At a signal from the photographer, the coroner knelt down next to the victim to begin his examination.

Greg saw Sam returning with Liam. Suddenly Liam stumbled, and the color and expression seemed to drain from his face. Greg followed the direction of Liam's gaze and saw the coroner carefully removing an anal thermometer from the victim's body. Glancing back, Greg saw Liam had turned away and was talking to Flores.

Liam had been the chief for five years. Previously he'd been a lieutenant in the Denver PD. Shortly after moving to Sonoma County, he and his wife, Karen, had scooped Greg under their wings and, despite his reticence, made him their local surrogate family.

A scrub jay swooped down to the ground, picked up an acorn, and flew back to a nearby oak tree. The bike path, running parallel to the tracks, was another ten yards away. Two small bikes stood next to it, propped on their kickstands. Fifteen yards from where the victim lay, Foss Creek flowed into a culvert under the tracks. A crude shelter, formed from small branches and dirt-encrusted pieces of cardboard, perched on the bank of the creek, just before the crossing. Greg could hear a faint drone of traffic from the city streets, but none of the cars were visible from their location. He rubbed his arms against the morning chill that persisted down in the shady depression.

Greg took a few steps toward the bike path to get his bearings. In the mid-nineties, after numerous landslides near the Eel River, the railroad discontinued freight service on the line north of Santa Rosa. Since then, vegetation had grown unchecked between and around the tracks, providing thick seclusion from the businesses and homes in the area.

The heavyset, grey-haired coroner braced himself on his right hand, struggling to stand up. Greg reached out to help.

"Thanks," the coroner said. "That gets tougher every year."

"Tell me about it," Greg agreed, smiling.

"You may be as old as me, but you're in much better shape," the coroner said, removing his nitrile gloves.

Greg shrugged. He exercised regularly—had to pass a fitness exam every year—but at fifty-nine, he had his share of stiffness and inflammation.

They both stepped out of the way to allow the evidence techs by them. Flores and Liam moved closer to hear the coroner's preliminary report.

"She appears to be in her early twenties. No identification, purse, or cell phone on or near the body. Clothing all seems to be intact. The only visible wound is the bruising on her throat. There are petechial hemorrhages on her conjunctiva."

Greg raised his eyebrows in question.

"Tiny hemorrhages in the white of the eye. They're generally a sign of terminal asphyxia. Trying to breathe against resistance causes the small end vessels of the capillaries to rupture. In other words, she's been strangled—probably with some type of rope." The coroner pointed to her neck. "See those fibers in the bruised tissue there? You may have noticed the broken nails and abrasions on her fingers. They were probably self-inflicted—trying to loosen the rope."

Liam's face had turned a decidedly sick shade of gray. All they needed was for the chief to have a heart attack out here, Greg thought. At least the paramedics were still on site.

"Because of the dirt and leaves on her hair and dress, and the marks in the soil, it looks like she was dragged to this spot. Based on temperature and the state of rigor mortis, I'd guess she's been dead eight to sixteen hours. The autopsy will tell you more."

They started walking up the slope as the paramedics loaded the body into a bag.

Greg caught up with Liam. "You okay?"

Liam looked around. "I'm fine," he said with a sad smile. "I thought for a moment I knew her—but I was wrong."

Greg was surprised to see Liam's face and neck turn red, making his dirty-blond mustache more visible. In their five years of working and socializing together, Greg had never seen him blush before. Liam turned and started walking again. Greg wondered who he thought she was.

A welcome warmth was radiating from the asphalt parking lot. Liam asked Sam and Ángela to coordinate a search for the victim's purse and cell phone and to organize a canvass of all the businesses and homes nearby. Then he went over to speak with the news crew and reporters, informing them the body of an unidentified young woman had been found, possibly the victim of homicide. He gave a brief description and requested that anyone with information please contact the Healdsburg Police Department.

Greg left him to it—public relations was Liam's responsibility. Hopefully, someone would come forward with a missing person report or recognize the victim from her description. He and Blake were heading over to interview the boys who'd discovered the body.

～

Matt Gilbert lived with his parents in one of the newer neighborhoods at the north end of Healdsburg. All the homes sported attractive wood siding, decorative stone veneers, well-manicured landscaping, and late-model family cars in the driveways.

At the front door, Blake introduced the woman who'd picked Matt up earlier in the day as Rhonda Gilbert. Greg felt her hand trembling as she shook his.

"Come in. We're in the living room. This is my husband, Scott."

The room was furnished in soft pastel colors. A large flat screen TV dominated the wall facing the couch.

A thin man, with a worried frown on his face, stood to shake their hands. "Matt's pretty upset about what happened today."

"I'm sure he is. This is our department counseling service." Greg handed him a business card. "The counselors are trained in working with children. I recommend you take advantage of them." Greg turned to look at the boy huddled on the sofa, hair awry and clothes rumpled. The freckles on his face stood out in stark contrast to his pale face. "We just have a few questions for Matt."

Scott sat down, put a protective arm around his son, and said, "These police officers need to ask you some questions. Is that okay?"

Matt nodded, giving Blake a shy smile.

Blake took out his notebook and pen.

"I'm Detective Davidson," Greg said. "You've already met Sergeant Maddox." Greg sat in a chair next to the couch. He considered his questions, not wanting to traumatize the kid any more than he had to. "How old are you, Matt?"

"Eleven."

"Can you tell us what happened today?"

Matt nodded.

"What time did you leave home?"

"Right after breakfast; Kevin came over and asked me to go bike riding."

Greg looked at Matt's mother, Rhonda.

"It was about seven forty-five when Kevin came over," she said.

Greg turned back to Matt. "Tell us everything that happened from the time you left here. Take your time and try not to leave anything out."

"Kevin and I rode to the skateboard park and then down the bike path to that spot near the tracks."

Blake looked up from his notepad. "Why there?"

"A few weeks ago we were riding around and discovered it. We hunt for frogs in the creek and we're building a fort. Sometimes we find stuff in old camps that we can use."

Greg knew he was referring to homeless camps, which accumulated along the overgrown tracks. But he wondered if the stuff the boys collected always came from abandoned camps and worried for their safety.

Rhonda broke in. "I had no idea they were playing back in there. I thought they were just riding on the bike path."

"When did you spot the woman?"

"We looked for frogs first, but there weren't any, so we started exploring. I was leading. First I thought it was some old clothes when I saw the red dress. I stopped when I saw it was a girl lying there. Kevin said I should check for a pulse, but I didn't want to touch her. She didn't look right. Her eyes were open and there were flies on her. I tried to move out of the way to let Kevin check her and I caught my shirt in a blackberry bush." Matt swallowed and his eyes filled with tears.

Greg gave him a few moments before gently asking him to continue with the story.

"Kevin touched her neck and said she was dead. He gave me his cell phone and told me to call 9-1-1 and then he threw up. The lady on the phone told us to walk up to the tire store and tell them we were waiting for a police officer, so we did." Matt started crying and Scott tightened the arm he had around his son.

"Did either of you touch her again or move her in any way?"

Matt shook his head no.

"Did you see any other items on the ground near her?"

"Like what?"

"A purse or cell phone or anything else?"

"No, but we didn't really take time to look around."

"Did you see any other people in the area?" Blake asked.

"There were some kids at the skate park and a few joggers on the bike path."

"Did you recognize any of those people?"

"No, sir."

"Did you see anyone in the parking lot of the brick building when you walked to the tire store?"

"No. Just a few cars. Did you bring my bike back?"

Greg explained that Matt's bike would have to be examined first, but eventually would be returned to him.

"We're also going to need your fingerprints and the clothes you were wearing, if that's okay."

Matt nodded.

After taking a description of the joggers on the bike path, bagging Matt's clothes, and taking his prints, Greg and Blake prepared to leave.

"Thank you, Matt. If you remember seeing anything else, please have your parents give us a call." Greg handed his business card to Rhonda. "And we'll be in touch if we need any more information."

"Do you think Matt might have to testify—if there's a trial?" Rhonda asked at the front door.

"Usually attorneys depose minors in the office, on video, rather than having the kids testify in the courtroom. But it might not even come to that since he probably didn't see the perpetrator." Greg pushed down the image of the police officer questioning him after his sister's accident when he was eight, and the irrational panic that always surfaced with the memory. "The DA's office will let you know if they need to talk to Matt, but it's unlikely."

"Thank God for that," Rhonda said, opening the door.

Greg looked back toward the living room. "Goodbye, Matt."

"'Bye." Matt looked a little happier. He'd perked up while Blake collected the prints. Still, Greg worried that the image of the dead woman's body would haunt Matt for the rest of his life. Shaking off the image of his own sister's torn and bloody face that popped, unwanted, into his mind, he unlocked his car with the remote.

Kevin's house was just a few streets away in the same neighborhood. His story matched Matt's exactly. After taking his fingerprints, clothes, and a DNA swab to compare to the vomit at the scene, Greg and Blake left. Discussing it on the drive back to the station, they were both convinced that the boys had told them everything they knew, which wasn't much.

Greg and Blake returned to the station mid-afternoon. There was still no identity on their Jane Doe. Ángela had put out a regional inquiry to see if any missing person matched the description, but there hadn't been any responses. No purse or cell phone had been uncovered in the ground search. No new information had turned up in the neighborhood canvass.

Tempers were a little short, reflecting everyone's frustration. Without leads, there was nothing to investigate. Liam dismissed everyone who was not previously scheduled to work on Saturday. Greg decided to head home, instructing the dispatcher to call immediately if any new information came in.

Pulling into his townhouse complex in east Santa Rosa a little before four in the afternoon, Greg vaguely registered a foursome playing doubles on the tennis courts and several scantily clad millennials lounging in the pool area. He'd lived in the same complex for fifteen years and had never once used the courts or the pool. For that matter, he barely had a nodding acquaintance with any of his neighbors.

He stopped by his mailbox, pulling out ads and catalogs he didn't want, then froze when he saw an envelope with a return address for Barrow, Alaska. *My God*, he thought. *After all these years*. He threw away the rest of the mail and carried the letter, unopened, to his unit.

Greg hadn't eaten since breakfast, so he made a quick sandwich. After starting a pot of coffee, he turned on his computer and checked to see if his son or daughter were online. He yearned to forge a closer relationship with both of them, but had no idea how to break down their barriers while keeping his own intact. Hana, his ex-wife, was much closer to both of them. And even she hadn't been able to penetrate Greg's walls.

Ray was online. Greg knew from Hana that Ray and his longtime partner had recently broken up. Greg had to hand it to her—she made every effort to keep him in the loop with their kids. After a few unsuccessful moments trying to decide what to say, Greg initiated a video chat. He hated talking online or on the phone. Hana did it so easily.

"Hi, Dad." Ray wore a sweatshirt. His hair, cropped short on the sides and longer on top, stood in spikes. He didn't look particularly distressed, Greg noted with relief.

"Did I interrupt anything?" Greg asked.

"No. I was just finishing up some work." Ray was a senior commercial loan officer at one of the big banks in San Francisco. He stretched and then scratched his head, disrupting his careful hairstyle. "What's up?"

"Just checking in to see how you're doing. Your mom told me you and Lucas broke up."

"I'm fine." Ray looked away from the camera for a moment, as if composing himself. "I was just getting ready to head to the Y for my basketball game."

"Well, I'm really sorry for both of you," Greg said, feeling inadequate to the task of offering any kind of wisdom or comfort. In desperation he asked, "Is Lucas okay?"

"Yes. It was the best thing for both of us."

"Would you like to talk about it?"

"I'm all talked out, Dad. But I appreciate the offer. Listen, I'd better get going—my game starts in half an hour."

"Okay." Greg tried to keep the hurt from his voice and face. "Have fun."

"Thanks. Talk to you later."

"Call me if you change your mind about wanting to talk…" but Ray had already disconnected.

Greg almost wished he hadn't called. He couldn't stand it when people pressured him to open up, and here he was, doing the same thing to his son. Ray was just like him—guarded about his life and feelings. *Wonder where he learned that,* Greg thought.

Christy, Ray's sister, was easier. At least she emailed Greg on a regular basis. Even though it was just the highlights—photos and updates—Facebook stuff—he wasn't hearing it all secondhand from Hana.

Greg looked at the picture on his computer screen—thirteen-year-old Ray and fifteen-year-old Christy standing in front of Yosemite Falls. Taken a few months before Ray came out, and about a year before Hana gave up on Greg, asked for a divorce, and moved to Santa Barbara with the kids.

He'd let them all down—been a lousy husband and father. Not because he didn't love them, but because he didn't believe he deserved their love. Everyone who ever cared about Greg ended up hitting the same wall. Greg didn't believe he could survive if they knew the truth of what he was hiding.

Marriage counseling hadn't helped—Greg couldn't even be honest with the counselor. When Hana asked if she could move to Santa Barbara and have primary custody of the kids, Greg didn't object. They all needed so much more than he could ever give.

He looked at the unopened letter propped against his desk organizer. When he started dating Hana, he'd begged his parents not to tell her anything about his sister Colleen's accident. His parents' shoulders slumped when he made them promise to keep the story a secret, making him feel even worse. But he figured Hana would dump him if she knew what happened. He told her Colleen worked at a mission school in Alaska and left it at that.

He sat there in front of his computer brooding about Colleen. During her senior year, she joined a popular Christian church. That had been a turning point in her life. She went from being an angry, troubled recluse to having dinner with the pastor's family and working weekends at the rescue mission. After high school graduation she announced she was going to work as a teacher's aide near Barrow, Alaska, serving the indigenous Iñupiat people. Their parents tried to talk her into at least getting a college degree first, but she was adamant. She wanted a clean break from suburban Marin County—and a chance to find some self-worth.

By all accounts, she'd made a successful life for herself above the Arctic Circle. Their parents visited several times and reported to Greg that residents of the small village were oblivious to her disfigured face. They said Colleen found the work fulfilling and was highly valued as a teacher's assistant. But she spent her summer vacations in Fairbanks, refusing to come home. And she made it clear she didn't want anything to do with Greg.

Why did she write now, after all these years, after their parents had both passed away? Was she expecting some kind of amends? How did she look after forty years? He'd never seen any pictures. Would the scars on her face have softened with age?

Tearing the letter open, he found a handwritten note:

Dear Greg,

I am retiring from the Mission Service and will be moving back to California. I'd like to see you after I finish my debriefing meetings in San Francisco. My schedule is still a little up in the air, but I think I can get up to Santa Rosa before the end of October. I'll be in touch soon.

Colleen

Greg couldn't refuse to see her. But he dreaded the thought of facing his sister and having to dredge up all the remorse and guilt he'd struggled fifty years to bury.

~

Later that evening, Greg parked his car in front of his girl-friend's 1920s Tudor-style cottage in east Santa Rosa. The setting sun gilded the facade. Large shade trees dwarfed the house, making it look like something out of a fairy tale.

Greg planned to put the gruesome murder, his awkward conversation with Ray, and his concerns about Colleen aside for a few hours. Julia didn't make any demands on his past or his emotions. She wasn't particularly interested in his cases or his troubles. She wanted him for a good time and sex —period.

He got out of the SUV, grabbed the bouquet of flowers he'd bought on the way, and hurried up the flagstone walk.

Julia opened the door with a wide smile, gave him a quick

kiss, accepted the flowers, and led him back toward the kitchen.

"Let me put these in a vase—they're beautiful." While she bent over to find one in a lower cupboard, Greg took the opportunity to admire her appearance. She wore a black dress covered with lace, cut very low in the back, and silver heels. Her long, dark brown hair was pulled up in a casual bun at the nape of her neck and diamonds dangled from her ears.

Walking up behind her, Greg slipped his arms around her waist and pulled her gently back against him. He moved his mouth next to her ear. "You look fantastic. What do you say we skip dinner?"

"No way! I want to show off my new dress and, anyway, I'm starving. Things were crazy in the lab today." Julia was a clinical lab scientist at Sutter Hospital. "One of the CLSs called in sick, so I had to work the blood bank. Between the emergency room and surgery I never had a chance to pee, let alone eat lunch." Holding the vase in one hand and the flowers in the other, she giggled when he kissed her ear. "I need to unwind first—besides, I've been looking forward to dinner at Sonoma Grill all week."

Greg released her, trying not to feel rejected. "Okay, but just so you know, I'll be thinking about pounding you the whole time."

She put the flowers in the vase and filled it with water. Placing it on her kitchen counter and grinning mischievously, she said, "Me too."

It had been a month since their last date. Julia worked long hours, her daughter frequently came to visit, and she'd recently attended a continuing education conference in Las Vegas.

"By the way, you don't look too bad yourself," she added.

They'd met at a party the previous summer. After a few dates that had gone surprisingly well, given Greg's dismal track record with women, she sat him down and said, "I love spending time with you. I'd like us to be exclusive. But I don't plan to get married again and I don't want to live together. My life is perfect, just the way it is. What do you think?"

"I'm in." Greg couldn't have imagined a more ideal relationship. It provided him with exactly what he wanted: companionship, good sex, and, most important, the freedom to live autonomously in between.

Seated in a comfortable booth at the restaurant, he watched her study the menu. A harpist played over the soft murmur of voices. After they ordered, the waiter returned with a bottle of sauvignon blanc.

Julia asked Greg how work was going.

"I'm investigating a murder."

"What happened?"

"Young woman—strangled. No identity yet. "

"I'm glad you didn't have to cancel our date because of it."

"So am I. But the only reason I could be here is that we don't have any leads—it's pretty frustrating."

"I can imagine," Julia said, squeezing his hand.

Greg asked her how the conference in Las Vegas went.

"I won over nine hundred dollars playing blackjack." Julia looked quite pleased with herself.

"How much of that did you give back?"

"All of it, but it paid for everything that wasn't deductible —my theater tickets, my bar tabs, the rest of my gambling, and this dress." Julia grinned.

"Not bad. Did you learn anything at the conference?"

She enthusiastically reported on advances in transfusion-transmitted Babesiosis, automated urinalysis systems, and other cutting-edge developments in her field, most of which went right over Greg's head. But he was impressed with Julia's knowledge and loved listening to her voice, watching the animation in her beautiful face.

After sharing an extravagant chocolate mousse, they

drove back to Julia's home. Greg pulled her down on the thick mattress. She didn't complain that he was wrinkling her dress when he pushed it up her thigh and ran his hands over her hips. He stayed focused on Julia's lovely, curved body and their mutual pleasure until she fell asleep. Then he lay awake a long time, wondering who the murdered woman was and why she was killed, and what in the hell Colleen wanted from him after all this time.

2

M ary's kitchen and backyard patio were crowded with people. She didn't know who most of them were. Standing at the kitchen sink, looking out the window, she could see Enzo, her husband, barbecuing hot dogs and hamburgers. He was having an animated conversation with Jake, her brother. Enzo was waving the spatula around, and Jake was laughing. She wanted to go out and give them both a big hug and tell them how happy she was that they came to her party, but she couldn't get out of the kitchen. Enzo and Jake were only a few yards away, but, no matter how hard she tried to push, she couldn't make a path through the dense crowd of strangers.

The struggle woke Mary up. Devastated, she wanted to crawl back into the dream where they were both still alive. Enzo had died suddenly, of cardiac arrest, six months before. Jake had been killed by a drunk driver two months after that. It was so unfair—they were both too young to be dead. And at sixty, she was too young to be a widow.

Her small spaniel, Lily, snuggled up against her stomach. Enzo's old sweatshirt lay on top of the comforter near Mary's chest. She hadn't washed it since he'd passed away. She realized that it smelled more of dog than of her husband now, but washing the sweatshirt would be like erasing one of the last tangible remnants of him from her life. Mary couldn't bear to lose what little she had left.

She reached over to rub Lily's head and belly. The dog had been an unexpected addition to their family. After they'd retired and had enough time to devote to a pet, Enzo developed an urge for a dog. Mary hadn't been too enthusiastic about the idea, but Lily was such a sweet creature, wanting nothing more than to follow them around like a little lamb, that Mary soon came around. Now, as much as Mary wished she would have died when Enzo did, she was also thankful, for Lily's sake, that she hadn't.

With a sigh, Mary dragged herself out of bed, then walked toward the kitchen. Lily went to the living room, where she stood on her hind legs, looking out the front window. Mary filled the kettle with water—the sight of Lily at the window, presumably waiting for Enzo to come home, broke her heart every morning. Mary could relate—she felt like her life was on hold too until he miraculously came back.

Later, she glanced through the Sunday newspaper while her oatmeal and coffee grew cold in front of her. Since Enzo's death, Mary had lost most of her appetite.

There was an article about a young woman in the paper who'd been found dead near the railroad tracks between the skate park and Healdsburg Avenue toward the north end of town the day before. She appeared to be in her twenties, hispanic, with long black hair. The police were asking for leads to her identity. Mary had no idea who she was, but she felt a stab of empathy for the poor woman's family. Once that woman was identified, she knew how they were going to feel.

Mary went to the hall closet and pulled on her jacket and boots for Lily's morning walk.

Outside, Lily pulled at the leash. There was a hint of wood smoke in the cold, foggy air. Once the fog burned off the temperature would warm up. Mary admired the leaves of the ginkgo tree down the street, just starting to turn gold. Enzo never got to see it.

Passing the yellow Queen Anne home on the corner, her thoughts drifted back to the early days of their marriage, when she and Enzo first started driving up from the East Bay to visit Jake and his wife, Zoey. Healdsburg's farming history, early twentieth-century homes, central plaza, and mom-and-pop businesses gave it an idyllic early-Americana feel, even though it was technically part of the greater Bay Area megalopolis.

She and Enzo bought a small Craftsman bungalow on North Street right before they retired and hired a contractor to renovate it. They moved in as soon as it was finished. Enzo died a month later.

Mary turned Lily toward the plaza. The tall redwood trees looked ghostly in the fog. A toddler in a tiny down jacket launched a rubber duck in the decorative fountain. His mom sat on the tiled edge, watching him closely. Lily peed near the base of a small World War I monument. Mary looked over toward the bookstore on Center Street. She used to love checking out the new titles displayed in the window. But since Enzo died, books, like food, had lost most of their flavor.

She and Enzo had looked forward to retirement—getting away from the congestion of the East Bay and the long hours of their respective work. They were going to devote more time to their hobbies and do some traveling. Enzo barely had a chance to experience retirement at all before his untimely death. And the thought of long, melancholy decades without him sat heavily on Mary's spirit.

As a family practice doctor, she'd been a pillar of empathy when her patients lost their spouses—carefully suppressing any tiny flare of impatience. Surely they knew their loved one would die someday? Now she understood. There was no way to prepare yourself for such devastating emptiness—for the whole foundation to drop out of your life.

Lily turned east, up Plaza Street to where it ended, then back down and around to Matheson and over to Badger Park. Mary gratefully sank onto one of the benches in the dog park. Two more dogs showed up with their owners, and Lily had a good run and play. Mary let her stay almost two hours. Talking to acquaintances at the dog park was better than sitting in her empty house.

When the park emptied out, she reluctantly told Lily it was time to head home. They took University over to North Street. The sun finally began cutting through the fog, creating a glare, which made it hard to see. Mary squinted her eyes. Her neighbor, Mabel, sat, slumped forward, at the top of her porch steps, wearing a pullover sweater and plaid pants. Her eyes stared unblinking. Something was wrong. A tingling surge of adrenaline shot into Mary's fingertips.

"Mabel," she called out, crossing the road and hurrying up the walkway. "Are you okay?"

Mabel's face was pale and her lips were blue. She wasn't moving. Mary wrapped Lily's leash around the rail and crouched on the steps, gently shaking Mabel's arm. Knowing it was already too late, Mary grabbed her hand and shook her harder. The hand was ice cold. Mabel's upper body fell back onto the wooden porch, exposing a thin rope and dark bruise encircling her neck. Mary gasped and climbed the last two steps. Unwilling to believe her eyes, she dropped to her knees and lowered her ear close to Mabel's mouth to check for signs of breath. Not hearing, seeing, or feeling anything, she placed two fingertips on Mabel's carotid artery. No pulse. Mary pulled the cell phone from her jacket pocket and dialed 9-1-1.

Greg walked across North Street and halfway down the block

to interview the woman who'd reported Mabel Garrity's death. A perfect blue sky and the gentle cooing of mourning doves belied the grimness of his task. Healdsburg averaged less than one murder a year. Now they had two strangulations in two days. What the hell was happening?

Mary Bransen sat in the shadows, under the eave of her front porch, the sunlight not quite making it to her rattan chair. Her slender build, pale skin, and sad expression gave her an ethereal appearance. Greg was reminded of the two boys from the day before—now he had another traumatized witness. At least this one was an adult—and a doctor at that, according to the first responding officer.

He had to remind himself that this woman was a suspect until proven otherwise, no matter how fragile she looked. A dog barked shrilly inside the house. Greg paused at the bottom of the steps.

"Doctor Bransen?"

"Yes, I'm she."

"Detective Greg Davidson, Healdsburg Police Department." He showed her his ID and badge. "I understand you called 9-1-1 about Mabel Garrity?" He climbed the steps to shake her hand. It felt cold.

"Yes, Detective, I did."

"Would you prefer to talk inside where it's warmer?"

"I'm fine." She looked down the street, toward Mabel's house, and took a deep breath. "They told me you'd want to speak to me, so I waited out here for you."

"Are you sure you wouldn't like to go inside and make yourself a warm drink?"

"No, I'm not cold." She shivered and her eyes brimmed with tears.

"Was Mabel a friend of yours?"

"More a neighbor—I only moved here seven months ago."

"You're a physician?"

"Retired."

"Well, you may not be cold, but I am. I'd really appreciate it if we could go inside," Greg said.

"Sorry, Detective. I'm not thinking straight. It's been a shock."

Greg followed her into the house. He looked around the sunny, airy space. Everything looked new—in stark contrast to the inside of Mabel's house. From the exterior architecture, Greg guessed Mary's house was built in the 1920s. "This is nice," he said. "Usually the rooms in these old Craftsmen are a lot smaller." A cute brown and white spaniel was sitting patiently at Greg's feet. He squatted down to pet it.

"We had it opened up." Mary took off her down jacket and hung it on a hook by the front door. "It lets a lot more light in."

"Nice." As they were sitting down, Greg took a moment to study her. She appeared to be about his age. Her lips trembled slightly and her eyes were moist. The dog jumped onto Mary's lap and she stroked its back absentmindedly.

"Can you tell me what happened?"

"She was sitting on her porch . . . She wasn't wearing a jacket . . ." A tear trickled down Mary's cheek. She paused and took a deep breath. "I'm sorry. My husband passed away recently. I'm a little emotional."

Greg made a mental note to find out how her husband died. He waited while Mary pulled a tissue from her pocket and blew her nose. "I'm sorry for your loss. Do you have someone you can call to come over?"

"Yes. My sister-in-law lives here in town. I'll call her as soon as we're finished."

"What happened after you saw Mabel sitting on her porch?"

"She didn't respond when I called out. She was slumped forward. Her face was white and her lips were blue. I knew she was dead before I touched her. I grabbed her hand. It was ice cold. She fell over backwards. By the way . . ." Mary leaned forward. "There was no rigor mortis at that point."

Greg was relieved Mary was gaining control of herself, taking on a more professional persona, as she described Mabel's condition.

"That's when I saw the rope on her neck. I checked for breathing and pulse—out of habit." She glanced toward the window. There was a thin gold chain around her neck, passing over her delicate collarbones, and disappearing into the top of her shirt.

"Had you heard or seen anything unusual prior to finding Mabel on the porch? Any arguments, strange noises, unusual traffic on the street?"

"Nothing. I was out walking Lily," Mary looked down at the dog, "and just saw her there."

"What time was that?"

"A little after nine fifteen."

"Did you move her?"

"Like I said, she fell over when I grabbed her hand. I positioned her head to check for breathing. That's all."

"Can you show me exactly how she was sitting?"

Mary looked up, her eyes widened, and she seemed to lose even more color from her face.

"Just so we have a record of her position before you moved her." Greg hoped that didn't sound too ghoulish.

Mary got up from her seat and led Greg back out to her porch, telling Lily to stay inside. She walked down to her second step and sat on the porch surface, letting her legs relax and her knees fall outward. She leaned her torso against the post beside her, her head fell forward, and she let her arms dangle loosely at her sides. "Like this."

"Do you mind if I take a picture?"

Mary hesitated again, obviously feeling uncomfortable.

"Sorry, I know it's an imposition. But it's important."

"Okay. Go ahead."

After he took the picture, Greg showed it to her. "Is this how she was sitting?"

Mary nodded. "I think so." She stood up and brushed the back of her pants.

They both remained standing on the porch.

"How did you meet Mabel?" Greg asked.

"She was always outside, working in her yard. You can see how beautiful it is . . ." Mary's head jerked up, searching his face. "She has two daughters—have you contacted them?"

"We will—soon. Do you have any idea why she was killed?"

Mary shook her head and rubbed her arms. "My first thought was that she committed suicide. But the rope looked too short—unless someone saw her hanging and cut her down?" Greg kept his expression impassive.

Mary looked back toward Mabel's house. "But then, why leave her sitting like that? It doesn't make any sense."

"Do you know if she had any enemies?" Greg asked.

"I have no idea."

"Do you know this woman?" Greg showed her a photo of their Jane Doe.

"Is that the poor woman they described in the paper this morning? I don't know who she is."

"Have you seen her in the neighborhood, talking to Mabel Garrity, or anywhere around town?"

"Not that I know of."

Greg glanced up the street, where the evidence technician was combing over the front yard and porch of Mabel Garrity's home. He had to get back.

"We'll need a complete statement. Sergeant Maddox will be by later to take one from you. Call me if you think of anything you'd like to add." Greg handed her his card from a small leather wallet. "For now, go back inside and warm up. I know this has been difficult."

Mary's eyes teared up again. "Thank you."

Greg watched her walk into the house. He wanted go inside with her, take the statement himself, and wait for her sister-in-law to show up. But he couldn't justify spending the time and didn't think it would move the investigation along.

Lily ran over to press her nose against Mary's leg before returning to her favorite chair by the window. She was excited about all the activity on the street—barking at every new vehicle and person that entered her line of sight.

Mary walked over and touched her muzzle, to quiet her, before pulling her cell phone out of her purse to call her late brother's wife. After four rings, Zoey picked up breathlessly. "Hi."

"Something's happened. Can you come over?"

"Are you okay? What is it?"

"One of my neighbors died. I found her body."

"Oh my God. Who was it?"

"Mabel Garrity."

"Oh, Mary, I'm so sorry. Give me fifteen minutes. I just got home from the store and have to put a few things away first."

"Thank you. You're an angel."

Mary walked into the kitchen and added water to the kettle. She put tea bags in the pot, then grabbed two mugs, the sugar bowl, and teaspoons and put them on the kitchen table. She brushed a few stray crumbs off the bronze-colored placemats that she'd bought from Zoey's gift shop on the town plaza.

Mary wondered why Mabel was strangled. Was death stalking her in some way? First Enzo, then Jake, then the woman in the paper, and now Mabel. Was she becoming some kind of harbinger of death? Zoey and her son Kyle, who lived in San Francisco, were the only family Mary had left.

What if something happened to them? She would be completely alone.

She watched a few chickadees fly from the roof of her small art studio in the backyard down to the bird feeder. A junco pecked at seeds that had fallen among the wet dogwood leaves on the ground. Enzo had always been the one to fill the bird feeder, because he was taller. Now she had to wrestle with a stepladder to get the job done—it looked like she'd have to fill it this afternoon.

The doorbell rang, setting off Lily's barking. Mary opened the front door and gave Zoey a big hug.

"What's with all the police cars?" Zoey asked. "I had to park two blocks away."

"Mabel was murdered."

"No!" Zoey and Mary both looked toward the blue-suited technician still moving around Mabel's yard.

"She had a piece of rope stuck to her neck. I think someone strangled her." Mary started shaking uncontrollably.

"Oh my God!"

"I know." Mary stifled a small sob. "Let's go inside." She led the way back to the kitchen table and they both sat down. Wiping her nose, she smiled at Zoey. "Thank you so much for coming over. I hope it wasn't too much for you."

Zoey picked up the pot and poured them each a cup of tea. Mary cradled the warm cup in both hands and wondered, not for the first time, how her fifty-five-year-old newly-widowed sister-in-law could look so fresh and bright after everything that had happened. Mary felt like the walking dead in comparison.

"Not to worry. I'm sorry you had to be the one to find her." Zoey reached for the sugar bowl, then stopped, eyes widening. "That woman they found yesterday was strangled too. Do you think it's the same killer?"

"I don't know." Mary took a sip of her tea. "The detective

did ask if I knew that other woman . . ." Did this mean there was a serial killer?

"How well did you know Mabel?"

"Not very." Mary played with her teaspoon. "She always seemed a little gruff, but when Enzo passed away, she brought me a casserole. And she sent a sympathy card. She was the only person on the street who did that."

"She's always had the most beautiful garden," Zoey mused. "I never really knew her either. But I got the impression people didn't like her. I heard she drove her husband to suicide."

"He committed suicide? No wonder she looked so unhappy." Poor old woman. Mary was beginning to regret she hadn't made more of an effort to get to know her.

"It all happened a long time ago. Doesn't she have some daughters? Do you think they know yet?" Zoey grimaced. "Can you imagine your dad killing himself and then having your mother murdered?"

"I mentioned her daughters to the detective when he interviewed me. He said he would contact them."

"Are you sure you're okay?" Zoey's eyes narrowed, studying Mary carefully.

"Not really. I feel like the grim reaper is following in my wake."

"Oh, honey." Zoey stood up and wrapped her arms around Mary. "You can't believe that. You didn't cause any of these deaths."

"I know. It's crazy." Mary got up to grab a tissue from the counter. "I'm feeling sorry for myself and overreacting. But, honestly, this feels like the last straw."

"Let's just hope it is the last straw, because I agree that neither of us needs any more grief for a long time. And I hope to God there's not a serial killer on the loose. Maybe I should spend the night with you here, just in case."

"You'd be more than welcome." Mary looked up

suddenly, feeling guilty. "Sorry, I'm going on and on about myself and it's just as hard for you. But you always seem so brave and look so good all the time. How do you do it?"

"Believe me," Zoey's face seemed to sag and, for a moment, she looked her age, "it's mostly show. It feels important to keep that stiff upper lip—for Jake's memory—and for Kyle. But just between you and me, I'm barely hanging on."

Mary reached over and squeezed her hand. "You won't believe this," she said, trying to lighten the atmosphere. "Do you know Steven Phillips, director of the Boys and Girls Club?"

"Kind of."

"He asked me to teach an art class at the club."

"What a fabulous idea."

"You've got to be kidding. I've never done any teaching, let alone to children. I'm sure I wouldn't be any good at it."

Zoey sat back in her chair and regarded Mary silently. "Remember when you used to do art with Kyle when he was little? He loved it."

Mary remembered the weekends when she and Enzo used to drive up to visit. The five of them would spend all day Saturday hiking in the redwoods or canoeing on the river. Then she and Enzo would babysit Kyle, while Zoey and Jake enjoyed an evening out to themselves. She and her nephew sat in the kitchen drawing while Enzo fixed dinner and then did the dishes. Kyle had channeled his love of art into becoming an architect. He held a promising job with a large firm in San Francisco now.

"That was different. We were just playing. I didn't have to make lesson plans and try to keep a whole bunch of kids under control for an hour." Mary shuddered.

"Teaching might not be your cup of tea, but you won't know unless you try. I know it probably feels too soon, but this is an opportunity to get involved in something. It's better than hanging around an empty house." Zoey paused.

"Believe me . . ." Her voice broke and Mary could tell she was trying not to cry. "I can barely drag myself out of bed and into the shop every morning. But once I'm there and busy, I always feel better. Without work to distract me, I don't think I could bear to go on."

Mary knew Zoey had a point. But she really didn't feel up to such a big commitment this soon after Enzo's death. "I get that. But teaching?" Mary wasn't going to be pushed into accepting the job just because Zoey thought it was a good idea.

3

Greg straightened up and stretched. He'd been on his hands and knees, looking under the couch in Mabel's living room. He thought longingly of the Calistoga mud baths Julia had coaxed him into trying earlier in the year. Amazingly, they had soaked the pain right out of his body. Wishing he were relaxing in one right now, he glanced around the room.

There was no sign of disturbance anywhere inside the house. Possibly the killer hadn't come inside, or was someone Mabel knew and trusted. The furnishings looked faded, but relatively clean—other than a thick coating of cat hairs.

The coroner and paramedics had left. Officers Sam Fry and Ángela Garcia were out canvassing the neighbors, to find out if anyone had seen or heard anything suspicious the night before or this morning. They were also showing the photo of Jane Doe in hopes that someone might recognize her, or know of any connection between her and Mabel. The evidence technician was still working on the front porch. Sergeant Maddox was searching one of the bedrooms.

Inexpensively framed, old-fashioned art prints decorated

the living room walls, along with photos of two girls, ranging in age from infancy to adulthood. Animal Control had come by to collect the two cats that had been found pacing back and forth in front of an empty food bowl in the kitchen.

Greg picked up a worn address book lying near Mabel's purse on the oak desk in the living room. Thumbing through the book, he noted the entries were handwritten in different colors of ink. Many of them had been scratched out with new addresses and phone numbers crammed in the small spaces between names. He located her daughters' names and addresses under "Emergency Contacts"—one in San Francisco and one in Medford, Oregon. Most of the other entries in the address book were local people and businesses in Sonoma County. Incongruously, given the modest nature of Mabel's home, he found the names of several older, prominent society women that he recognized. He wondered what her connection had been with them.

Her wallet was still in her purse, containing several credit cards and a little under one hundred dollars in cash. Nothing appeared disturbed or missing that Greg could tell. It didn't look like robbery had been a motive for the homicide.

He rifled through a few unpaid bills stacked neatly in a wire tray. None were overdue, nor for very large amounts. The property tax bill was much lower than Greg paid for his condo—probably because she'd lived here so long. Greg opened the desk's only file drawer and scanned the contents of the folders. There was a small white envelope in the bank file, containing another two hundred dollars in twenty-dollar bills.

He moved over to a small bookcase. Most of the books were on gardening. Greg pulled a couple from the shelves and flipped through them. Published back in the sixties and seventies, they were well-used with bent corners, a few apparent smears of dirt, and lots of handwritten notes.

Photo albums, stacked in the same bookcase, were filled with carefully labeled pictures. Greg studied a younger version of Mabel; a man, Cliff—obviously her husband from the wedding shots; and the two girls he'd seen in the wall photos, Charlotte and Isobel. There weren't any current pictures of Mabel, so he removed her driver's license from her wallet and put it in a separate evidence bag.

Blake Maddox walked into the room and shook his head to indicate he hadn't discovered anything significant in the bedrooms. Greg asked him to copy and enlarge the DMV photo back at the station. He also asked him to call both the San Francisco Police Department and the Jackson County Sheriff's Department in Oregon to inform Mabel's daughters of her death. After those tasks were done, he asked him to head back to Mary Bransen's home and take her formal statement.

Something nagged at Greg, something he should know about the Garritys, but he couldn't remember what it was. And Mabel looked familiar. He wasn't sure if he'd just seen her around town—it felt more like he'd interacted with her in the past.

He could hear the evidence tech moving around on the porch. Earlier Greg had pointed out scuff marks on the painted surface, leading all the way from the door to the step where Mabel had been found sitting. He walked to the window and watched the tech for a few moments, through the living room window. He imagined Mabel, up and dressed for the day, opening her front door in response to the doorbell, stepping out on the porch, and looking around. The perpetrator could easily have hidden where the porch curved around to the side of the house. He or she could have crept up behind Mabel before she knew what was happening. Once the rope tightened around her neck, Mabel wouldn't be able to scream. She would have struggled, shuffled forward, scuffing the paint with her shoes and trying to break the rope's stranglehold with her fingers, until the moment she lost consciousness.

The coroner—the same guy who had examined Jane Doe's body—estimated the time of death to be sometime between 0600 and 0915, as rigor mortis was just beginning to set in. The coroner also pointed to broken nails and abrasions on her fingers, indicating a frantic attempt to loosen the rope. The rope, partially embedded in her neck, was unlikely to show any fingerprints, but the coroner assured Greg it would be sent it in for processing.

Greg stretched again, pulled the gloves off his sweaty hands and rubbed his face in a futile attempt to relieve his fatigue. The evidence tech stuck his head in the front door and told him he was done and heading back to the station. Greg thanked him and instructed the remaining patrol officer to secure the house.

Greg felt sure that two homicides involving the same modus operandi, both victims female, and so close together in time and location had to be related. The question was, were these random serial killings or were the two women connected to the murderer in some way? Finding where Jane Doe's and Mabel's worlds intersected might provide a critical clue they needed to solve these cases. Every name in Mabel's address book would have to be followed up. Greg started his car and made a U-turn back toward Center Street.

"Charlotte Garrity on the line for you, Greg," the receptionist announced as soon as he walked into the station.

"Ask her to hold for a minute until I get to my office."

Greg poured a cup of coffee in the break room and walked down the hall to his office, took off his jacket, and hung it behind his door. He walked around his desk and dropped into his chair. He took a sip of coffee, grabbed a notepad and ballpoint pen, then picked up the phone.

"Ms. Garrity?"

"The San Francisco Police asked me to call you . . . about my mom, Mabel Garrity?"

"Yes. Thank you for getting back to me so fast. Do you feel up to answering some questions?"

"I just spoke to her on the phone last night." Charlotte had the confused, disbelieving tone most family members exhibited when first learning of a loved one's sudden death.

"Did you look at the photo we faxed to the SFPD?" Greg asked. "Was that your mother?"

"Yes. But what happened?"

"I'm sorry for your loss. We're still investigating. I'm hoping you can give us some information."

"Of course. What do you need?"

"Did she seem worried about anything last night? Or nervous?"

"No . . ." Charlotte drew the word out.

Greg waited for her to collect her thoughts.

"She talked about her garden—normal stuff."

"Do you know of anyone who would have wanted to kill your mother?"

"No."

"People that don't like her, people she doesn't like?"

"That would be half the town," Charlotte blurted out. "Sorry—I'm being sarcastic."

Everyone dealt with unexpected death differently. But Greg thought the rapid switch from disbelief to sarcasm indicated a lack of profound grief.

"She wasn't well liked?" he asked.

"She had a habit of rubbing people the wrong way."

"Anyone in particular?"

"No. In general. But I don't know of anyone that disliked her enough to kill her."

"When was the last time you saw your mother?"

"Last weekend, on Saturday. I drove up and took her out to lunch."

"Did the two of you get along?" Greg didn't want to make Charlotte feel like a suspect, but after the initial shock she seemed pretty unruffled. From her demeanor on the phone, Greg expected her to give a straightforward answer. She didn't disappoint him.

"We had the normal mother-daughter disagreements about how the daughter should be living her life, and we didn't see eye-to-eye on politics, social issues, or religion." Charlotte paused. "And my mother wouldn't talk about the past or her feelings. Other than that, we got along fine."

Typical family relationship, then, Greg thought, deciding he could be blunt with her.

"Your mother was strangled."

"Like the other one?" Charlotte seemed to realize her question might confuse Greg. She quickly added, "Mom mentioned her on the phone last night."

"Did your mother know who she was?"

"No. But I got the impression she was going to snoop around."

"What?"

"I don't mean to sound heartless, but Mom was a bit of a gossip hound."

"What did your mother say about the other homicide?"

"Not much. She was just curious, as far as I could tell."

"She didn't seem worried or frightened?"

"No." There was another pause. "Maybe she should have been. Do you think the same person killed her?"

"We don't know yet," Greg said. "Did she mention anything else?"

"Halloween . . . how much candy she should buy for the

trick-or-treaters." Another pause. "She asked how my job was going. I think that's everything."

Greg skimmed back through the notes he had made earlier in the day while he was searching Mabel's house.

"By the way," he said, "her cats were taken to the Sonoma County Animal Shelter. Let me give you their number."

"Oh God, I forgot all about the damn cats." Charlotte sounded a little more subdued, like the reality of her mother's death was starting to sink in. "Can I see her . . . her body?"

"I can meet you at the morgue in Santa Rosa. When can you get there?"

"Around six tonight?"

Greg gave her the address of the morgue and his cell phone number. "Thanks for your help." Even though Charlotte seemed more surprised by her mother's death than distraught, he repeated, "I'm very sorry for your loss."

Greg and Liam met at the door to the stairwell, both headed to the briefing in the upstairs conference room that had been scheduled for 1500. Liam smoothed his mustache and asked, "Is this second homicide going to be too much for you to handle?"

Greg was the only detective on the small Healdsburg force. He knew Liam could ask another detective from one of the neighboring community police forces, most likely Santa Rosa, to help out. These were high-profile cases. There was going to be a lot of media scrutiny. It was important that everything be properly coordinated. Greg chose his words carefully. "I think these cases are related. I think I should investigate them together. It's the only thing that makes sense."

Liam opened the door, waving Greg through. As they started up the stairs he said, "Okay. I expected as much.

You'll be the official investigator of record on both. But you'll need assistance. You can have Blake, Sam, and Ángela. Will that be enough manpower?"

Greg nodded, relieved that Liam had agreed so easily. "For now."

"Unless there's a third victim," Liam cautioned. "Then we have to bring in outside help."

Greg hoped to hell there wouldn't be a third victim.

On the second floor, they entered the large room containing laminated desks and whiteboards. Every person on the force who wasn't on patrol had been called in for the briefing. Most of the officers had laptop computers open in front of them. Someone had ordered a pizza and Greg helped himself to a slice before moving to the front of the room and raising his voice. "Listen up, everyone."

He waited until all the extraneous conversations died down. "Second victim: Mabel Garrity. Seventy-four years old. Also strangled. This time the perpetrator left the rope garrote around her neck. Mabel lived alone on North Street. She had two daughters. One lives in San Francisco. I just spoke with her—more on that later. The other lives up in Oregon. We haven't heard back from her yet."

Blake Maddox raised a hand and Greg nodded toward him. "Do we think the two cases are related?"

"We're working under that assumption for the time being," Liam answered, nodding toward him. "You, Garcia, and Fry are going to assist Greg in the investigation."

Greg watched a grin spread across Blake's freckled face. He'd recently taken the detective exam. This would be his first murder investigation.

Greg continued. "Mabel was discovered by a neighbor, Mary Bransen, while she was walking her dog. Coroner estimates time of death between 0600 and 0915, when she was found. It appears that she was strangled on her front porch.

The neck wound looks very similar to our Doe case. We have no obvious motive at this time."

"Maybe Mabel was a copycat killing," Ángela Garcia suggested. She was sitting on top of one of the desks, using a napkin to wipe her mouth and hands. "Someone heard about the Doe case and used the opportunity to get rid of Mabel."

"We have to consider every possibility," Greg said. "If we do have a copycat killer, he or she acted fast."

"You don't need much preparation to strangle someone," Sam said. Short and stocky, he sat in the back of the room, near Blake.

Sam had transferred to Healdsburg from the Chicago Police Department two years before. Greg had a hunch Sam had a crush on Ángela, which was a bad idea for many reasons, not least that they were patrol partners.

"Good point," Greg said. "Interestingly, Mabel mentioned the Doe case to her daughter, Charlotte, on the phone yesterday. But Charlotte said Mabel didn't know who our Doe was." Greg looked directly at Blake. "Charlotte is driving up to the morgue later tonight, so we'll be able to question her."

Blake nodded. "What were your impressions when you spoke to her on the phone?"

"She's not too broken up by her mother's death. Said her mother had a habit of rubbing people the wrong way. And get this: she said her mother planned to snoop into the Jane Doe murder."

"That's interesting," Blake said.

Greg asked Sam what he had learned from the neighbors. He thumbed through his notebook. "They didn't see or hear anything out of the ordinary. They didn't know Jane Doe or remember seeing her with Mabel. They were alarmed about the murder, but not necessarily sorry that Mabel was the victim. I got the impression that she wasn't the most popular woman in town."

That confirmed Charlotte's statement about Mabel not being well liked, Greg thought.

"Noreen James lives across the street," Sam continued. "She drove her kids to a sunrise church service up in Alexander Valley at 0600. Didn't see anything unusual at Mabel's house when she left.

"Next door is Bud Morris. He didn't see or hear anything. He knew Mabel pretty well. Their kids grew up together and the families were friends for years. He has no idea who would've wanted to kill her. He read about Jane Doe in the newspaper this morning, but didn't know of any connection to Mabel."

While Sam was giving his report, Greg started a schematic map of the street on one of the whiteboards and was jotting notes about the occupants of each house. He put an asterisk after Bud Morris's name.

"Any reason to suspect the Bransen woman might be the perpetrator?" Liam asked from the side of the room.

Greg knew it was irrational, but he felt irritated that Liam was directing suspicion toward Mary. "We don't have enough information to rule out anyone at this stage," he forced himself to answer diplomatically. It felt like a betrayal, but he added, "Her husband died three months ago."

Blake looked up. "She didn't mention that when I took her statement this afternoon. Any idea what the cause of death was?"

"No. Would you check that out?"

"So, if the statements we have are correct, no one saw Mabel on her porch between 0600, when Noreen left with her kids, until 0915, when Mary found the body," Blake said, picking up his pizza slice. "Unless it was too dark to see her. What time did the sun come up? Wasn't her porch light on? How about streetlights in the area?"

Sam did a quick search on his laptop. "Sunrise was at 0717 today. Hold on a minute . . . I have the crime scene photos here. The porch light was on . . . and there's a streetlight right in front of her house, so I think she would have been visible, no matter how early."

"People don't pay that much attention," Ángela said. Her shoulder-length dark brown hair was pulled military-style into a bun at the back of her head. "None of the neighbors I spoke with heard or saw anything helpful either. Except Calvin Roberts. He lives down the street. He may have spotted our Jane Doe a few times at the Redwood Bar."

Ángela was referring to one of the upscale bar/restaurants on Healdsburg Avenue.

"He didn't know her name and couldn't remember any exact dates. I asked him if he'd seen her this past week. Negative. I asked what made him notice her. In his words, she was stunning and impossible to miss."

One of the younger, macho officers turned around to look at Ángela with raised eyebrows. "'Stunning'? Is he gay?"

Ángela stared him down. "What difference does that make?"

Greg shot a quick glance at Liam. They'd all had diversity training. This was the kind of thing Liam would normally jump on quickly and diplomatically. It appeared Liam hadn't even noticed the exchange. He seemed to be lost in thought.

"Check out the Redwood Bar this afternoon to see if any of the employees recognize her," Greg told Ángela. "See if you can find out who she was with, especially in the last month or so. Liam, as soon as we speak to Mabel's other daughter, I'd like to put out a media announcement about Mabel's death."

"What do you want to say?"

"That we are treating the death as a homicide. Remind them of our Jane Doe. Ask anyone with information about either victim to get in touch with us right away."

"Sam, go back and check with the neighbors you missed earlier," Greg continued. "Hopefully, some of them will be home by now. I'll call the Jackson County Sheriff's Department and see if they've been able to notify Isobel Davis. If they have, I'll do a phone interview with her."

Greg looked at Liam, to see if there was anything else.

Liam shook his head no.

"Oh, and Blake, do a search of similar crimes, especially in Sonoma County," Greg said. "How about we meet back here at 1700?"

There were a couple of groans. It was Sunday afternoon and Greg knew most of the force would prefer to be home, enjoying their day off. But unlike the day before, they actually had some lines of investigation to follow. They couldn't afford to let things slide while memories were still fresh in the minds of potential witnesses. Besides, this killer might strike again.

The Jackson County Sheriff's deputy in Oregon confirmed that he had driven to the Davis goat farm and informed Isobel about her mother's death. He stated that Isobel and her husband, Ben, had received the news together. He said that Isobel seemed pretty upset. It was a little after 1600. Greg dialed Isobel's number.

A woman answered the phone and Greg established she was Isobel Davis, Mabel's daughter. "I'm very sorry about your mother."

"Thank you," Isobel said. "It's such a shock. I talked to my sister, so I know some of the details. I guess you're still considering it a homicide?"

"Yes. Do you feel up to answering some questions?"

"Go ahead."

"Was your mother worried or frightened about anything recently?"

"No," Isobel answered.

Greg could hear a little sniffle.

"We spoke on the phone last Thursday, and she seemed fine."

Isobel was showing more emotion about Mabel's death than Charlotte had. Greg wondered why there was such a difference between the two sisters' reactions. "What did you talk about?"

"The holidays," Isobel answered. "Then she asked a bunch of questions about the farm and our finances, like she always does—did. She always seemed to expect the worst—that the farm would fail, or at least that I'd get tired of the life."

"Did that bother you?"

"Yes. But that was Mom—always the pessimist."

"When did you last see her?"

"Ben and I drove down for a weekend in September."

"Isn't that a long way to come for such a short visit?"

"When you run a farm, you can't be away very long."

"And everything seemed normal that weekend?"

"Yes."

"Did your mother have any enemies you know of?"

"She wasn't the easiest person to get along with, but I don't know of anyone who would want to kill her."

"Did you get along with her?" Greg kept his tone friendly and encouraging. He didn't want Isobel to feel he was accusing her of anything.

"Better after I left home."

Greg wrote her words down exactly as she said them.

"And before that?" Greg asked.

"Ben and I wanted to get married and establish this farm right after I graduated from high school. We'd dreamed about it for years. Mom was against the whole idea. She thought I should go to college. That I was way too young to get married. She refused to pay for a wedding, so we eloped. Charlotte drove to Carson City with us. Mom didn't even acknowledge the marriage at first. But she gradually came around."

Greg gave that some thought. Didn't sound like a reason for Isobel to kill her mom. He decided to change tack.

"Were you aware that we had another homicide in Healdsburg yesterday morning?"

"Charlotte mentioned it, but I don't know anything about it."

"Are you able to come down to Healdsburg in the near future?"

"Yes. I'm driving down next weekend. Charlotte told me about the cats. I'll take them back to Oregon with me."

"Okay, please check in with me while you're here. In the meantime, I'll have Deputy Rinehart of the Jackson County Sheriff's Department take written statements from you and your husband. And please call me if you think of anything else that might pertain to this investigation."

Sam Fry was the last one to return to the squad room at 1709 and the first one to report.

"Mabel's next-door neighbor on the other side, Amanda Turner, teaches at the elementary school. She left for an early hike at 0550. Didn't see Mabel on the porch. But two weeks ago, on Sunday evening, she saw Mabel in a heated discussion with Frank James, who lives across the street. She was putting her trash out for the Monday morning collection. Frank was over in front of Mabel's house and they kept their voices low, but they both looked angry when they parted."

Blake looked over at the whiteboard. "That would be Noreen James's husband?" he asked.

"Yeah."

Greg put asterisks by Frank and Noreen James's names.

Blake's search of the National Crime Information Center site hadn't helped. "Ten percent of violent deaths in the US each year are due to strangulation," he said. "Most of the victims are adult women. Our killer doesn't have a unique signature, at least that we're aware of, to help narrow down the search."

Greg didn't expect much help there, but they had to check.

"Mary Bransen's husband, Enzo, died of a heart attack," Blake added. "Autopsy confirmed genetic heart disease. No suspicion of foul play."

Greg glanced at Liam, who was sitting impassively. Greg didn't want Mary involved in the investigation any more than she already was, but he had to be careful about this unprofessional desire to shield her.

Sam concluded his report by saying there were a few more neighbors he hadn't been able to contact.

"Try to reach them tomorrow," Greg said. "Ángela?"

"The bartender at the Redwood Bar recognized Jane Doe's photo. He said she came in frequently. Her first name is Sofia, but he doesn't remember her last name or know where she lived. Two of her friends are called Olympia and Patrick. No last names. I asked him to get their last names and call us immediately if either of them shows up again."

Greg thought Ángela looked beat. They'd all worked overtime this weekend and the lack of rest was starting to show. Her alcoholic ex-husband had beaten her severely, killing their unborn child, a year before. Supposedly, she'd recovered physically, but Greg wondered if there were some residual problems.

Ángela never spoke to any of them about the incident, other than asking Liam for time off to testify at her husband's criminal trial. She maintained a stoic front at all times and it wasn't Greg's place to counsel her—he left that to Liam. And, as far as Greg could tell, she performed her duties faultlessly. He was glad Liam had assigned her to assist him with the case.

"Do an in-depth investigation of Mabel Garrity's finances, including her will," Greg told Ángela. "Then do background checks on her, her daughters, her son-in-law, and all the neighbors.

"Blake and I will conduct follow-up interviews with Frank and Noreen James and Bud Morris. Anything else before we call it a day?"

"Yes, actually." Sam looked up from his computer screen. "Cliff Garrity, Mabel's husband, committed suicide in 1992."

4

"Why didn't we hear about this from her daughters or any of the neighbors?" Blake asked, turning to look at Greg.

"I knew there was something familiar about that name," Greg said, thinking back. "I was on vacation when it happened, but as I remember, there was never any question of murder."

"That's right," Sam continued, scanning the report. "It was pretty straightforward. Shot himself in his backyard. Left a note addressed to Mabel and his daughters that said 'I'm so sorry, but I can't go on.' Gunpowder on his hand—gun and body position consistent with suicide—no reason to suspect otherwise."

"Could this be a motive for Mabel's murder?" Ángela asked.

"After more than twenty years?" Greg asked. "I don't know. Okay, you guys go home and get some rest. Blake and I are headed down to the morgue to meet Charlotte Garrity."

Ángela stood up, stretched, and started walking to the locker room. Several conversations picked up around the room.

Greg raised his voice to be heard over the buzz. "I'll be at the morgue first thing tomorrow morning. The autopsy on Jane Doe is scheduled for 0700."

∼

Charlotte Garrity looked to be in her forties, tall and buxom, with auburn hair pulled tightly into a French braid and green eyes. Greg could see a resemblance to her mother's photographs in the grim set of her mouth.

She apologized for keeping them waiting, but Greg reassured her they'd only arrived a half hour before she did and had been getting everything set up for the viewing. He offered Charlotte a cold bottle of water and led her into a private room. A shaded window separated them from the body.

Greg warned Charlotte that Mabel's face would show signs of strangulation. Charlotte nodded that she was ready. Greg pushed a small buzzer and the window shade opened to reveal Mabel on a gurney. The morgue attendant had pulled the sheet right up to her chin, covering the bruises and indentations on her neck. But the sheet didn't hide the blue lips and gray pallor of her face.

Charlotte gasped and then nodded

"Just for the record, is that your mother, Mabel Garrity?" Greg asked.

"Yes. That's my mom." She unscrewed the bottle cap and gulped some water, keeping her eyes on her mother the whole time.

"Do you feel up to answering some more questions?" Greg asked, glancing at Blake to make sure he was ready in case Charlotte fainted. She looked a little pale.

"Sure. I'm okay."

Charlotte tried to smile, but there was a sheen of sweat on her forehead.

Greg led her down the corridor to an interview room and gave her a few moments to compose herself while Blake started the video recording.

"We were reminded earlier today that your father committed suicide," Greg said softly.

Charlotte's eyes widened, then her face crumpled into an expression of grief and her eyes filled with tears. "In the early nineties," she said.

Interesting, Greg thought. She seemed more distraught about her father's death twenty-two years ago than her mother's death today.

"You didn't mention it on the phone earlier," Greg said. "Neither you nor your sister brought it up."

"It didn't occur to me that it would be relevant."

She seemed unaware of any implication that she'd been withholding information.

Greg took note of her guileless response. "Do you have any idea why he did it?"

"I was away at school when it happened. He didn't leave much of a note. My mother wouldn't talk about it."

"That doesn't really answer my question."

Charlotte stared him right in the eyes. After a few moments, she gave a tiny shrug. "Mom had a chip on her shoulder about almost everything. I'm sorry to say this about her, but she treated my dad like shit. He, on the other hand, was a saint. He let her walk all over him. I think he reached a point where he just couldn't take it anymore. In the end, I think he saw suicide as his only way out. But I don't see how this could have anything to do with Mom being murdered now."

Okay, he thought. This gal clearly blamed her mom for her dad's death.

"You think your mom was responsible for his suicide?"

"Ultimately. But Dad had other choices." Charlotte gave a sad smile.

Greg studied her face, waiting. She looked directly back at him as if trying to decide how much information she wanted to disclose. Then, as he hoped, she continued.

"Mom was a bitch. Dad was passive-aggressive. She nagged and bullied him their entire marriage. I think they were happy in the early years—at least that's how I remember it. But Dad never lived up to Mom's expectations. The older she got, the more resentful she became. Dad couldn't stand up to her. Isobel and I had both moved out by the time he killed himself. He never gave either of us any hint that things were that desperate. It was a tragedy, but I don't know what we could have done."

She sounded defensive. Survivor guilt? Greg changed the subject. "How did your mother get along with her neighbors?"

"She was always complaining about something. Lately, it was the Jameses' cat. Mom hated the neighbor cats coming into her yard, pooping in her flower beds, and fighting with her cats. I'm pretty sure she confronted the Jameses about it on multiple occasions. And I know she antagonized other neighbors about other issues over the years, like barking dogs or kids riding their bikes into her flower beds. But nothing serious enough to make anyone want to kill her."

Blake consulted his notes. "I understand Bud Morris was pretty close to your family?"

Charlotte crossed her long, shapely legs, rested against the back of her vinyl chair, and looked around the plain morgue interview room.

"He's practically an honorary uncle. They lived right next door. We were all good friends in the early days." Charlotte took another sip of water and appeared to be lost in thought, frowning. "Then relations between our two families went downhill. When I was about ten, Mom did something . . ." Charlotte held up her hand to stop Greg from asking. "I never knew what it was. After that, the Morrises barely spoke to Mom or Dad."

"Morrises . . . ?"

"Bud and Genny. She died a while ago of cancer."

"Do you think Bud could have a reason to kill your mother?"

"No! He might not have liked my mom, but he wouldn't do anything to hurt Isobel or me."

Greg couldn't think of any further questions.

"Can I start clearing out her house on Wednesday?" Charlotte asked. "There are some things I have to take care of at work in the next couple of days, but Isobel and I want to get the house on the market as soon as possible."

"Sure," Greg answered, a little taken aback. "We should be finished over there by tomorrow afternoon. When you have a chance, check around and see if anything is missing or disturbed. If you find anything out of place, or think of anything you want to add to your statement, no matter how insignificant, please let me know immediately."

"Do you think it's safe to be there by myself?"

"I'll ask the patrol officers to check in periodically while you're working there."

"Okay, thanks. I'll be staying at the Healdsburg Avenue Inn. When can I make arrangements with the mortician?"

"We can't release your mother's body until the investigation is concluded, but give us the name of the funeral home and we'll contact them as soon as possible."

"Isobel and I just want a simple cremation. She wasn't religious, and I'm not sure many people would come to a service. I don't think she had a lot of friends in the end." Charlotte frowned, a wistful look in her eyes. "It was different with my dad; there were at least a hundred people at his memorial."

∾

Greg took a shower and climbed into bed. He lay awake, analyzing Charlotte's interview. Her eagerness to put her mom's house on the market seemed cold in light of the fact that her mother had been dead less than twenty-four hours. Would his kids be as anxious to cash out his assets and get on with their lives if he died suddenly?

They hardly knew him. He'd spent most of his life guarding his vulnerability. Hana, his ex-wife, never understood. How could she? She'd tried to break down his barriers, find out what troubled him, but was repeatedly rebuffed until she finally gave up. Greg never blamed her—neither for trying nor for giving up.

Greg's parents had been overwhelmed by Colleen's problems. At a very young age, he learned to suppress his feelings to avoid adding to their burden. It became an ingrained habit that he couldn't break. In the seventh grade, he never told his parents he was going to try out for baseball. That way he didn't have to tell them when he failed to make the team. He didn't want them to feel guilty that they never had time to play catch or take him to the batting cages. In high school and college he stayed up late almost every night studying, hoping good grades would give his parents some comfort and reassurance. He avoided talking back or asking for money or attention.

Colleen had been robbed of a normal childhood, so Greg didn't feel he deserved one. Instead of playing hopscotch, giggling all night at sleepovers, hogging the phone, and shopping for prom dresses, she slogged her way through school, friendless and resentful. Greg offered to help her with homework. He invited her to go out with him and his friends. But Colleen refused to have anything to do with him.

It wasn't until she was sixteen, right before Greg left for college, that their parents finally found a good psychologist who broke through her barriers, and she began to show signs of improvement.

Greg fell into an uneasy sleep sometime after two in the morning.

Greg returned to the morgue Monday morning in a heavy, wet fog. He parked in front of the facility, turned off the windshield wipers and the headlights, and quickly dabbed a little Vicks VapoRub on his upper lip and around each nostril in an attempt to counteract the smells of decay. He was buzzed into the autopsy suite by the forensic assistant.

Dr. Ronnie Harvey, one of several rotating pathologists working for the Sonoma County Coroner, was shrouded in a gown, gloves, booties, cap, and face shield. She once confessed to Greg that she'd been interested in forensic pathology ever since discovering crime fiction in her preteens. She added that she might have thought twice if she'd realized how uncomfortably hot it would be working in all that gear, despite the morgue's icy air-conditioning.

"Hi, Greg," she said, pulling off her headgear. "Come on in. I'm just finishing up." Dr. Harvey asked where Greg wanted the DNA scrapings, blood samples, stomach contents, hair, fingernail scrapings, and victim's clothing sent.

"Forensic Science Associates in Richmond. Thanks."

"Do you have an ID on her yet?"

"No," he answered.

Dr. Harvey pulled off the rest of her protective gear and left it in the autopsy suite for cleaning, washed her hands thoroughly, then led Greg down the hall to her office. There were large wet patches on her scrubs under her arms and down the middle of her back. She grabbed a small hand towel from a neatly folded pile inside her office door and wiped her face.

"The cause of death was asphyxia. No surprise there. Broken nails on each hand and rope burns on her fingertips.

Fingernail marks on her neck. Rope fibers embedded in the skin of her neck. Petechial hemorrhages in the conjunctiva, small hemorrhages in the larynx and surrounding tissues—all consistent with strangulation. No signs of any other disease or injury."

Greg nodded. The coroner had mentioned many of the same signs.

"Her clothing was intact. But there was evidence of recent vaginal intercourse."

"How recent?" Greg asked.

"Within two to three hours before she was killed. No semen, unfortunately, but traces of lubricant, and a pubic hair, which was a lighter color and finer texture than hers. We're sending it in with the other samples."

Greg jotted a few notes, encouraged to hear there was at least one new clue.

"Lividity indicates she was lying on her back within thirty minutes after she expired."

"That's how we found her. But it looked like she'd been moved after she died."

"She ate approximately eight to ten hours before she died…" Dr. Harvey scrolled down her computer screen, checking the computer-generated transcript of her dictated notes. "We'll run her thumbprint through the DMV records and get back to you on that. And I'll fax my full report to your office after I've studied the organ samples."

Greg thanked her and walked out to his vehicle. The sun was starting to break through the fog, so he pulled on his sunglasses. They were making some progress now. They would have an ID soon. The pubic hair would be helpful for comparison once they found a suspect.

Finding a connection to Mabel would also be instructive.

~

While Greg was finishing up at the morgue, a young woman, Olympia Kontos, walked into the Healdsburg police station and announced her roommate was missing. Blake thought she looked to be in her early thirties. She was short and a little overweight, and was wearing a fleece pullover and leggings. Her long, dark hair was pulled into a careless ponytail and her wide smile seemed forced. She held a large coffee cup in one hand. She raised her eyebrows and hesitated a bit when Blake immediately led her into the interview room. He asked her to wait and called Greg on his cell.

"Get up here fast. We've got a missing person report."

As soon as Greg arrived, they went into the interview room. Olympia, who'd been standing, studying the art prints on the wall, turned around anxiously.

"I need to ask you some questions about your missing roommate." Greg pointed toward the sofa. "Have a seat. What did you say her name was?" He sat across from her in a chair.

"Sofia Molina," Olympia said. "Thanks for taking such an interest. I was expecting you to tell me I had to wait another forty-eight hours to even file a report." Her smile was more of a grimace. Her hand shook when she raised her coffee to her mouth.

"Do you have a picture of her?"

Olympia put her coffee on the table, pulled a smart phone from her sweatshirt pocket, punched a few keys, then passed the phone over to Greg. "This was taken a few weeks ago at a party."

Blake looked over Greg's shoulder. Sofia was laughing, holding a glass full of amber liquid and wearing a low-cut top and tight jeans. She looked like a match for their Jane Doe. Blake caught Greg's eye, knowing he'd want to get more information out of Olympia before he broke the news that her roommate was probably dead.

"What would you say her height and weight are?"

"Maybe five-three, and 110 pounds?"

"When did you first notice she was missing?"

"Last night. I was away most of Saturday and Sunday, visiting my parents at Sea Ranch. When I drove home yesterday her car wasn't in the parking lot. And there was no sign she'd been in the apartment since I left." Olympia took another sip of coffee, staring at the wall. "It's hard to tell, because she's very neat. Looking back, I don't think I noticed any sign of her having been there Friday night or Saturday morning either, but it didn't register until today. I work night shift at the hospital." Olympia searched their faces.

Greg waited quietly. Blake followed his lead, making notes.

"She works days at a local winery. Sometimes we don't cross paths for several days at a time. Anyway, when I got home last night, I realized I hadn't seen her since Friday morning. I tried texting her, but she didn't respond. This morning I called Dry Creek Cellars—that's where she works. They said she hadn't come in all weekend." Olympia looked at Greg expectantly. Blake stole a glance at Greg's face, which remained impassive.

"I wondered if she had an emergency at home," Olympia said. "Her family's in LA. But I don't have any contact information for them and she hardly puts anything on Facebook. I tried calling and texting a few more times, but she never answered. That's when I started to worry. She's never disappeared like this before."

"What did she tell you about her plans on Friday morning?" Greg asked.

"That she was going to be working all weekend . . . and that she'd left me a check for the phone bill. Then she left."

"Did she seem worried about anything?"

Olympia shook her head. "No."

"What type of car does she drive?"

"A blue Honda Fit."

"Have you seen it since Friday?"

"No."

"Where were you on Friday night?"

"At work." Olympia's brow wrinkled. "Do you know something I don't?"

"Possibly."

Blake knew it was cruel to lead her on like this, but he understood that Greg needed more information before he broke the news.

"Please bear with me."

Olympia nodded. The worry lines stayed on her brow.

"Do you know what time you got home Friday night?" Greg asked.

"Midnight?" Olympia shrugged. "Around then."

"And her car wasn't in the parking lot?"

"I don't think so."

"And what time did you leave home Saturday?"

"Ten."

"How long have you been roommates?"

"Three and a half years."

"How well do you know her?"

"Not that well." Olympia said, turning her cup in her hands. "She's a good roommate. We hang out together when I have a night off. But she's guarded about her personal life. And as I said, I don't see that much of her."

Olympia seemed more confused and distressed than wary. "Why are you asking all this?"

"It's standard procedure," Greg said. "She works at Dry Creek Cellars?"

"Yes, in the tasting room. She's keen to learn about the wine industry—taking classes at the JC. She wouldn't miss work—that's why I'm worried."

"Does she have a boyfriend?"

"Not that I'm aware of, but she doesn't like to talk about

that stuff." When she spoke again, her voice trembled. "Has something happened to her?"

"Has anyone been causing her problems?"

"Not that I know of."

"Would anyone have any reason to harm Sofia?"

"I don't know!"

Blake could tell from her exasperated tone of voice that Olympia was reaching her limit. "I'm sorry to tell you this," Greg finally relented. "We have an unidentified murder victim . . ."

"Oh, no! Is it Sofia?"

"I think it may be. She looks like the woman in your photo."

"What happened?"

"She was strangled to death sometime Friday night or early Saturday morning."

Olympia started crying. Blake passed her a box of tissues.

"You don't have contact information for any of her relatives?" Greg asked.

Olympia shook her head no, blotting her tears and blowing her nose.

"Do you know a Mabel Garrity?"

"I don't think so."

"Did you ever hear Sofia mention her name?"

"Not that I can remember."

"Olympia," Greg said gently, "I know this has been a shock, but thank you for coming in."

Olympia tried unsuccessfully to stifle a sob.

Blake gave her what he hoped was an encouraging smile. There was no easy way to break the news of a death. That was one part of police work he'd never gotten used to.

"If it turns out to be Sofia," Greg added, "we're going to need access to your apartment. In the meantime, I need you to write out a statement and we need your fingerprints. And a list of her friends."

As soon as the forensic lab was able to confirm that Jane Doe's thumbprint matched Sofia Molina's DMV record, Greg called Olympia and made arrangements to search her apartment.

Sofia and Olympia lived in a new, four-story building on Healdsburg Avenue. A wine-tasting shop faced the street on the ground floor. The elevator was in a breezeway that led to an open courtyard and an Italian restaurant. The upper floors contained luxury apartments.

Greg and Blake rode the elevator to the third floor.

Olympia invited them in.

The spacious living and dining areas were decorated in a stark, urban style. Greg wondered how people lived like this. The place was spotless. The furniture looked angular and uninviting. He couldn't picture lounging in front of the TV with a beer and chips. In fact, there was no TV. No ottomans, no magazines, just a couple of big, heavy books stacked in a small, precise pyramid on the glass coffee table next to a bowl of glass fruit. It looked like a cover photo from *Architectural Digest* or some other glossy, overpriced magazine—too perfect, too neutral.

Even though Julia was meticulously neat, you could still find a comfortable chair in her house. And a TV. Not that he spent much time at her house.

Greg turned his attention back to Olympia. "Who's your housekeeper?"

She gave a wry smile and a shrug. "Sofia wanted it this way. She couldn't stand clutter."

Greg looked around again, amazed.

"Does anything seem out of place, missing, or disturbed, that you've noticed?"

Olympia shook her head no.

The evidence technician arrived. Olympia showed them all into Sofia's bedroom and bath suite. She assured them that, other than a quick, fruitless search through the desk for an address book, she hadn't touched or moved anything. The technician started taking photos while Greg and Blake looked around. At Greg's request, Olympia remained standing in the doorway and didn't enter the room.

Like the common area, the bedroom was decorated in a sparse, minimalist style, the color scheme a serene green and off-white. Greg pulled on a pair of vinyl gloves and opened the door to a large walk-in closet. The clothes looked clean, pressed, and relatively new, the hangers evenly spaced. He quickly searched all the pockets of the garments, finding them empty. Opening drawers, he found neatly folded items arranged carefully by purpose and color.

Back in the bedroom itself, there were a few framed photographs on one wall and a large abstract print on another.

"Do you know who the people in these photos are?" Greg asked Olympia, who was still standing in the doorway.

"I asked her if they were her family. Sofia said yes, but she never told me their names or how they were related to her. It's like she didn't want me to know any more about her life than I absolutely had to." Olympia looked sadly around the room, shaking her head.

Greg walked closer to study the photographs and Blake joined him. There was a middle-aged Hispanic couple in a formal studio photograph. Another photo of what looked like the same couple, taken when they were younger adults, with a young child that must have been Sofia, standing on the rim of the Grand Canyon. The last one showed a large wedding party with Sofia off to one side in a bridesmaid dress.

A closed laptop sat perfectly centered and aligned with the front edge of her desk. The only other objects on top of the desk were a sleek, contemporary lamp and a vase filled with wilting white flowers. The water reeked of decay and several petals had fallen to the desktop. The drawers contained office supplies and well-organized files of paid bills, Sofia's college transcripts, receipts, and tax returns. Like Olympia, Greg was unable to find any diaries or address books.

The technician's digital camera was clicking away. Greg turned around. The bedroom had the impersonal air of an expensive hotel. No books, nothing on the bedside tables except lamps. Nothing in the drawers except tissues and foot cream. An upholstered chair in the corner looked like it would force you to lean back at an uncomfortable angle. No half-finished cup of coffee with a lipstick stain on the rim, no Post-it notes with reminders to pick up the dry-cleaning or buy milk, no discarded jewelry, shoes, or jacket—no sign of life at all.

The section of the bathroom counter Greg could see from his vantage point held nothing but a decorative container of liquid hand soap. He walked to the bathroom doorway. Everything was sparkling clean. The towels were precisely aligned on the racks; the vanity countertop and shelf in the shower contained neatly arranged cosmetics and hair products. Birth control pills and an industrial-size box of condoms were stored in the vanity drawers, but no other medications, not even a bottle of aspirin. The trash can was empty. No evidence of a struggle, let alone anything to indicate why she might have been murdered.

The tech turned on a black light and began moving through the bedroom and bathroom, looking for signs of blood spatter or other bodily fluids. They still didn't know where Sofia was murdered, and, although she'd been strangled, she might have wounded the perpetrator in a struggle. Unfortunately, the light didn't turn up any evidence.

"Go ahead and bag the laptop and start dusting for prints," Greg said to the tech. He turned to Olympia. "I'm sorry about the mess the fingerprint dust will make."

Olympia shrugged and gave a wry smile. "It can't bother Sofia now."

They walked back into the living room. Olympia plopped down on the couch, grabbed a small, decorative pillow and pulled it against her waist. Greg took an almost perverse pleasure in her willingness to disrupt the perfect decor.

"Are you okay?" he asked, still standing.

"I don't know. I just can't believe she's dead. Why would anyone kill her?"

"We're going to do everything we can to find out. Is your apartment always this neat? It hardly looks like you guys live here."

"Well, you haven't seen my room." There was that wry smile again. "Sofia insisted everything be kept just so. It upset her if I left stuff lying around or even changed the order of the spices or canned goods in the pantry."

"How could you live this way?" Blake asked.

"It was a pain," Olympia conceded. "But she always paid her share of the rent and bills on time. That's better than most roommates I've had. Plus, I've been working so many hours, I wasn't around much to mess the place up—neither of us were."

"Did Sofia have friends over?"

"No way! She hated having other people here. I got the impression that this place was a sanctuary and she didn't want anyone disturbing her safe zone. If I brought someone over and they moved something, like the books on the coffee table, she'd immediately get up and shift them back to their original position. After my boyfriend and I broke up about a year ago, I stopped inviting people over."

Greg watched Olympia carefully. She looked sad, even worried, but he didn't sense any animosity toward Sofia.

"It seemed kind of pointless to keep the place looking so good if no one was ever going to see it," Olympia continued, brushing some loose strands of hair off her face. "But it wasn't that big a deal. We went out whenever I had a night off."

Olympia suddenly frowned and looked from Greg to Blake. "You know, when we were out—at a bar or a party—she became a completely different person."

"In what way?" Blake asked.

"It was like she lost all her inhibitions. She drank a lot, danced, struck up conversations with total strangers. She was always the center of attention. And not just with our friends…"

"Are these the friends you made a list of at the station?"

"Yes." Olympia looked toward the living room window, a thoughtful expression on her face. "Everyone in the place would have their eyes on her. And she went home with a lot of guys—to their home or wherever—not here." Olympia looked back at Greg expectantly, her voice picking up speed. "I tried to warn her about high-risk behaviors, but she blew me off. Told me to stop being such a nurse—that she knew what she was doing."

"Did she?"

Olympia shrugged again. "I figured she was old enough to make her own choices." She sat silent for a moment, then continued in a sadder tone. "I wonder if that's what got her killed—going home with the wrong guy."

5

Olympia was probably feeling guilty that she hadn't done more to protect Sofia from unsafe practices. Greg could relate to her overdeveloped sense of responsibility. But they needed to move on.

"Can you give me the names of any of the guys she'd been with lately?"

"Not really."

Blake raised his eyebrows, glancing toward Greg, probably wondering who she was trying to protect.

Olympia must have caught his gesture. "She never introduced them or told me who they were."

"Would you recognize them if we showed you pictures?"

"I don't know . . . maybe. It was someone different every time we went out. I kept hoping that she'd get into a real, lasting relationship—and then maybe she'd open up."

The more Greg heard about Sofia, the harder it was to understand why Olympia wanted to live with her. But then, Olympia seemed pretty laid-back. And it sounded like Sofia was financially responsible, which was a bona fide asset in a roommate.

"Thanks, Olympia. You've been a big help. Could we take a quick look at your room?"

Olympia nodded and led them down the hall. Her bedroom did look more normal—some discarded clothes on a chair, a wet towel carelessly draped over the towel bar in the bathroom, makeup scattered around the vanity in a haphazard pattern, even some used tissues in the trash can.

"Thanks," Greg said. "The tech will finish checking for fingerprints in all of the rooms. Call me if you think of anything else or if you discover anything missing or out of place."

Greg and Blake spent the rest of the afternoon interviewing the other tenants of the building, both residential and commercial. Most of them recognized Sofia's face and some of them knew she lived with Olympia and worked at Dry Creek Cellars.

One young man with a fashionable three-day growth of beard, just emerging from a BMW sports car in the parking lot, told them Sofia was a tease. "She wore all these revealing clothes, but when I asked her out she turned me down."

"Why do you think that was?" Greg asked, trying to keep from laughing at the guy's indignation.

"I don't know. Maybe she only dated older guys?" the young man said, glancing at his Rolex watch.

"What makes you say that?"

"I saw her talking to some old dude at Juan's Place a few weeks ago," the guy said, referencing a popular new Mexican restaurant in town. "Looked like she was coming on strong to him."

"Do you know who he was?" Greg asked eagerly.

"Nope."

"What did he look like?" Blake asked, making notes.

"About his age," he said, pointing at Greg. "Not as tall. A little heavier. Darker hair—looked like maybe he dyed it."

"Have you seen the man since?"

"Nope."

~

Ángela Garcia and Sam Fry were working patrol Monday afternoon. She rode shotgun, carefully scanning the streets, homes, and businesses they passed for any signs of suspicious activity. They were both wearing sunglasses. In spite of that, Ángela was forced to shade her eyes with her hand. The visor wasn't low enough and the coastal mountain range wasn't high enough to block the sun's direct glare as they drove west on Matheson. Sam made a right on Center Street and Ángela lowered her arm with a sigh of relief. Sam gave her a quick smile, before turning his attention back to the traffic.

Ángela noticed a slight, middle-aged man come out of a small Hispanic grocery with two full carrier bags. He climbed into a dirty, beat-up Ford F-250. His worn work clothes and the condition of the truck indicated he was probably a migrant farm worker from one of the surrounding vineyards.

"Reminds me of my dad," she said, nodding toward the man.

"What's that?" Sam asked.

"He used to drive up from Oaxaca every January with a couple of other guys. In an old truck held together with duct tape and a prayer. Winter pruning, harvest, crush. Sleeping in undeveloped camps or the back of the truck. Bathing in the river . . . or going without for weeks at a time. Only saw his parents and my mom for two short months before he had to leave again."

"I thought you grew up here in Sonoma County," Sam said.

"I did—my dad got a permanent job right before I was born. The owners let my parents live in a cottage on their estate. Mom started working as their nanny. My parents became naturalized citizens. We were lucky."

"You still have family in Oaxaca?"

"Lots—on both sides."

"You ever visit?"

"A few times." Angela wondered what Sam would think about the impoverished town with its dusty alleys, mongrel dogs, and air of poverty. The few American tourists that accidentally stumbled in quickly left when they realized there weren't any fancy hotels, shops or restaurants.

The dispatcher came on the radio, reporting an abandoned car in the Healdsburg Market parking lot. The Honda Fit was registered to Sofia Molina, identified earlier in the day as their Jane Doe. Detective Davidson was requesting they meet the forensic technician in the parking lot to oversee what evidence might be found in the car. He and Blake were still canvassing Sofia's apartment complex. Ángela grinned at Sam and gave the thumbs-up sign, delighted to abandon patrol and do a little detecting. Sam made a U-turn and hurried back toward the market.

Typical for late afternoon, the parking lot was a mess, cars circling for open spots, full carts being pushed out of the store by tired-looking mothers with schoolchildren in tow, a homeless couple with a mangy dog begging for handouts at the entrance on North Street.

Sam stopped in the fire lane in front of the store and Ángela went inside to find the manager. They came out together and walked to the far back of the lot, Sam driving slowly behind them. A grassy knoll topped with large pine trees separated the lot from the sidewalk and street. There were cars on either side of the Honda, so Sam double-parked.

A woman carrying two full shopping bags starting running toward them.

"Is there a problem?" she asked anxiously.

"No, ma'am," Sam answered. "Are we blocking you in?"

"No. But I left my dog in the car. Is he okay?" She pushed her cart toward a dirty white Camry. Ángela could hear the little Yorkie inside barking furiously.

Sam helped the woman load her groceries into the car while she gathered the dog in her arms from the backseat. Ángela listened to their conversation while she pulled on a pair of gloves.

"I know it's not safe to leave him in the car. But it was an emergency. We got home from Santa Rosa so late and I was desperate for groceries," she apologized.

"Well, it looks like he's fine," Sam reassured her. "Just try to avoid doing it in the future. The car turns into an oven pretty fast, even with the windows cracked," he added gently, before she drove off.

The Honda Fit's doors were locked. Sam radioed the dispatcher. She reported the evidence tech and a tow truck were on the way. Sam took photos of the rest of the cars parked nearby, in case any of the owners needed to be contacted later. The sun finally dropped below the redwood-covered hills to the west, throwing the parking lot into shadow. Without touching the glass, Ángela looked through the car windows. She could see a purse on the backseat and canvas grocery bags on the floor behind the passenger seat.

"How long has the car been here, sir?" she asked the manager.

He shrugged. "Hard to say. My assistant manager noticed it yesterday when she came to work. It was still here when she left last night, so she left me a note. I waited most of the day, in case someone came to move it. Finally decided I'd better call it in."

It was a wonder no one broke the window to steal the purse, Ángela thought.

As the cars on each side of the Fit pulled away, Sam put cones out to keep the spaces free. The evidence tech arrived soon after. He dusted the door handles for prints before popping them open. The smell of spoiled milk and rotting vegetables wafted out of the car. Ángela and Sam looked around inside, careful not to touch anything. Ángela pulled the purse open with two pencils. She could see a smart phone nestled inside.

She nodded to the tech, letting him know he could close the car back up and prepare it for towing down to the forensic garage. She asked the manager if he would show them his CCTV tape beginning Friday morning. They found footage of Sofia walking into the store at 2048 and leaving at 2059, alone each time.

Ángela and Sam met Greg in his office fifteen minutes later. He'd just returned from Sofia's apartment and was typing notes on his computer. A large Ansel Adams photo of Half Dome in winter dominated one wall. Ángela sank into one of the spare chairs while Sam leaned against the door frame.

"Looks like the car's been there all weekend," she said. "They're towing it to the garage in Richmond."

Blake knocked on the wall outside the door and Sam moved over to let him enter. Blake sat in the other chair.

"Any sign of a struggle in her apartment?" Ángela asked.

"No. The tech's still there," Greg said, using his mouse to show them photos of Sofia's apartment. He clicked on the picture of the canned goods precisely lined up and alphabetized in the pantry.

Ángela leaned forward, fascinated. She'd majored in psychology at Sonoma State University. "Maybe she had OCD."

"Obsessive-compulsive personality disorder," Blake said. "Undoubtedly."

Angela continued, "Everything has to be just so—in its place, clean, uncluttered." She studied the pictures, thinking. "They don't like other people coming into their space because they disturb the order."

"That fits," Greg said. Then he switched to Olympia's Facebook page. A couple of bar and party scenes showed Sofia, dressed in low-cut tops surrounded by good-looking men and women. "And this fits with the party personality that Olympia, her roommate, described."

Ángela and Sam filled Greg and Blake in on the contents of the car.

"This fits, too," Greg interrupted.

"What's that?" Sam asked, moving back around so he could look over Greg's shoulder.

"Olympia said Sofia hardly posts anything on her Facebook page. A few pictures of the winery. That's it."

Greg turned his chair around to face them. He reviewed Sofia's autopsy results and quickly summarized the interviews he and Blake had conducted with Olympia and her neighbors.

They were all quiet for a few moments, Ángela thinking about everything they'd learned. "How does any of this tie in with Mabel Garrity?"

"That's the sixty-four-thousand-dollar question," Greg said. "Ángela, first thing tomorrow I want you to conduct preliminary phone interviews with Sofia's friends from the list Olympia provided. Find out what they can add about Sofia's personality and her recent activities—especially where she was on the tenth."

Ángela nodded.

"And call Olympia's parents. Make sure she went to Sea Ranch this past weekend like she said." Greg looked around. "Anything else?"

They all shook their heads no.

"Okay," Greg said. "See you tomorrow."

Sam high-fived Ángela as they started down the hall. "Would you like to get a drink after we finish our reports?" he asked hopefully.

She was tempted. It had been a good day, probably one of

the best days since she'd returned to work. If anyone else was going she wouldn't hesitate, but she didn't like the idea of going out alone with Sam. Not that she didn't like him, because she did, very much. And she felt like celebrating and discussing the case with him. But she didn't want to lead him on. "Sorry," Ángela reluctantly declined. "I can't."

Luckily, Sam never pressed the point.

The forensic lab called Greg before he left for work Tuesday morning. Olympia had given the tech Sofia's smart phone passcode and they had a list of all of her contacts and recent calls. The phone had last been used Friday, the tenth, at 2031 to call a Valentina Molina in the 213 area code. The call lasted a little over eight minutes. There were voicemails from Dry Creek Cellars left on Saturday, Sunday, and Monday. There were texts and calls from her roommate, Olympia, on Sunday evening and Monday morning.

Sofia didn't have many contacts in Sonoma County—just the three guys and one woman Olympia had already listed, a few people listed as coworkers at Dry Creek Cellars, and a number of businesses. There were more numbers in the Los Angeles area code, including one for Valentina and José Molina.

The lab gave Greg a list of her credit card numbers, but they were still working on the laptop recovered from Sofia's apartment and her email accounts. The only fingerprints found on the laptop were her own. Not surprisingly, most of the fingerprints in the apartment were Olympia's and Sofia's. They did pick up other partial prints, but they were still unidentified. The only recoverable fingerprints in and on her car seemed to be her own.

As soon as Greg arrived at the station, he called the Los Angeles Police Department, faxed them a copy of Sofia's photo, and asked them to contact the Molinas. LAPD would confirm their relationship to Sofia and inform them of her death.

He grabbed a muffin and called Sam and Blake over to Ángela's desk in the squad room. She was typing up notes on her computer. Greg reported on the latest forensic findings. The morning sun, coming in through the mini-blinds on the east-facing windows, cast stripes of light across the desks. Greg could hear one of the police technicians and a dispatcher chatting outside in the hall.

Ángela had come in at 0700 to call Sofia's friends before any of them left for work. They'd all heard about her murder from Olympia, and they'd been expecting a call from the police. None of them had seen her on Friday. They'd all been in Sofia's apartment at one time or another and were aware of the excessive neatness.

One of the guys said every time he put down his beer, Sofia would reach over and re-position it on the coffee table, so that it was always in the same spot. Every time he took a sip he'd put it down in a different place, just to mess with her. He said she didn't understand or appreciate the humor in his teasing.

Asked about Sofia's relationship history, most of them repeated what Olympia had told Greg. "We'd all go to some bar or club. Next thing we know she's flirting with some new dude. Half the time she'd just abandon us. Didn't even say goodbye."

They didn't know the names of the men and were only able to give vague descriptions. The last time any of them had seen her was at Juan's Place, two weeks before she was murdered.

One friend, a nurse who worked with Olympia, told Ángela she should talk to Patrick Weiss, indicating he might have had something going with Sofia about a year ago. He was on the list, but Ángela hadn't called him yet. When she did, she asked him to come in to the station. "I figured you'd want to interview him face to face," she told Greg. She glanced up at the clock. "He should be here in about ten minutes."

Greg could sense the heightened energy in the room, now that there were leads to follow.

"That last phone call on her cell narrows the time of death," Greg said. "We know Sofia had sexual relations shortly before she was killed. According to Olympia, Sofia had multiple partners. We need to pin down who she was with Friday night."

"One more thing," Ángela said. "I called Olympia's parents. They're faxing over time-stamped photos of her in Sea Ranch Saturday and Sunday. She has an alibi for Sunday morning at least."

Patrick Weiss had spiked hair, like Greg's son Ray. Must be the style now, Greg thought. Patrick wore jeans and a jacket with a Healdsburg Dynamics logo embroidered on the front.

"Thanks for coming in. Have a seat." Greg motioned him toward a chair and introduced himself and Blake.

Patrick looked around the interrogation room. His eyes lingered on the video camera before he turned back and reached across the table to shake hands. His palm was clammy. "I still can't believe Sofia's dead." He pushed thick, black-rimmed glasses up the bridge of his nose.

"I'm sure it's a terrible shock." Greg started the recording and identified everyone in the room. "Could you give us your address for the record?"

"802 Vineyard Creek Drive, Santa Rosa." Patrick went on to state he was an engineer and had been working at Healdsburg Dynamics for the past four years.

"What can you tell us about Sofia?" Greg asked.

"Not much," Patrick answered. He tried to maintain eye contact, but his eyes kept drifting away. His legs were jiggling below the table—the top half of his body was vibrating from the movement. "Sorry, I'm a little nervous. I've never known anyone who was murdered and I've never been interviewed by the police before. I don't really know the protocol."

Greg advised him he was welcome to have an attorney present, but they just wanted to find out a little more about Sofia, especially any recent relationships she may have had.

Patrick looked around a little wildly, before he blurted out, "I don't know about her other relationships, but I hooked up with Sofia for a short time last year."

"Why didn't Olympia mention this?" Greg asked.

Blake looked up from his notes and watched Patrick's reaction.

"She didn't know. Before that, I was with Olympia."

Greg sat up a little straighter. "I see."

"Olympia and I were together before Sofia ever moved in with her. The three of us started hanging out with a couple other guys from work and another nurse Olympia knows." Patrick paused to take off his jacket.

"Around a year and a half ago, Sofia started to pay more attention to me. She'd look at me more, make eye contact, smile. It was a little weird. She'd make an effort to sit next to me and touch me when we spoke. Olympia didn't seem to notice, so I tried to ignore it, and hoped Sofia would stop." Patrick took a deep breath.

"To be honest, I guess I was flattered. But I had no intention of getting involved with her—I was happy with Olympia. Then, at a party one night in September last year, Sofia and I ended up alone in the kitchen together. She walked right up and grabbed my dick."

Greg wondered if Patrick was bragging—his face and neck had turned bright red. Patrick's story fit with the reports about Sofia's promiscuous sexual activity, but not with the neighbor's claim that Sofia only went after older guys.

"She caught me off guard and I froze. Right then, some other people came into the kitchen, so she backed off and walked away without a word. After that, I couldn't stop thinking about her, which pissed me off. I hated her taking up space in my head. One night she showed up at my apartment. When I opened the door she was all over me."

Blake paused again in his note-taking and stared at Patrick, which made Patrick falter. Greg slowly moved his leg to nudge Blake, not wanting Blake's body language to interrupt Patrick's story. Greg didn't want Patrick to think he was a suspect or that they didn't believe him.

"Maybe I should get a lawyer," Patrick said, leaning forward in his chair and looking from Blake to Greg.

"That's your choice," Greg said calmly. "Would you like to call one now?"

Patrick thought for a moment. Greg figured the young man didn't have a lawyer and had no idea how to find one. Since he hadn't been arrested, he wasn't entitled to a public defender.

"Oh, forget it," Patrick said, shaking his head. "Let's get this over with." He frowned. "Where was I?"

"Sofia showed up at your apartment and threw herself at you," Blake said, with a sarcastic tone.

Greg shot him a stern look. Blake had to learn to hide his personal feelings. The key was to appear to be on the witness's side.

"Okay. I never should have let her stay. But you saw what she looked like . . ." Patrick's voice faded. He took a deep breath and continued. "The next morning, I tried to tell myself that it didn't mean anything, but she came back a couple more times that week. Like a complete asshole, I had sex with her every time."

"And where was Olympia while all this was going on?" Greg asked.

"Working mostly. I starting lying to her when she asked me what I'd been doing. I was disgusted with myself. I couldn't keep lying to Olympia and cheating on her. I had to choose between them. I stupidly chose Sofia and broke up with Olympia."

"What reason did you give her for the breakup?" Greg asked.

"I told her there was someone else." Patrick sounded sad. "She didn't ask me who it was and I didn't want to hurt her by telling her it was her own roommate."

"Didn't you think she'd find out pretty quick?"

"I wasn't thinking very clearly. All I knew was Sofia was hiding it from Olympia, so I figured I should too." Patrick paused, his mouth in a grim line. "Olympia was amazingly gracious about the whole thing. Looking back, I don't think she was that serious about me." He paused again and shrugged. "Anyway, right after I broke up with Olympia, Sofia dropped me."

"Are you sure Olympia didn't know about you and Sofia?" Greg asked.

"If she did know, she did a great job of covering it up. And after Sofia broke up with me, there didn't seem to be any reason to tell her what happened between us. At least not until Olympia called me last night to say Sofia was dead. I told her the whole story. She said she never knew, but that I should tell you guys everything." Patrick had calmed down. His body was still and his gaze steady. "So here I am."

"Sofia broke up with you?" Greg asked.

Patrick nodded.

"Please give us a yes-or-no answer for the recording."

"Yes . . ." Patrick seemed to hesitate, then continued. "She stopped coming over, didn't return my calls, ignored me when we got together as a group, and acted like nothing had ever happened between us. I got her alone at the Redwood Bar a few nights later and told her I had broken up with Olympia. She got a self-satisfied smile on her face and said, 'Too bad. It's over between us. Leave me alone.' Then she walked away like I was some obnoxious pest." Patrick's face turned red again.

"How did that make you feel?" Greg asked.

"How do you think? She started coming on to other guys right in front of me. Up until that point, I hadn't realized what a manipulative narcissist she was. I tried to let it go—chalk it up to experience. But I couldn't stand to be around her anymore."

"Can you give us some names or descriptions of these other guys?" Greg asked.

"Sorry. They were just guys that happened to be in the same places we were. Different ones every time, as far as I could tell. But for all I know, she could have screwed every one of my friends as well."

"Can you tell us who Sofia has been seeing recently?" Greg asked again, suspecting they were rapidly approaching another dead end.

"No. I felt guilty every time I was around Olympia, for cheating on her, and for not telling her about it. Sofia would hardly say a word to me—acted like I wasn't even there. After a week or so, I made excuses to stop hanging out with any of them." Patrick took a deep breath. "Last night was the first time I'd spoken to Olympia in months."

"Did Sofia ask you for money or payment for sex?" Blake asked.

"She wasn't a prostitute," Patrick stated flatly.

"Did you kill Sofia because you felt used?" Greg asked, carefully watching Patrick's reaction.

"You said I wasn't a suspect!"

"Answer the question."

"No." Patrick looked Greg directly in the eye and spoke

slowly, as if he were trying to stay calm. "But someone else might have, if she played the same game with him." Patrick shrugged his shoulders and leaned back in his chair. "Look, I volunteered this information, because Olympia asked me to. That's all I know."

"Can you tell us where you were this past Friday evening through Sunday morning?" Greg asked.

"I was at work until six forty-five Friday. I was working on a project with two other guys. We went out to dinner afterward and I got home about nine. I worked all day Saturday and Sunday."

"Is it normal for you to work on the weekends?" Blake asked.

"Not if I can avoid it," Patrick said with an irritated frown. "But we're on deadline with this project and we've been working seven days a week for the past month."

"Did anyone see you when you got home Friday night or when you left Sunday morning?" Greg asked.

"I don't know." Patrick seemed sullen at this point.

Greg thought it was time to wrap up the interview. "We'll need the names of the people you worked with on Friday night and Sunday morning." As an afterthought he slipped in one more question. "What do you know about Mabel Garrity?"

"Who the hell is Mabel Garrity?" Patrick looked flustered and a little wild-eyed.

Greg showed him a photo of Mabel.

Patrick said he didn't recognize her.

"Don't you read the paper or watch the news?" Blake asked.

"Sure. I read *The New York Times* online," Patrick replied with finality. "And if you want to ask me any more questions, I want an attorney."

Greg thanked him again for coming in and escorted

Patrick out to sign a statement and leave a sample of his fingerprints.

"Can you believe that guy?" Blake asked, when Greg returned to the interview room.

"What do you mean?"

"Why on earth would Sofia throw herself at a nerd like him?"

"Why didn't Olympia see what was going on behind her back?" Greg countered. "If it really went down like Patrick described it, she'd have to be blind."

"You think Olympia was lying?"

"For the sake of argument, let's assume Patrick and Olympia both had a reason to be angry at Sofia," Greg said. "Would it be a good enough reason for either one of them to kill her?"

At that moment, Liam walked into the interview room. "Were you watching?" Greg asked, nodding toward the video camera.

"Yeah," Liam said.

"What was your impression?" Greg asked.

"He's one stupid bastard for dumping his girlfriend for that tramp. And he's still pissed about the way she used him," Liam said. "But that doesn't mean he killed her."

"So where do we go from here?" Blake asked.

"We need to learn a hell of a lot more about Sofia—find out who she was screwing Friday." Greg patted Blake on the shoulder as he stood up. "Let's drive out to Dry Creek Cellars and talk to her employers."

O n weekends Dry Creek Valley was crowded with bicyclists and tour buses, but on Tuesday morning traffic was light, except for several large trucks delivering late-season grapes.

Greg's cellphone rang shortly after they left town. The LAPD reported they had contacted Valentina Molina and her husband, José. They had confirmed Sofia was their daughter.

Greg called the Molinas immediately. He introduced himself and expressed his condolences. José informed him they were headed for LAX and would arrive in Healdsburg sometime in the late afternoon or early evening. Greg gave him directions to the police station.

He could smell fermenting grapes as soon as Blake pulled onto the crushed granite drive of the winery. The post-and-beam-style tasting room was empty when Greg stepped out of the vehicle and peeked in, but Blake beckoned him to a corrugated metal building off to the side, where a door displayed an "Office" sign. A ruddy-faced man with a friendly smile, wearing jeans, a flannel shirt, and a down vest, came from behind a reception counter to greet them.

"Ted Billings. What can I do for you gentlemen?"

Greg introduced himself and Blake before asking Billings if he was the owner of the winery. He nodded, so Greg continued, "I understand that Sofia Molina was one of your employees?"

"She still is, but she's been AWOL since Saturday. We're very concerned about her."

"I'm afraid I have some bad news for you, Mr. Billings. Sofia was found dead on Saturday morning."

Ted Billings's brow wrinkled. "My God! What happened?"

"We don't know, sir. But it appears to be a homicide. We'd like to ask you some questions."

"Of course." Ted led them behind the counter and through a door into a large, crowded office space, containing several desks. A glass partition separated the office from the wine-making area. Greg could see presses, fermentation tanks, barrels, and a half dozen workers in a large warehouse space. Cold emanated through the glass.

A woman with long blond hair in a ponytail looked up from her computer. Her tanned face was crazed with fine lines around the eyes and mouth.

"My wife, Sigrid." She stood up as Ted introduced Greg and Blake. Greg noticed dirt under her fingernails when she shook hands.

She looked down at her hands and brushed them against her jeans. With a Swedish accent, she said, "Sorry, Detective. I was working out in the vineyard earlier. Are you here about Sofia?"

"She's dead, Sigrid. They think it's a homicide." Ted said.

"Oh, no." Sigrid looked shocked and her eyes filled with tears. "It was not like her to just not show up without a call or anything." Sigrid pulled a tattered tissue out of her pocket and wiped at her eyes and blew her nose loudly. "When her roommate called yesterday, to ask if we'd seen her, I thought something terrible must have happened. But I wasn't expecting this." Sigrid stepped closer to Ted and wrapped her arm around his waist.

"You didn't see any of the news reports about the unidentified body we found Saturday? We were asking for information. We didn't even know who she was at that point." Blake looked from Sigrid to Ted.

"It's the tail end of our crush, Sergeant," Ted said. "We've been busy from before dawn to late evening every day. There hasn't been time to do anything else." He pulled out a chair. "Sit down. Can we offer you water or coffee?"

"No thanks, Mr. Billings, We're fine. How long had Sofia worked here?"

"Over three years. We hired her to pour in the tasting room. She was perfect for the job. She kept the clients laughing and she had a knack for selling wine. Within her first week she'd completely reorganized the tasting room shelves and storage areas. Then she expressed interest in learning more about viniculture and winemaking."

Greg and Blake exchanged a quick look when Ted mentioned her organizational skills. Ted explained that he'd recommended Sofia enroll in classes at the community college. He and Sigrid started introducing her to different aspects of growing and production. As far as they were concerned, Sofia was a natural for the business. Losing her was a blow.

"How'd she get along with the other employees?" Greg asked.

"Fine," Ted answered. "At one point we worried Sofia and the head winemaker might start a relationship . . ." Ted broke off and looked at Sigrid, who nodded emphatically.

"It can cause so many problems if there's a breakup in a small business," she added. "We don't have a policy against it, but we did not want to lose our winemaker—he's one of the best. Luckily, it seemed to fizzle out without any animosity."

"Did she date anyone else that you know?" Greg asked hopefully.

"No," Sigrid answered. "She never talked about her personal life and never brought a date to any of our parties. It was a little odd, because she was so pretty."

At Greg's request, Ted printed a list of all their employees and indicated which ones had worked with Sofia on Friday. Sigrid showed Greg and Blake into a small storage area at the back of the office. Although it was crowded with boxes of wine bottles and labels and dusty metal file cabinets, she was able to squeeze three chairs around an old refectory-style table so Greg and Blake could interview each of Sofia's coworkers privately.

They learned that Sofia joined several of them for lunch in the picnic area on Friday around 1230. She left for the day a little after 1700, without disclosing her plans to anyone.

"I walked her out to the parking lot," one man stated.

He was dressed in a button-down oxford shirt and pressed chinos. His hair was neatly cut and combed and his fingernails had been professionally manicured. Greg wasn't surprised to hear that he worked the tasting room and sales as well.

"I saw her get into her car and drive away." He drove out right behind her, heading north to Ukiah for a family party, and could provide a solid alibi.

Everyone else had worked late, until after 2100. None of them saw or heard from Sofia after she left work.

All of her fellow employees expressed admiration for her work ethic. "Although I didn't like the way she was flirting with my husband at our summer picnic," one middle-aged and overweight woman in denim overalls said. "She was always leading men on."

"But she was a good worker?" Greg asked.

"As far as I know," the woman admitted grudgingly.

When Greg dismissed her, she returned to the wine production section.

"Sofia always lined up the wine bottles in alphabetical order," a college kid who helped out weekends in the tasting room said. "Every time I put one back in the wrong spot, she'd immediately go over and move it. I feel kind of bad now, because I started doing it on purpose—I knew it would drive her crazy. It was just a joke—she was so easy to tease," he added sadly.

Greg thought about the guy who purposely kept putting his beer down in the wrong spot on her coffee table. People could be cruel.

All the employees expressed shock when told them of Sofia's death and had no idea who would want to kill her. They all drew a blank on her relationship history and her activities away from work, agreeing that she kept her personal life to herself.

Finally, they interviewed Henry, the winemaker.

"I understand you dated Sofia at one time," Greg said.

"If you mean did I ask her out a couple times, the answer's yes. She turned me down. And after I saw her with Logan Johnson, I left her alone." Henry was a good-looking, bearded man in his late twenties. He seemed relaxed and unconcerned about the direction the interview was going.

"Who's Logan Johnson?" Blake asked.

"Owns a winery a half-mile down Dry Creek Road—Johnson Family Winery."

"Sofia had a relationship with him?"

"I'm not sure, but I saw her flirting with him." Henry tilted his chair back, balancing on two legs. "The Johnsons had a big party for their daughter's twenty-first birthday. They invited all of us. I asked Sofia to go to the party with me and she said no. I probably wouldn't have noticed her talking to Logan, except I was still a little pissed that she didn't want to go with me. Not to mention he's old enough to be her father, and he's married."

Another available young man she rejected, choosing a married man instead, Greg thought. She seemed to have a pattern of going after unavailable men.

"Were you pissed enough to kill her?" Blake asked.

Henry let the chair fall forward. "No! Shit! More like irritated and confused." He glared at Blake, then turned back to Greg. "It all happened a long time ago. It never was that big of a deal. I met my fiancée, Stephanie, at that party. That wouldn't have happened if I'd been there with Sofia. Everything worked out for the best."

"When was this party?" Greg asked.

"Summer before last. August."

"Do you know if she continued to see Logan Johnson?"

"She never said anything about it and I never saw them together again."

"Did her behavior at the birthday party affect your working relationship with Sofia?"

"Not at all," Henry answered emphatically.

"Where were you last Friday evening until Saturday morning?" Greg asked.

"Working here until a little after nine on Friday. Home by nine thirty—Stephanie was there and can confirm I didn't leave again until four thirty Saturday morning when I came back to work."

"I'm going to need Stephanie's contact information to verify your alibi."

"No problem. Are we finished here? I really need to get back to the wine."

Greg watched Henry leave. He seemed likable, confident. Greg looked at Blake and raised his eyebrows in question.

"I don't think we're going to get anything more here," Blake said, standing up and stretching.

"What do you think their answers say about Sofia?"

"Seems like people either loved her or hated her. My guess is it was one of the latter that killed her."

"Good guess." Greg got up too. "We'd better get back to the station. Sofia's parents should be there by now."

~

Mary looked away from her painting and out the window to watch Lily. She was sniffing around the backyard, her paws wet and muddy from the damp ground. Smiling, Mary turned her attention back to the watercolor of the Russian River, seen from the Healdsburg Ridge Trail. She and Enzo had hiked up there the year before. The leaves in the surrounding vineyards were just starting to turn burgundy and gold. A red kayak floated in the bend of the river. She paused to compare her painting to several photos she'd taken on the hike.

Before heading to the ridge, they'd walked through their new house, checking on the renovations, in preparation for their upcoming move. After a light lunch in town, they drove to the trail. It was a warm, sunny afternoon.

They'd gone out to dinner with some friends in Oakland the night before. Their friends' house had been uncomfortably cold. Enzo was joking around on the hike, saying, "They had all those tiny candles burning, but they weren't giving off any heat at all." Mary laughed so hard she had to stop and bend over to catch her breath. Enzo hugged and kissed her when they reached the overlook. "Are you happy?" he asked.

"Totally. I can't wait until we move up here full time."

Less than a year later, Enzo was dead.

She dropped into a chair. She missed him so much. His silly, dry humor occasionally went right over her head, but usually caused her to burst out laughing at the sheer absurdity. She missed the way he'd patiently tackle life's myriad little difficulties—like spending hours on the computer to figure out why the printer wasn't working, methodically going step by step through help menus and internet searches until he had the problem solved. The way he'd become wholly absorbed in new math textbooks or science fiction novels. His calm demeanor in almost any crisis.

Mary wondered for the umpteenth time if Enzo had felt chest pains prior to his heart attack. Did he just ignore them, assume they were nothing? Or did he know they were serious, but not want to worry her?

She started crying again. Why were their lives torn apart so abruptly? How did other people who lost spouses bear it? How did anyone function when they were wracked with self-pity and despair like this? She knew she should attend a bereavement group. Everyone told her how helpful it would be. But she couldn't stand the thought of all that grief in one room.

After she was all cried out, she took a deep breath, blew her nose, and looked at her painting again. It really was good. The fall colors glowed. She'd captured the afternoon sparkle on the river perfectly. Mary had always been artistic, but during her medical career she'd only had time to dabble at drawing and watercolor. Now that it was a full-time vocation, she could see she was improving.

One of these days she'd have the courage to gather a portfolio together and show it to one of the art galleries in town. She abruptly decided to call the director of the Boys and Girls Club back and tell him she'd teach the art class. Zoey was right. She needed to stop wallowing in sorrow and get out of the house.

∼

The Molinas were waiting in reception when Greg and Blake entered the station that Tuesday afternoon. Greg guided them into the comfortable interview room—the one with the couches, artwork, and soft lighting. He brought them each a bottle of water and made sure the tissue box was handy. He expressed his condolences again and told them they were welcome to view Sofia's body at the morgue at any time. A positive ID would not be necessary, as it had been made from her thumbprint. José was anxious to answer any questions Greg might have first.

"I want you to catch the *cabrón* that killed my daughter."

Greg nodded. "We plan to." He studied the Molinas for a moment. They appeared to be early middle age, prosperous, well-dressed and groomed, but their eyes were red and their lids swollen.

"What led Sofia to Sonoma County?" Greg asked after Blake had started the recorder and opened his notebook.

"She couldn't wait to get out of LA when she graduated from high school." José's voice choked. "She got into San Francisco State, but she didn't take school very seriously. She kept changing majors. We got the impression she attended more nightclubs than classes. When she dropped out of college to work full time, we thought it was a good idea. We hoped that after a year or two of hard work and low pay, she might go back to college and finish her degree."

Greg nodded. His son, Ray, had experienced a lot of bullying in high school, affecting his grades. And Christy struggled to keep up with her classes in college and had to drop out for a semester because of stress. Eventually, they both completed their degrees, in spite of his deficiencies in guiding them. All parents want their kids to succeed, but they don't always know the best way to steer them.

"It turned out to be the best thing she could have done," José continued. "She found her calling at the winery and started taking winemaking classes at the junior college."

Valentina cut in. "I'd never seen her so excited since she was a little kid. Her goal was to own her own winery some-day." Her voice started to break. "I just don't understand why this happened." She reached for one of the tissues. José took her free hand in both of his.

"When you spoke to her on the phone last Friday, what did she say?"

"All she ever talked about these days was wine," Valentina said. "It was the crush, how good the wines were going to be this year, how hard they were all working . . ."

"Did she mention anyone by name?"

"Let me think. She mentioned Ted, her boss—that he was letting her help at all the stations and teaching her as much as he could. Sofia planned to work all weekend. And she told me Olympia, her roommate, was going to Sea Ranch. We only spoke for a few minutes. I didn't know it would be our last conversation . . ."

Greg waited. Both of the Molinas were crying. José put his arm around Valentina's shoulders. It was too horrific to even think about being in their shoes. And God knows how he would react. He couldn't remember crying since he was eight years old—flashing on an image of his mom pressing blood-soaked towels against Colleen's face while he stood to the side, sobbing uncontrollably.

After a couple of minutes, the Molinas apologized for the delay.

"Take your time. We're not in a hurry here,"Greg said. "Do you know if she had any problems with anyone at work? Anyone who was giving her a hard time or didn't like her?"

"Not as far as we know. She had nothing but nice things to say about the Billingses and everyone she worked with," José answered.

"For what it's worth, they felt the same way about her." Greg hoped that would give them some small comfort. "Did she have a boyfriend?"

"She had a lot of friends," Valentina offered. "She was always going to parties, out on dates, but she said there wasn't anyone in particular. She said she was too busy for a serious relationship."

"Do you have any idea who she was meeting Friday night?"

"Do you think that's who killed her?" José's fists tightened and Greg watched Valentina shoot him a worried glance.

"We don't know yet, sir." Greg looked over to Valentina. "Did she sound worried or upset when she spoke to you?"

"No. She sounded happy." Valentina was adamant on that point.

Greg was hesitant to ask, but he had to know. "Did she have any history of mental illness?"

"Absolutely not!" José said.

Valentina just shook her head no and started crying again.

Greg waited until she had herself under control. "Can you think of anyone else she might have mentioned recently?"

"Olympia and her coworkers are the only ones I can think of." It was clear to Greg they were both tired and emotionally drained. He had just one more question, then they'd wrap up for now.

"Does the name Mabel Garrity mean anything to you?"

"No," Valentina said.

"No," José added.

Greg suggested they return to their hotel for the evening. At their request, he offered to have someone drive them down to the morgue the next day. They could come back into the station afterward to sign formal statements and provide a list of all of Sofia's friends and relatives in LA.

One of the forensic scientists, Bob Montgomery, from the lab in Richmond left a phone message while Greg was talking to the Molinas. "We have something interesting from Sophia's computer. Call me ASAP."

Greg called him back as he walked toward his office. Blake had gone home for the night.

"She's been booking hotel rooms at various places around the county over the last year. The most recent was this past Friday."

"Give me the names and dates of the hotels." Greg had reached his desk and eagerly pulled out a notebook.

He wrote down over a dozen hotel names and dates, then asked Bob to hold on, and scrolled through his computer to Patrick's statement. He'd told them his relationship with Sofia had ended over a year ago and he never mentioned that they went to a hotel. She must have been meeting a married man—otherwise, why not just go to his place, like she had with Patrick? No wonder she was so secretive about her dating history.

"Sorry," Greg said. "I had to look something up. Go ahead."

"Switching to the Garrity case," Bob continued, "we found traces of what appears to be black leather near the ends of the rope. Could be from gloves. If you find them, they should be damaged where the rope scraped them. And, if the perpetrator pulled the rope tight enough to scrape some of the leather off the gloves, he might have some bruising on his hands from the pressure."

"Good."

"We found a couple of small fibers in the rope—navy-blue nylon, which could be from the perp's clothing."

"Anything else?"

"We've recovered several different fingerprints from the porch rails and around the front door and doorbell. We have matches with Mary Bransen and Mabel Garrity. The rest are unidentified so far. Lots of hair on the porch, mostly cat. Some from Mabel. But one from a different human source on the shingle siding. It was around the corner from the door, seventy-three inches above the surface, near a light. It's short and light brown."

"Can you run a comparison between all the unidentified fingerprints found in the Molina case and the ones from the Garrity case?" Greg asked.

"Already done—no matches."

"Any similar hairs in the Molina case?"

"Negative. I'll fax these reports up to Healdsburg right now."

Greg walked down the hall to see if Liam was still there. His office was empty and the light was turned off. Greg gathered his things and drove to The Windsor Inn, where Sofia had booked a room for Friday, October tenth.

The receptionist on duty thought he recognized her photo. He thought he remembered her coming in and registering alone, asking for a second key for her husband, who would be joining her later. He was able to confirm that she had made the booking online and secured it with the same credit card she used to pay for the room. Sofia had also requested an online checkout. The hotel no longer had security camera footage for that evening. For their clients' privacy, as well as storage limitations, they erased all digital recordings after seventy-two hours. He was twenty-four hours too late.

Greg met with similar results at each of the hotels she'd booked. He left messages and a photo of Sofia for the manager at each one, asking them to call if any employee remembered seeing her with another person. Five hours later, exhausted and discouraged, he drove home.

Walking into his condo, he threw his jacket over a chair and pulled a beer, cheese, and bread out of the refrigerator. While his grilled cheese sandwich was browning in the frying pan, he logged into his computer. There was an email from his daughter, Christy, in Portland.

She said her husband, Rick's, dental practice was doing well and he had hired an associate. She also sent photos of

Tiffany's first dance recital at her small ballet school and of Emily's most recent soccer game. Greg smiled at the images of his granddaughters, wishing they lived closer so he could see them more often.

Then she invited Greg and Julia up to Portland for Thanksgiving. He accepted for himself and said he'd let her know about Julia. He hadn't seen his daughter since June, when the whole family stopped by to visit with him for two days before driving down to Santa Barbara to see Hana, his ex-wife.

After he finished eating, he pulled out his guitar and settled down in the living room and started playing Tom Paxton's "The Last Thing on My Mind." The song always made him think of his sister, Colleen, and that time before her accident when he still believed in living happily ever after.

7

Ángela brought freshly baked bread to the Wednesday morning briefing. Greg cut a slice heavy with whole wheat and cornmeal.

"One of my favorites," he said, slathering it with butter.

Ángela laughed. "They're all your favorites."

"True," he said, glad she seemed to be in a good mood.

She made bread regularly, saying it helped get her mind off things. Greg knew those things had to do with her abusive ex-husband and her dead baby. He thought she was doing a remarkable job of coping with the loss.

Liam called the briefing to order and Ángela gave the first report, stating that she and Sam had spent time Tuesday afternoon calling all the LA contacts listed in Sofia's phone. None of them had any idea who she'd been dating the previous Friday night, let alone at any time since she'd left for college. Ángela glanced at Greg when she announced none of the contacts recognized Mabel Garrity's name or knew of any connection with Sofia.

After checking the contacts, Ángela and Sam had interviewed staff at the bars and restaurants Sofia had frequented with her friends. Most of the bartenders, hostesses, and wait staff recognized the photos of Sofia and her friends, and even knew some of them by name, but they couldn't or wouldn't tell Ángela and Sam who Sofia had met while she was there, nor who she left with when the partying wound down.

Greg filled everyone in on the interviews at Dry Creek Cellars, the forensic findings, and his unproductive canvass of the hotels the night before.

"Damn," Blake said. "If only we'd been able to check those CCTVs sooner."

"At least the recordings for Friday night," Greg agreed, sharing Blake's frustration.

Greg asked Liam to put out another media bulletin with Sofia's photo, asking if anyone had seen her Friday evening, either in the Healdsburg Market parking lot, at the Windsor Inn, or elsewhere in the county. "Include a list of the other hotels on the nights she stayed there. Someone must have seen something," he said.

A number of phone calls had been trickling into the station about possible sightings and there were speculations about Sofia's and Mabel's murders. But, so far, nothing had panned out. Why were they both killed? Greg wondered again if an opportunist with a grudge against Mabel copied Sofia's murder, knowing a copycat killing would confuse the investigation. But the similarities in the murders were too striking—the same person must have killed both of them.

"Anything else?" Greg asked.

Ángela raised her hand. "It sounds like Sofia might have been a sex addict."

Liam's head jerked up from his laptop. "What do you mean?"

"She seduced her roommate's boyfriend," Ángela said, "had sex with him, and then dropped him shortly thereafter. That guy at the winery said he saw her flirting with a married man at the birthday party. Her roommate told us she'd been picking up strangers in bars, and now it looks like she may have been taking some of them to hotels. She didn't mention any of these men to her parents or her friends. If she wasn't a prostitute, it's the only explanation that fits."

"You mean like a nymphomaniac?" Blake asked.

"Mind you, not everyone agrees that it's an addiction," Ángela said with a worried frown.

Greg picked up a pencil and started tapping it on his notebook. "What would that mean? If she was addicted."

"Well, it's a compulsion to repeat certain patterns of behavior." Ángela looked around the room. "As a way to relieve stress or uncomfortable feelings."

"Her parents said she didn't have any mental health issues," Greg reminded her.

"She's lived away from home since high school," Sam said. "They might not have been aware of her more bizarre habits."

"Is it possible to have both OCD and a sex addiction?" Greg asked, leaning forward.

"I'm not an expert," Ángela cautioned. "But I think it's common to have multiple addictions and compulsions, because the underlying causes are the same."

Greg nodded. "Okay."

"Maybe the thrill of luring men away from their wives or girlfriends is the addictive aspect. In that case, it would be normal to dump them once she had sex with them—mission accomplished." Ángela frowned, as if questioning her own conclusions. "The problem is," she said thoughtfully, "so many people behave that way, how do you know where to draw the line between morally questionable and outright pathological behavior?"

"So many people?" Liam asked.

"People do it all the time," one of the female police technicians who was sitting in on the briefing spoke up. "I've encountered a couple of men like that. Not that I was in a relationship at the time, but they courted me until I was hooked, then dropped me"—she snapped her fingers— "just like that. It's fun while it's a challenge—then it isn't. Just another feather in their cap."

From what he'd heard and observed, there was no way Greg thought Sofia had been normal, but she might have appeared that way to her family.

"This is pure speculation," Ángela said. "I'm not a psychologist. But if Sofia didn't want to do what she was doing and felt compelled to do it anyway, then she may have had an addiction. And she might have felt ashamed of her behavior. Just like a food addict who hides the candy wrappers or an alcoholic who hides empty bottles, she wouldn't have wanted her parents or friends to know about these conquests."

"It could explain a lot of her behavior," Greg said.

"One more thing we should consider," Ángela added. "It's not unusual to have a traumatic sexual event triggering this type of pattern."

"Getting back to the night she was killed," Blake said. "Did she seduce the wrong man?"

"Don't jump to any conclusions about that," Liam said. "At this point it could just as easily be a random killer that caught Sofia in the wrong place at the right time. Follow up on her date Friday night, but keep an open mind. And keep looking for a connection between Sofia and Mabel, because I agree, the homicides are too similar to not be related in some way."

Heading out to Dry Creek Valley again, Greg asked Blake how his son was doing. Blake's wife, Sydney, was a bitch. Greg didn't like her. At the last department picnic, she took offense at something he said, Greg never knew what. She stormed out of the gathering early, dragging Blake and

Jeremy with her. But Jeremy was a cute kid and Greg hoped he was doing well.

Blake made some vague statement about him being fine before pulling onto a stamped concrete driveway at the Johnson Family Winery. A large Mercedes SUV and a convertible Audi Spyder, with its top folded down, were parked in the lot. A majestic oak shaded the Spanish Revival building. A fountain in the center of the entrance patio provided a soothing trickle of water.

In the spacious tasting room, a beefy man in his late sixties and an anorexic-looking woman, expensively coiffed and in a designer pantsuit, broke off what appeared to be an argument. They both turned to glare at Greg and Blake, clearly miffed at being interrupted.

After establishing they were the Johnsons, Greg asked Logan Johnson if they could speak privately.

Logan glanced at his wife, who shrugged and walked outside without another word. Greg heard one of the cars start up and drive away.

Logan gestured toward another door. "Come through here." He led them into an office with an antique Spanish desk, a leather sofa, and a sideboard covered with liquor and wine bottles. The opposite wall had arched windows above open French doors leading out to the patio. The elegant decor was in sharp contrast to the stark, utilitarian furnishings of the Dry Creek Cellars office they'd visited the day before. Pointing toward the sofa, Logan said, "Have a seat. Can I offer you coffee, water?"

"No, thanks," Greg said. "I'm sorry to inform you, but Sofia Molina was found dead last Saturday here in Healdsburg."

"Yeah, I heard. Hell of a thing."

"We understand you knew her," Greg said.

"She worked at my friends' winery."

"Didn't you read her description in the paper? We were

having trouble identifying her," Blake said, with a hint of accusation.

"I only read the sports section," Logan said, managing to avoid the question.

"We understand that you might have known her a little better than just as an employee of your friends," Greg said.

"What are you implying?"

"We have a witness who saw the two of you together at your daughter's birthday party a year and a half ago."

"We were just having a good time. I may have had a little too much wine that night. It was harmless."

"Would your wife corroborate that statement?" Blake asked.

Logan turned his gaze to Blake. "I'd rather you didn't involve my wife in this."

"Why not?"

"Okay. Listen. I'll tell you everything. But I don't want my wife to know about this. She's very suspicious—probably because I left my first wife to marry her. I think she lives in fear of history repeating itself." Johnson flashed a self-satisfied smirk.

Greg took a slow breath to keep any irritation out of his voice. He would let Blake play bad cop. "What, exactly, was your relationship with Sofia?" he managed to ask calmly.

"There was no relationship. We had a quickie at the party."

"How did that come about?"

"Like I said, I had a little too much wine that night. Sofia came on to me. While my wife and daughter were distracted by the other guests, she lured me out back, behind the winery buildings, and we had sex out there. You probably won't believe me, but it was all her idea. I had no intention of hooking up with her or anyone else that night—I mean, it was my daughter's birthday party, for Christ's sake. But on the other hand, why not? She was hot and I'm a healthy man."

Why would she choose an arrogant pig like this? Greg thought. *She must have had a compulsion to seduce married men to make her want to have sex with this asshole.*

"I felt a little guilty afterward—even a little foolish that I was so easily manipulated. And maybe a tiny bit infatuated—like I say, she was hot. But whenever I ran into her after that night, she acted like nothing had ever happened between us, as if she hardly knew me. I was a little disappointed at first, but then, I figured it was for the best."

"Where did you run into her?"

"I'd see her around town. But like I say, she pretty much ignored me. I was definitely a one-off for her."

"Did you kill her?" Blake asked.

"Why would I do a thing like that?"

Logan didn't seem upset by the question or even Sofia's death. He was taking pleasure in the opportunity to brag about his little peccadillo, Greg thought.

"Jealousy? Hurt pride? Fear of her telling your wife?" Blake suggested.

"None of the above. I didn't kill her and I wasn't jealous or hurt. I was a little worried my wife might find out, but she didn't. Anyway, if I was afraid of her telling my wife, why would I wait over a year to kill her?"

This guy probably wanted his wife to find out—he was the type that would enjoy rubbing it in her face. Greg didn't doubt for a moment that Logan had indulged in other extramarital affairs—that's probably what he and his wife had been arguing about when they walked in. "Do you know of anyone else who might have felt some animosity toward Sofia?"

"I don't know anything about her other than the fact that she was a looker and worked at Dry Creek Cellars. We never actually talked to each other except the night of the birthday party and we didn't even say much that night, if you know what I mean."

"Are you sure your wife didn't know about your little rendezvous?"

"Believe me, if she'd suspected anything, I would have caught an earful."

"Any idea who Sofia had been seeing since?"

"No idea," Logan said, shaking his head. "Ask Ted and Sigrid at Dry Creek Cellars."

"Can you tell us where you were on Friday evening?" Greg asked.

Logan paused and looked off to his right. Then he answered, "I was working here until eleven. I had a lot of paperwork and my wife and daughter were in San Francisco, shopping for wedding dresses. My daughter's getting married in December."

"Was anyone here with you?"

"Just until eight thirty, then I was alone—here and at home."

"Would you be willing to give us fingerprints and a DNA sample?"

"Yes. All I ask is that you don't discuss this with my wife."

"I'm afraid that won't be possible," Greg said with satisfaction. "We're going to need to verify *her* alibi."

Charlotte carried a bag of groceries into the kitchen of her mother's house. After placing them on the counter, she took a quick look around to see if anything looked out of place or missing. As far as she could tell, the only disturbance was fingerprint dust everywhere. Charlotte grimaced, hoping it wouldn't get on her clothes, and pulled out the card Detective Davidson had given her for the crime scene cleanup firm.

A full pot of coffee on the counter felt cold to the touch. An empty mug sat beside it, along with an opened loaf of bread. Charlotte could see mold starting to form through the bag. Her mom must have been fixing breakfast when she was killed. For the first time since entering the house, Charlotte felt uneasy. She called the Healdsburg Police Department and requested that a patrol officer come by and check on her and the home as soon as possible. They asked if it was an emergency and she said no.

The only thing missing from the kitchen was her mom, bitter and critical, impatient to get outside and work in her yard. Feeling a little safer after speaking with the dispatcher, Charlotte left her groceries on the tiled kitchen counter and walked down the hall to the bedroom she and her sister, Isobel, had shared growing up. It still contained their twin beds, the wobbly nightstand with the single lamp, and the two small scratched and battered dressers they'd used as children and teens. The frilly pink curtains and bedspreads had been replaced years ago with fading blue-and-green plaids from Walmart. Isobel and her husband, Ben, stayed in this room when they visited from Oregon. Isobel had secretly moaned to Charlotte that the forty-year-old mattresses were saggy and miserable to sleep on.

Charlotte moved down the hall to her parents' room. Memories of an Easter Sunday, when she was four, flashed through her mind. Waking up to find baskets filled with plastic grass, candy, and toys on their nightstand. Running into this room to show their sleepy parents the treasures the Easter Bunny had delivered. Dad pretending he was going to eat their chocolate bunnies while Mom grudgingly grabbed her robe, muttering about being woken too early, and started down the hall to make coffee.

Back in the small kitchen, Charlotte noticed how run down and shabby the place looked. The enamel on the stove and sink was chipped, the grout between the pale yellow tiles was stained or missing in places, and the mid-century furniture was so old it was coming back into style. Too bad it wasn't very good stuff to start with and hadn't been well maintained. The TV was an old boxy tube type, still hooked up to a rooftop antenna.

Why hadn't she noticed this before? It all happened so gradually while she was off in San Francisco, living her dream. This wasn't her home anymore, and she hadn't given it much thought on her obligatory visits. But looking at it through the eyes of a potential real estate agent, she could see it was a tear-down. The rooms were small, with stingy windows and low ceilings. Charlotte had neither the money nor inclination to renovate the place herself.

Mabel always wanted something bigger and better than this two-bedroom, one-bathroom bungalow. But Charlotte's dad had loved their cozy little house. And Charlotte doubted they had enough money to upgrade. The home's one redeeming feature was its large lot. Many of the properties in the neighborhood had added granny units and even small apartment buildings behind their homes.

The garden was Mabel's pride and joy. Unlike her husband and daughters, the garden never disappointed her. Any new owner would probably subdivide and destroy it. Charlotte didn't care. She just wanted to sell the place and be done with it. Her only truly happy memories of the place, like the one from Easter, were vague—from her earliest years.

She'd called Isobel the night before to ask if she wanted anything from the house. Isobel had been more concerned about being considered a suspect and having to provide an alibi than she was about mementos from their childhood home.

"I'm sure it's just standard procedure," Charlotte had said, curling up on her hotel bed, the TV on mute, trying to reassure her sister. "We're the ones who'll benefit financially from Mom's death. They have to suspect us. Better not mention that you've been hoping to expand the barn and buy those new goats."

"Oh, God!"

"Just kidding—sorry. Luckily you were up in Oregon when it happened, so you don't have to worry."

"Still, it feels so ugly."

Charlotte heard Isobel blow her nose.

"It's awful to think she was murdered," Isobel said. "But even worse that they think one of us might have done it."

"Apparently we look even more suspicious because neither of us mentioned the fact that Dad killed himself," Charlotte added.

"Do they think that had something to do with her murder?"

"I'm not sure what they think. But try not to worry. Everything will be fine in the end."

Mabel's doorbell rang, disrupting Charlotte's thoughts. She opened the door to find two uniformed patrol officers on the front porch. She thanked them for coming. The woman, Officer Garcia, asked if she was okay.

"Have you found anything out of place or missing from the house?" the man, Officer Fry, asked.

"No," Charlotte replied. "Sorry to waste your time. I just got really uneasy when I first came in."

"No problem," Fry said. "Would you like us to do a quick search around, just to set your mind at ease?"

"That would be wonderful," Charlotte said with relief, knowing she'd been too spooked to open all the closets and look under the beds. "There's a garage out back as well, if you don't mind."

Feeling much better after the police officers had completed a very thorough search, while Charlotte followed them around, peering over their shoulders, she decided to make a trip to the packing store to get boxes.

Bud Morris, the next-door neighbor, startled her by walking over the lawn from his yard and suddenly speaking right behind her back. Even in his mid-seventies, he still had thick gray hair and no excess body fat. He was wearing tan slacks, a navy pullover sweater, a light blue shirt, and well-polished black wing-tip shoes.

Charlotte quickly recovered and gave him a big hug. She reluctantly moved away from the comfort of his arms. "Hi, Bud."

"I'm so sorry about your mother. It's terrible for you and Isobel."

"Thanks," she said, stepping back. "It is pretty horrible. I still can't figure out why anyone would want to kill her." Charlotte studied Bud's kind face, wondering how much he knew about her parents. "Did you and Genny have some kind of fight with Mom when I was a kid?"

"We did have a falling out, honey. But it was a long time ago. It's all water under the bridge now. You don't want to know about it."

"Actually, I do. Mom wouldn't ever answer any of my questions."

"I don't blame her," Bud said. "She probably didn't want to burden you kids with our adult problems."

"I'm not a kid anymore, Bud. I'd really like to know."

Bud looked at her for a moment, obviously uncomfortable with the topic. Finally, he seemed to give in. "I don't like to speak ill of the dead, but your mom spread a damaging rumor around town regarding Genny's work at the law firm. It really hurt Genny."

Charlotte frowned, as she considered the implications. "Why did she do it?"

"That I can't answer. She never offered an explanation and we pretty much stopped talking to her."

"Do you know why Dad committed suicide?"

"Sorry. He never said anything to me about it," Bud said, shaking his head.

Charlotte let out a big sigh, frustrated and disappointed.

"Is there is anything else I can do to help?"

"There is one thing—can you recommend a good real estate agent? I want to put the house on the market."

"I was hoping you and Isobel might keep it for a vacation home. That way I could still see you from time to time."

"I know." Charlotte loved Bud. He'd always been so nice to her and Isobel, even after her parents stopped socializing with the Morrises. And he was probably lonely with Genny dead and all his kids moved out of the area. But she couldn't see herself coming back now that her mother was gone. "Isobel really doesn't have much time to get away, and with both our parents dying here, the house holds too many sad memories."

"I understand." Bud patted her on the shoulder. "Let me make a few calls—I'll get the names of some good agents and be over with the information later today."

Hugging him again, Charlotte said, "Thanks, Bud. You're a dear."

Bud walked back toward his house and Charlotte started toward her car in the driveway. Why would her mom start a rumor about Genny? They'd been good friends at one time. Charlotte paused with her hand on the car door and looked up and down the street.

Everyone raved about Healdsburg—the surrounding vineyards and redwood forests, the turn-of-the-century houses, the unique shops around the central plaza. But, to Charlotte, a miasma of disappointment and secrets hovered over the neighborhood. And Bud was the last one left alive who was old enough to know what happened back when she was growing up.

Driving down the street, Charlotte was glad she'd left this sleepy little town the first chance she got. She went to college in San Francisco and stayed there. She worked hard to become a highly respected paralegal at Cooper-Severson. She'd been cavalier about romance and marriage, figuring that would come in good time. Her parents' unhappy relationship made her dubious about commitment anyway. Whatever the reason, she found herself in her forties, complacent with her single status.

Many of the men at the firm had asked her out at one time or another. She discouraged the married ones immediately, and confined her dates with the others to firm-related activities or charity events. She had no intention of getting involved with any of them and becoming a target of corporate gossip.

~

Sam and Ángela sat at adjacent desks, working on reports. Except for the two of them, the squad room was empty. Sam stopped typing and leaned back in his chair, arms crossed above his head. "I'm leading a hike at Point Reyes on Saturday for the Sonoma County Hiking Club. If you promise not to make a pass at me, you're welcome to join us."

Ángela froze for a split second. Then she forced herself to relax and reply in the same lighthearted tone Sam had used, "I don't know, Sam. It's probably not a good idea."

"Okay—you can make a pass, but don't expect me to marry you just because you come on to me."

"That's exactly why it's not a good idea." Ángela laughed, in spite of her misgivings. He was funny, and the dimples on each side of his mouth were cute. She'd never tell him that—but she didn't want to hurt him, either, so she tried to play along. "You and I might start dating and then we might fall in love and then we might get married."

"Yeah, you're right. That would be a disaster."

"Seriously, it's too soon. I'm not interested in a relationship right now."

"I know I'm irresistible, Ángela, but you really have to control yourself."

She tried to smile, but her lightheartedness evaporated.

Sam meant well, but after her disastrous marriage to Felipe, she just couldn't face another relationship right now. "I seem to lack the right instincts when it comes to men."

"So you can't even go on a hike?"

Sam wasn't smiling anymore; she could tell he was irritated.

"I know you think you're protecting yourself," he said. "But it looks more like punishment to me."

"I'm sorry." Ángela really was—for both of them.

"I'd just like to see you get out and have some fun."

"I'm not ready to have fun." She turned off her computer and stood up, angry herself.

"Wait," Sam said. She stood there reluctantly, holding the back of her chair. "The offer still stands—I won't consider it a date. You don't even have to drive down with me—you could meet us at the trailhead. You'd just be one of the group. They're nice people…"

Ángela walked out of the room without answering. She didn't want Sam to see the tears spilling down her face.

Dr. Ronnie Harvey, shrouded in her protective gear, was just about to start Mabel Garrity's autopsy when Greg arrived at the morgue. The smell of decay made him feel a little nauseated, in spite of the Vicks VapoRub. He never got used to it. But as they had so little to go on, he was hoping for more information.

Ronnie looked up from her examination of the body. "Two homicides in one weekend? In *Healdsburg*?"

"I know," Greg said, glad for the rubber coveralls they made him wear in the autopsy suite. It felt like a refrigerator in there on Wednesday morning.

"Are they related?"

"We're hoping you can answer that."

Ronnie removed the paper bags from Mabel's hands, took fingerprints, then collected nail scrapings and clippings. "Abrasions and torn nails on both hands, consistent with struggling against the rope around her neck. The bruising looks very similar to the other one." She carefully loosened the rope from Mabel's skin. "There should be a lot of cells on this. We'll check them for DNA. We'll also compare the fibers to the one we removed from Sofia."

"I'd be way ahead if I knew the same rope was used to strangle both of them," Greg said. "Any chance of finding Sofia's skin cells on there as well?"

"That's more of a stretch—but you never know."

Ronnie pulled out a magnifying lens to do a careful search of Mabel's clothing. She tweezed a hair from Mabel's pants, laid it on a slide and covered it with a piece of cellulose tape before placing it under a microscope. "As I suspected: feline. The outer cuticle layer is spinous. Present in cats but not humans."

"She had two cats."

"Not much of a clue then."

Greg nodded.

Ronnie's assistant helped her cut Mabel's clothing and remove it. The front of her body was carefully examined before they turned her over. Ronnie pointed at Mabel's buttocks. "Note the lividity here. She must have been sitting when she died, or placed in that position shortly afterward."

The autopsy continued for another hour.

Because her stomach and small intestine were empty, Ronnie determined Mabel's last meal was eaten at least twelve hours before she was killed. She had been in relatively good health. The cause of death was asphyxiation from strangulation.

~

After three hours of sorting her mother's items for the charity bin, the trash, Isobel, and herself, Charlotte needed a break. The backyard was sunny, so she took her lunch to a small table on the patio. Unlike the neglected interior of the home, the yard was straight out of *Better Homes and Gardens*. The slightly uneven brick patio gave way to a thick, green lawn surrounded by perfectly groomed perennial beds and ornamental plum trees with deep maroon foliage. Charlotte sat soaking up radiant heat from the sun and watching a large bumblebee work the Japanese anemone and chrysanthemums. That was another reason to get the house on the market ASAP—before the last flowers of the season faded and dropped.

Charlotte finished her tuna sandwich and was walking up the back steps when she felt a faint dizziness. Suddenly, she was six years old, standing in this very spot, looking into the kitchen through the glass door. Her four-year-old sister was beside her, trying to get her attention by tugging on her shirt. Charlotte was watching her mom and the Morrises, seated at the kitchen table. Her father leaned against the stove with a puzzled frown on his face. Her mother looked furious. Genny Morris was crying. Bud was talking. Charlotte didn't know what was happening, but, somehow, she knew she was at the root of their distress.

As suddenly as the scene came to her, it disappeared. She was standing on the back porch, one hand on the kitchen doorknob, the other holding her lunch plate. She opened the door and went in. As hard as she tried, she couldn't remember anything else about that day. But whatever happened back then, she knew it wasn't good.

8

C harlotte heard a knock on the door and slowly got up from where she sat cross-legged on the floor, putting books in a carton for the library book sale. When she opened the door, Bud stood on the porch, a piece of paper in his hand.

"I brought over the names of three Realtors," he said, holding up the paper. "I've been told they're all pretty good."

"Thanks. Have a seat. Sorry about all the mess." Charlotte quickly pulled three boxes off the couch and set them on the floor.

Bud handed her the list of names. Charlotte glanced over it, then shoved it into the pocket of her jeans.

"How's it going?" Bud asked, looking around the room.

"It's turning out to be a much a bigger job than I thought it would."

"It's too bad you have to do it all by yourself," Bud said. "Let me know if there's anything else I can do."

"There is something, Bud." Charlotte hated to nag, but there wasn't anyone else who would know. "Did you and my parents have some kind of fight when I was about six years old? Maybe because of something I did? Different from the rumor my mom started about Genny?"

"What do you mean, honey?"

"I'm not sure." Charlotte twisted her lips in an apology. "But earlier today I had this weird memory of being in the backyard and seeing you and Genny and my parents in the kitchen, arguing. I remember being really scared and feeling responsible for the situation, but I don't know why."

"Well, nothing comes to mind right off the top of my head, but I promise to think about it." Bud stood up. "I'd better get going."

After he left, Charlotte quickly called all three Realtors. She made appointments to meet with each of them the next day. She also called the charity shop. The earliest they could send out a truck was Tuesday, so she called her firm and arranged to take off Monday and Tuesday as well.

She felt disappointed that Bud hadn't been able to shed any light on her mysterious flashback. She got the impression that he didn't want to remember. Was it because he didn't care or because it made him uncomfortable? Or had it really happened? Was she reading too much into what she had seen as a child? With a sigh, she went back to sorting and packing.

Greg and Blake sat in Blake's car, checking out the Jameses' large renovated farmhouse, right across the street from Mabel's small shingled bungalow. The white siding, wraparound front porch, flowering perennials, and lawn all looked immaculate. *Good advertisement for Frank's construction business,* Blake thought. He'd love to move from his generic 1960s stucco at the north end of Healdsburg to one of these beautifully restored places in the original town grid.

Noreen answered the door when they knocked. Blake studied her androgynous face, one that would have been attractive on either a man or a woman but for the worry lines on her brow and around her mouth. Greg introduced himself and Blake and asked if they could come in to question her about Mabel. Blake watched her restless hands fiddle with the zipper on her dark blue down vest. Her eyes darted swiftly from Blake to Greg, as if looking for a way out. *Something's going on here,* Blake thought. She reminded him of domestic abuse victims he'd questioned in the past. Sam reported that Mabel had been seen arguing with Frank two weeks prior to her death. Was Noreen worried about that?

She led them into a large, light-filled living room with hardwood flooring and built-in cabinetry around a tiled fireplace.

"Thanks for your time, Ms. James," Greg said, lowering himself onto a large sofa. "We really appreciate your help."

Noreen remained standing. "What's going on? I already told you guys we didn't see or hear anything. I need to pick up my kids from practice."

Her voice was unusually deep and raspy. Blake wondered if she had a cold.

"Please sit down, Ms. James," Greg said. "We won't keep you long. We just need to verify a few things. What time do your kids finish? We could send a patrol car to pick them up and bring them here."

"Not until four," she answered, looking at her wristwatch. "I guess it will be okay, as long as I get out of here by three fifty." She dropped onto a wingback chair and took a deep breath, shoving her hands into the pockets of her vest.

"Could you just go over your morning Sunday?" Greg asked, while Blake opened his notebook and started writing. "Tell us everything that you remember, from the time you woke up until nine thirty."

"We got up at five thirty," she said, looking toward the front window where Blake could clearly see Mabel's house across the street. "At six thirty I drove the kids up to the Alexander Valley campground, for a sunrise service and canoe trip with their youth group. Everything seemed normal over there when we left." She nodded in the direction of Mabel's house. "I dropped the kids off, then I went to my health club—Park Point. I was there for a little over two hours. I drove to the market for groceries. When I got back, the street was full of emergency vehicles. I couldn't get to my driveway, so I parked down the street and carried my groceries to the house." Noreen paused. "One of your officers came by about eleven and questioned me. That's all I know."

"How did you get along with Mabel Garrity?"

"She was a mean old bat," Noreen said, smiling for the first time, as if remembering a funny incident. "She hated our cat, Buster." As if on cue, a huge orange tabby with part of an ear missing walked into the room and jumped onto Noreen's lap, kneading her legs and purring loudly. Noreen started petting him. "We try to keep him inside, but he's fast and sneaky. We had him neutered, but he still insists on fighting with every cat in the neighborhood. Mabel was always complaining about him. I was constantly apologizing and offering to pay any vet bills." Noreen shook her head and leaned forward in her seat. "We tried to be nice. Frank helped her with little repairs around her house. She was pretty old and her daughters didn't come around very often."

"Do you remember a confrontation between your husband and Mabel on September twenty-eighth?"

"I know she caught him in the front yard one Sunday night to complain about Buster. It might have been that day."

"Do you know of any other incidents when Frank and Mabel might have exchanged angry words?" Greg asked.

"No." Noreen was adamant. "Frank never got angry at her. At least, not to her face. It was always one-sided."

"You mean Mabel was always angry?" Greg asked.

"Yes. The kids called her The Wicked Witch behind her back."

Greg changed the topic. "Do you know anything about Cliff Garrity's suicide?"

"Not really." Noreen's expression shifted from amused to contrite. "It happened before we ever moved here. Mabel never mentioned him. But that might explain why she was so negative."

Greg glanced through his own notebook. "And you stated Sunday that you didn't know our first victim, later identified as Sofia Molina?"

"That's correct."

"And you're not aware of any connection between Sofia and any of the Garritys?"

"Not that I know of," she replied.

"Thanks, Ms. James," Greg said. "May we contact you in again if we have any further questions?"

"I'm happy to help, but I really don't think there's anything more I can tell you."

Greg put his notebook away. He and Blake left the house.

"Let's sit in the car and see if Frank comes home anytime soon," Greg suggested.

Sure enough, Frank drove up in a white truck twenty minutes later. "Think she called him?" Blake asked.

"Probably."

"Think she briefed him on her story so their accounts would agree?"

"Maybe." Greg smiled at Blake. They got back out of Blake's car and met Noreen and Frank on the front walkway.

Frank and Noreen James both turned toward them, anxious looks on their faces. Frank was dressed in a plaid flannel shirt, Levi's, and scuffed-up construction boots. He was tall, muscular, and tan, with light brown hair. Greg asked if he had time to answer a few questions. Noreen said she had to go get the kids, gave Frank a quick kiss on the lips, and she hurried over to her Ford Explorer. Blake made note of her personalized license plates: "HBGMOM."

Frank invited them back into the house, this time to the kitchen. He pointed toward chairs at a large, wooden farm table and offered them something to drink. Greg asked for water and Blake declined. Frank took a bottle of water out of the refrigerator along with a bottle of beer. While Frank's back was turned, Blake pointed toward his own hand, then toward Frank. The backyard, visible through French doors, had a large patio area, a basketball hoop and raised planting beds.

Greg complimented him on the house. Frank thanked him, ducking his head in a surprisingly humble way before taking a long swallow of beer.

Blake guessed Frank was in his mid-forties. He tried not to be obvious about checking out Frank's hands—they looked roughed up, possibly bruised a little.

"How long have you known Mabel Garrity?" Greg asked.

"Seventeen years."

"Would you say you had a good relationship with her?"

"I'd say we were neighborly."

Interesting way to avoid a direct answer, Blake thought, *and give a lot of information at the same time.*

"We have a witness who claims that you and Mabel had a heated discussion on the evening of Sunday, September twenty-eighth. Do you recall that occasion?"

"I would hardly call it heated. She spoke to me about our cat. I was putting our trash cans out, trying to hurry, because dinner was ready. I told her I had to run."

"What were you doing this past Sunday morning?"

"I drove over to one of my construction sites. I hadn't been there for a few days. I wanted to check the progress before my crew came in Monday morning."

"What time did you leave your house?"

"Soon after Noreen and the kids left—around six fifty-five."

"And you didn't see Mabel out on her porch when you left?"

"I'm positive."

"Where is this work site?"

"Sunrise Avenue."

"Are those bruises on your hands?"

"Yes . . ." Frank looked down at his hands and splayed his fingers.

Greg remained silent. Blake figured he was allowing Frank time to explain.

"I was hoisting some heavy supplies up to the second story of a house I'm renovating and the rope started to slip. I had to twist the rope around my hands until one of my crew could get over and help me."

"When did this happen?"

"Monday."

"Can anyone confirm that?"

"Sure," Frank said slowly, frowning. "Two of my employees."

Blake, who was busy taking notes, felt Frank's head turn to look at him. Blake paused and looked up, wondering what was going through Frank's mind.

"Were you wearing gloves at the time?" Greg persisted.

"Canvas work gloves." Frank looked confused, like he didn't understand where the questioning was going.

"And where is this worksite located?"

"On Dry Creek Road."

Blake resumed writing.

"Did you know Cliff Garrity, Mabel's husband?"

"No. He died before we moved in." Frank's confusion seemed to ease up as the questioning shifted back to Mabel.

"Are you aware that he committed suicide?"

"Yeah, we heard."

"How well did you know Mabel?"

"Not that well. She was elderly and all alone. I helped her around the house and tried to be a good neighbor."

"Do you have any information that might pertain to her murder?"

"No."

"Did you know Sofia Molina at all?" Blake asked nonchalantly.

Frank hesitated a moment and looked off to his left. "Wasn't she the young gal that was found dead Saturday?"

"Yes. Did you know her?"

Frank shook his head no.

"Would you mind telling us where you were Friday evening?"

Frank's eyes narrowed. "What's that got to do with Mabel?"

"We aren't sure," Greg replied evasively. "We're just trying to get as much information as we can at this point."

Frank hesitated. Finally he said, "Creek Brewing. Then home. Noreen was at a meeting Friday night—I think she got back about ten. The kids were at slumber parties."

Greg looked at Blake, who shook his head, indicating he had no further questions.

"Would you be willing to give us the addresses of those two work sites you mentioned and contact information for your employees?" Greg asked.

Frank shrugged. "No problem."

"Frank's the right height. He's got short, light brown hair. He's got bruising on his hands. He had the opportunity to kill Mabel after Noreen and the kids left Sunday morning. And he could have killed Sofia Friday night before Noreen got home from her meeting."

Blake and Greg were walking across the street to interview Bud Morris. Blake kept his voice low so that no one could overhear.

"Okay," Greg said. "But why?"

"He was having an affair with Sofia? Then she dumped him? He murdered Mabel because of the cat?"

Greg gave a short bark of laughter. "What did you think about Noreen?" he asked.

Blake shrugged. "She seemed a little nervous. Do you think she's afraid of Frank?"

"Maybe she suspects Frank killed both women," Greg said. "Do you believe the Jameses didn't know Sofia?"

Blake thought for a minute. "I don't know. But Frank's hiding something. He could have let that rope slip Monday on purpose to explain the bruising that was already there from strangling both of 'em."

"Let's see what Morris has to say," Greg said.

Bud lived in a small stucco bungalow—about the same size as Mabel's. He invited Greg and Blake inside. The living room had a dingy carpet and darkly upholstered furniture. The floor plan looked like a mirror image of Mabel's. Bud sat, smiling and expectant as if Greg and Blake were making a social call. The old widower must be lonely, Blake thought.

"I understand that you and the Garritys were pretty close," Greg began.

"We bought these homes around the same time," Bud replied, gesturing toward Mabel's house next door. "In the late sixties. Our kids all played together. We were friends for years."

"Did something happen to change that?"

"Yes—Mabel happened."

"What do you mean?" Blake asked, perking up.

"They're all gone but me. The kids have all moved away. It all happened a long time ago." Bud stared at the wall behind Blake's head; the corners of his eyes and mouth sagged. Blake had to admire the way Greg gave Bud space to tell the story.

"Mabel started a false rumor about my wife, Genny," Bud

said. "We tried not to make a big deal about it, because we liked Cliff and the girls so much. But it pretty much severed our relationship with the whole family."

"What kind of rumor?"

"Genny worked for Mitchell and Andrews—they're attorneys here in town. She was the receptionist and secretary. She worked for two generations of Mitchells and they never had reason to question her loyalty."

Greg nodded.

"I don't know if you remember Luigi Romano," Bud said. "He died in the eighties?"

"I vaguely remember all the media coverage," Greg said.

Blake shook his head no. "Before my time."

"He had a huge wine estate up in Alexander Valley and a lot of money," Bud explained for Blake's sake. "He also had four kids who were fighting over the money and control of the winery. There was a lot of speculation about the will. Mabel starting telling everyone that Genny had leaked information about the will to the press. It was a lie, but Genny was distraught. She was afraid Mitchell or Andrews might believe the rumor. Of course they didn't and it all blew over. But from that time on, neither of us wanted anything to do with Mabel."

"Were you angry about what Mabel had done?" Blake asked.

"What do you think? I wanted to punch her right in the face. But, because of Cliff and the girls, I just let it go. Genny did too."

Greg resumed the questioning. "Did you ever discuss it with Mabel or Cliff?"

"No. I didn't know how to bring it up without hurting him and I didn't know how to confront her without blowing up, so I just let it slide. In the end, there wasn't any real harm done."

"Do you have any idea why Mabel would have made up a rumor like that?"

"No, it didn't make any sense. We'd all been such good friends."

Greg waited a few seconds before his next question. "What can you tell us about Cliff's suicide?"

"Not much," Bud answered. "I was just sick when I heard. Cliff was one of the best friends I ever had."

"Do you have any idea why he killed himself?"

"I don't know, but I have my suspicions."

"Would you share them with us?"

"I heard Cliff was having an affair with another woman. I think Cliff felt trapped in an unhappy marriage. I don't think he had the financial resources to divorce Mabel and support her as well as a new wife. I think he just lost interest in living."

"He didn't talk about any of this with you?" Greg asked.

"We had drifted apart by then." Bud shrugged. "And— you know how it is—men don't talk about stuff like this."

"How did you hear about the affair?" Greg asked.

"Gossip. I heard that Mabel found out, confronted Cliff and the gal, and put an end to it."

"Who was the woman?"

"I think her name was Gail. I think she worked as a bartender at Tristan's, on the Plaza."

"Did you know her at all?"

"Not really."

"Did you believe the gossip? Or did you think Mabel might have made up the affair?"

"God, I never thought of that. But I wouldn't put it past her."

"Why's that?" Greg asked.

"I know she started another rumor about a teacher, Frederick Hart, at the middle school. I only heard part of this from Frederick himself, so I may not have all the facts completely right. But she claimed he sexually assaulted one of his students."

"That's right," Greg said, narrowing his eyes. "I remember that case. When did it happen?"

"I don't remember exactly. Maybe ten years ago?"

"Wasn't it all a hoax?"

Bud nodded.

Blake underlined Frederick Hart's name on his notepad.

"What type of work did you do?" Greg asked, shifting gears again.

"I was a high school teacher, in Santa Rosa, speech and drama."

"Can you tell me what you remember about this past Sunday morning?" Greg asked.

Bud looked down at the floor and thought for a few moments. "I always wake up around six. I went outside for the paper. Made coffee. Sat in my kitchen about an hour reading." He looked up at Greg. "Got dressed and worked on my computer until I heard all the sirens and went out front to see what was going on."

"Did you notice anything happening on Mabel's front porch at any time before you heard the sirens?" Greg asked.

"I can't see her porch from anywhere in my house. And I didn't look over there when I got the paper."

"Is there anything you'd like to add about Mabel, her murder, the other neighbors?"

"Not that I can think of."

"At your initial interview you stated that you didn't know our other murder victim, Sofia Molina, other than what you read in the newspaper?"

"Correct."

"Do you know of any connection, no matter how minute, between any of the Garritys and Sofia Molina?"

"No."

Walking back across the street to the car, Blake asked Greg about the sexual assault case at the middle school.

"I'd forgotten Mabel had been involved in that case too. No wonder the Garrity name sounded so familiar. I interviewed Mabel. As I remember, she seemed bitter—like she wanted Hart to be guilty, and was disappointed he wasn't."

~

As soon as Greg and Blake walked into the station, Liam waved them over to Sam Fry's desk.

"Listen to this," Sam said, clearly excited. "Jon Zimmerman lives two blocks down from Mabel Garrity. He was arrested in 'ninety-seven for the murder of his neighbor in San Mateo. An elderly woman who was strangled and robbed."

Greg leaned over to look at the report on Sam's screen.

"Was he convicted?" Blake asked.

"Acquitted. I spoke to one of the arresting officers. The DA believed they had a case, but couldn't produce enough evidence to convince the jury. And they never recovered the stolen goods. I've requested copies of the murder book and trial transcript."

"What's Zimmerman have to say about Mabel?" Blake asked.

"Nothing," Sam said. "We haven't been able to reach him. No one's seen him or his wife since Sunday, but I did find out they both work at the pharmacy here in town. The manager said that they'd been planning a vacation for some time. They're due back at work this coming Monday. I left messages on their cell phones."

"Shouldn't we put out a BOLO on him?" Blake asked. "He could be dangerous."

"Not enough cause at this point," Liam decided. "We have

to wait for him to come back. But then we definitely bring him in for questioning."

Greg reported the gist of their conversations with the Jameses and Morris. Then he asked Sam to search for the file about the sexual assault hoax at the middle school.

"Both Bud and Frank had an opportunity to walk over, ring the doorbell, strangle Mabel, and be back home in five minutes," Blake said. "They don't have alibis. Bud even has a motive."

"The rumor Mabel started about his wife?" Greg asked. "Why wait thirty years?"

"Maybe he wanted to wait until Cliff and Genny were gone," Blake said. "So they wouldn't be hurt further."

"When did Genny die?" Liam asked

"I don't know. Let me look that up." Blake walked over to his own desk to use the computer.

"What if Bud had something going with Sofia?" Sam looked up from his screen. "Maybe Mabel saw them together and threatened to spread rumors about that."

"Why would Bud mind?" Liam said. "Shoot, if I were a seventy-year-old widower and a beautiful, young woman like Sofia wanted to have sex with me, I'd spread the news myself."

"Not if you killed her," Greg said, looking up from Sam's monitor toward Ángela. "Let's get pictures of Bud Morris, Frank James, Logan Johnson, Jon Zimmerman, and Patrick Weiss and put them in a series of photo lineups. We can show them around the hotels Sofia booked. Maybe someone will recognize one of them."

Sam found the report on the middle-school assault and got out of his chair so Greg could read it.

"What's in there about Mabel?" Blake asked.

Greg skimmed through the file, stopping to read some sections more carefully. "I was right—it was all a hoax. Mabel named Hart initially . . ." He scrolled down. "Turned out he wasn't the intended target . . . but he was the first person to report the incident to the principal . . . The story was directed against another teacher . . . retaliation for a D on a book report . . . The child who started the hoax received a three-day suspension . . . Mabel said she overheard two of the students talking about the assault, thought they were talking about Hart, so she called him . . . Claimed she wanted to get his side of the story, which didn't make any sense. Why give him a heads-up if she thinks he's guilty?" Greg shrugged. "In the end it was a big shake-up over nothing. Damn kids."

"Okay. Check in with Hart," Liam said, looking at his watch.

Greg nodded. "I got Mabel's preliminary autopsy report. No surprises. Looks like the same type of rope that was used on Sofia. That can't be coincidence. They're sending it for further tests. Sam, did you learn anything else from the neighbors on North Street?"

"Nothing pertinent."

"What about Mabel's finances?" Greg asked.

"Between her bank account and her investment portfolio she only had a little over sixty-eight thousand dollars," Ángela reported. "No other assets except the house. She had twelve hundred coming in from Social Security every month. That's it for income."

"That's not much to live on," Liam said.

"What about a reverse mortgage?" Blake asked.

Ángela shook her head no.

"A will?" Greg asked.

"She had a revocable living trust. Everything goes equally to the two daughters. Charlotte is the executor."

"Genny died in 2011," Blake said from his desk.

"In that case, why not kill Mabel right afterward?" Liam asked. "It still doesn't make sense to wait another three years."

Greg was thinking. "A house in that part of town with a

large lot is probably worth a million dollars." He turned around in Sam's chair and leaned back, yawning. "We can't rule out money as a motive. Charlotte seemed awfully eager to put the house on the market."

"The Jackson County Sheriff confirmed Isobel's alibi," Ángela said.

Greg thought she seemed subdued this afternoon.

"They're faxing her statement, along with the husband's and the ranch hand's."

"Anything else?" Greg asked. Everyone shook their heads no. Greg looked at Blake. "Let's see if we can catch Tristan McMahan at his bar this evening. Maybe some long-simmering fury from Cliff Garrity's affair precipitated Mabel's murder."

As they left the station, Greg wondered if something was bothering Ángela. It had been only a year since her husband assaulted her and she lost her baby, so it was understandable if she was feeling a little blue. Greg hesitated to ask. As far as he could determine it wasn't affecting her work, and he certainly didn't want to make her feel self-conscious. His ex-wife always knew what to do in these situations, but Greg didn't have a clue.

Which reminded him of Colleen's impending visit. The thought of his sister gave him a horrible sinking feeling in his gut. The skin grafts never matched the color and texture of the rest of her face. What would she look like now? Greg tried to push it out of his mind.

9

Tall redwood trees cast long, cool shadows on the walkways and lawns of the plaza. The late-afternoon sun was still hitting the facade of Tristan's Bar. Reggae music, punctuated with the sound of clacking billiard balls, greeted Greg and Blake as they walked in. After his eyes adjusted to the gloom, Greg could see three guys gathered around the pool table in the back. Tristan stood behind the bar, polishing glasses with a white towel. Otherwise the bar was empty.

"What can I do for you?" asked the light-skinned barkeeper, with a Jamaican accent and big smile. Small, with short, kinky silver hair, he wore a loose, short-sleeved shirt and white chinos.

"Is there somewhere we can talk?" Greg asked, showing his badge. "We need information about one of your former employees. We heard she worked here in the nineties and may have had a relationship with Cliff Garrity."

"I'm the only one here right now," Tristan said, putting down the glass and towel and coming out from behind the bar. "We'll have to stay out here. I was wondering if your lot would be coming 'round to ask about Gail. Have a seat." He pulled a chair from one of the tables.

"So you know who we're talking about?" Greg asked, sitting down.

"This in relation to Mabel Garrity's murder?" Tristan asked, raising an eyebrow.

Greg nodded.

"You're talking about Gail Jones. Ain't no other employee of mine had an affair with Cliff Garrity—that I know of."

"Sounds like the person we're interested in," Greg said, happy they were in the right place.

"She didn't kill Mabel. I can tell you that much."

"How do you know?" Blake asked.

"She wouldn't do anything like that. She's a good woman and has more integrity than anyone I know."

"But she did have an affair with a married man?"

Greg shot Blake a sharp glance.

"I didn't say she was a saint." Tristan sounded a bit huffy.

"What do you know about her relationship with Cliff?" Greg asked, hoping to smooth the interaction out.

"Not much." Tristan appeared to be mollified. "Except he didn't have the gumption to divorce Mabel and marry Gail."

Greg gave that some thought. Was Gail just a fling? Or did Cliff stay with Mabel because of the financial constraints Bud had mentioned? "How did it end?"

Tristan tightened his jaw and seemed reluctant to say more. Blake shifted impatiently and Greg glanced at him again. Rather than rush or redirect witnesses, Greg liked to give them free rein. You never knew what they might reveal if you gave them enough space. He could sense Blake forcing himself to sit still. Patience wasn't his strong suit.

Tristan looked back toward the pool players, as if checking that they didn't need anything or make sure they weren't listening. "Cliff and Gail were seeing each other. Mabel found out. She showed up here demanding I fire Gail. I refused, but Gail felt terrible about the situation. She decided to resign and leave town. I tried to talk her out of it." Tristan shook his head. "I lost the best bartender I've ever had, Cliff ended up killing himself, and Gail eventually lost her son."

Blake and Greg both leaned forward.

"What do you mean by 'Gail lost her son'?" Blake asked.

Tristan's mouth twisted. "She and her thirteen-year-old son ended up moving back to Tracy. That was her hometown and she didn't have much money. She lived with her parents for awhile down there. The boy got mixed up with a rough crowd. Overdosed on heroin about ten years later." Tristan held up his hands, as if to ward off any questions. "Gail never blamed Mabel. She took full responsibility for the way things turned out."

"How do you know?"

"We've stayed in touch. She's living in Sebastopol now. And she hasn't changed."

Greg was dubious about that. How could she have avoided changing, after her son died? She could easily have blamed that on Mabel and harbored a grudge all this time. Anyway, since she was local, they could question her as well.

"Can you think of anyone else who would have a reason to kill Mabel?"

"No," Tristan answered, "but from the way she went ballistic on Gail, I'm not surprised that someone wanted her dead."

After dinner, Blake dressed to go out with his friends. He'd asked his wife, Sydney, to join them, knowing what she'd say. She declined, as usual, not wanting to leave Jeremy with a babysitter. He'd expected that response—and felt irritated and relieved at the same time.

They'd been married about a year before he realized it was her insecurity, bordering on paranoia, that made her so aloof and defensive around other people. He had no idea why she thought everyone disliked her, but she compensated with hostility and sarcasm. Blake kept hoping she'd warm up to his friends and family. God knows they'd made plenty of efforts—but Sydney was unyielding. Gradually, they all started giving her as much distance as possible, while remaining outwardly polite. Everyone had a better time when she wasn't around.

"Don't stay out too late," Sydney said from her seat in front of the TV.

He bent over to kiss her. "I promise. See you in a few hours."

The tavern in Sebastopol was crowded and noisy. The first thing Blake noticed was Denise sitting next to her older brother, Aaron, Blake's best friend. She'd been a skinny little pest when the boys were in high school—always trying to hang out in Aaron's bedroom with them, asking annoying questions, wanting to know what they were doing and where they were going.

When he saw her earlier in the summer, newly graduated from college, Blake's jaw dropped in astonishment. It wasn't just that she'd grown taller and filled out. She had a degree in computer engineering and seemed much smarter than anyone else in their crowd. Even Aaron said he couldn't understand half the things she talked about anymore. Suddenly the tables were turned—Aaron and Blake wanted to hang out with her.

A country singer was performing on stage, so conversation was difficult, but Blake greeted everyone with a smile and a few handshakes. He managed to convey his order to the harried waitress and sat back to enjoy the show.

During the break everyone in the place started talking at once, so it was still hard to hear anyone except those sitting directly on either side of him. Blake found his eyes straying toward Denise. She was laughing and talking with Aaron and a woman Blake didn't know. Denise's friendly, outgoing personality was the polar opposite of Sydney's tight, hostile attitude. Blake wondered if his life would have been different if he had married someone like Denise. Who was he kidding? Someone like Denise wouldn't have looked twice at someone like him. To this day he had trouble figuring out what Sydney ever saw in him.

Denise caught his eye and smiled, lifting her beer in a toast. He raised his in response and finished it off, deciding to head home. It was too noisy to carry on a conversation and he was too tired to sit through another set.

When Blake got up Thursday morning, his son, Jeremy, was sitting at the kitchen table, working on his activity book.

"Daddy! Look! I'm doing dot-to-dot!"

"So I see, little buddy. What's it going to turn out to be?"

"A robot!"

"A robot? But isn't that a zoo book?"

"It's going to be a robot that feeds the animals at the zoo."

"A robot zookeeper? That's a clever idea." Blake smiled up at Sydney. He breathed an inward sigh of relief when she smiled back and didn't bitch that he'd stayed out too late the night before. "Do the animals like having a robot zookeeper?"

"Yes! They would eat the mens, but they love the robot."

"Actually, Jeremy, it looks like it's turning out to be a zebra."

"It's a robot pretending to be a zebra."

"That's a pretty clever disguise for a robot. Is that so the animals won't be afraid of it?"

"Yes! The animals aren't afraid of a zebra. So it can go next to them."

Sydney interrupted. "Jeremy, put your book away now. I need to set the table. Go use the toilet and wash your hands before breakfast."

"But Daddy and me want to work on my dot-to-dot."

"Daddy and I. You can do it after breakfast. Go on."

Jeremy reluctantly closed the book and took it to his bedroom. He came running back into the kitchen two minutes later, explaining how the robot cleaned all the enclosures.

Blake and Sydney had taken him to the San Diego Zoo the previous summer and he had been fascinated with the animal handlers' jobs. Ever since, he'd been saying he wanted to be a zookeeper when he grew up.

After they ate, Blake and Jeremy spent a few minutes on the activity book while Sydney did the dishes. She followed Blake down the hall to the bathroom when he went to brush his teeth.

"I wonder how long this zoo phase will last," he said.

"Probably as long as the robot phase."

"You have to admit, a zoo-bot isn't a bad idea. Probably much safer and more cost-effective than human keepers. But I wonder if Jeremy realizes that by inventing them, he's putting himself out of a job." Blake ran a comb through his hair, then gave Sydney a quick kiss.

"Well, he could supervise the robot keepers or he could design and build the robots, which would be even better." She gave him a longer kiss at the door. "Love you. Have a good day."

He held her against his chest, inhaling the perfume of her shampoo, thinking: if she could be this nice all the time, life would be perfect.

His cell phone rang while he was walking to the car. Not recognizing the number, but thinking it was probably work-related, he answered as he climbed into his SUV.

"Sergeant Maddox."

"Hi, Blake, it's Denise."

She'd never called him before. "What's up?"

"I hope I'm not calling too early, but you left last night before I had a chance to talk to you."

"No problem—I'm just leaving for work. What do you need?"

"I was wondering if you'd like to meet for coffee today. I need to talk to you."

"What's it about?"

"I'd rather not tell you over the phone."

"Is it urgent—a police matter?" Blake asked, concerned.

"No—nothing like that. It's personal. About Aaron."

Blake thought he detected a tiny sniffle. Did she have a cold? "Would after work be okay? Say six? Vineyard Roasters?" He was going to be wondering all day what was going on, but with this murder investigation in full swing, it would be difficult to get away sooner.

Greg pulled on his sunglasses. The sun rising over the eastern hills reflected off his rearview mirror and directly into his eyes as he drove north. Crossing the Russian River, he glanced toward the 1920s metal strut bridge that connected Healdsburg Avenue with Veterans Memorial Beach on the other side. The bridge was temporarily closed for refurbishing and stabilization.

His parents used to bring him and Colleen to Healdsburg every summer until Colleen's accident. They would stay in one of the motels on Healdsburg Avenue, walk across the bridge to the beach, rent canoes, jump off the diving boards, buy hot dogs at the snack bar, and eat Italian food at Chiara's just down the road. After the accident they couldn't risk infection in her wounds. As far as Greg knew, Colleen never swam again. Just one more way he'd ruined her life.

At the station, he found Blake waiting in his office.

"Fax just in from forensics," Blake said. "Rope fibers found on Sofia's neck definitely match the rope embedded in Mabel's neck."

"Great," Greg replied.

Blake hesitated, looking around the office aimlessly. Finally he said, "Is there something going on with Liam? He seems to be acting a little weird."

Greg didn't want to voice his own doubts to Blake until he understood what was going on. "I don't know." Greg looked at his watch. "Briefing's due to start. We'd better get in there."

The department's administrative assistant was in the conference room adding hard copies of yesterday's interview transcripts to Mabel's case book. As soon as the team had assembled, Greg began by summarizing the interviews with the Jameses, Bud Morris, and Tristan McMahan.

Sam had the full report from San Mateo on the Jon Zimmerman case. In 1997, an eighty-three-year-old widow living on Zimmerman's street was manually strangled to death and robbed. She hadn't been wealthy, but she did have some valuable jewelry, art, and stamp collections in her home, insured for a total of three hundred and fifty thousand dollars according to records that her children later produced. All of those items were missing and never recovered. There was no sign of forced entry or disturbance in her home where she was found, leading the detectives to suspect the perpetrator was someone she knew.

Most of the surfaces in the house had been wiped free of fingerprints. After an extensive investigation, Jon Zimmerman seemed the most likely suspect, primarily because one of the other neighbors swore she saw him go into the victim's home the night of the murder.

"Several neighbors testified Zimmerman had gone out of his way to befriend the victim," Sam read. "He had no alibi for the night in question—his wife had been out of town visiting relatives. He was arrested and the judge refused bail. But he was acquitted for insufficient evidence.

"Apparently the jury was convinced the neighbor couldn't accurately see who walked into the victim's house that night.

Afterward, Zimmerman refused all interviews. The case was relegated to the cold files and never solved."

Sam went on to explain that upon his release from jail, Zimmerman and his family moved to Coeur d'Alene, Idaho, to start a new life. But recently, they had relocated to Healdsburg. Zimmerman had no criminal record prior to the San Mateo incident, nor any since.

"He's got to be our man," Blake said, giving Sam a thumbs-up. "Let's put out a BOLO on him now." Blake grabbed his notebook and stood up.

"Hold on," Liam said, motioning Blake to sit down. "Any unsolved murders in the Coeur d'Alene area while he was living up there?"

"Nothing," Sam answered.

"You haven't been able to contact him yet?" Greg asked.

"Negative."

"Let's give him until Monday," Liam said. "If he doesn't show up for work we'll put out the BOLO then."

"But he's probably on the run," Blake said. "We're just going to let him get away?"

"At this point he's just a witness," Liam said calmly.

"What would his motive be?" Ángela asked. "Nothing's missing from Mabel's house, as far as we know. Plus, Mabel was strangled with a rope, not manually."

"You're right," Greg agreed, relieved to see Ángela looking and acting more animated and engaged than she had been the day before. "But, the Zimmermans do live on Mabel's street. We have to talk to them for that reason, if nothing else."

Greg held up his hand to stop Blake from interrupting. "And, I agree, it's quite a coincidence—two elderly women, living on the same street as Zimmerman, strangled to death." Greg looked back toward Sam, sitting next to Ángela. "Where are we with the rest of the neighbors?"

"We've contacted everyone except Zimmerman. Nothing

else of significance to report." Sam looked toward Ángela, who nodded and started her report.

"I reached the rest of Sofia's relatives in LA. None of them know who she's been dating. But, I found out that when Sofia was seventeen, she was raped."

Greg knew her parents hadn't mentioned that in their interview.

Several people started to speak at once. Ángela waited until they were quiet again. "The only person who knew was *la tía*—her aunt—Lupe Juárez. Sofia made her promise not to tell anyone. I don't think she would have told me, except Sofia's dead—so it didn't matter anymore. According to Lupe, the perpetrator was a boy by the name of Luis Berra. Sofia knew him from school. They were at a party and she thought he'd slipped something into her drink."

"Did she press charges?" Greg asked.

"No—against Lupe's advice. She kept it secret from everyone and tried to get on with her life. Lupe said she noticed Sofia getting compulsively neat a few months after that." Ángela looked up from her notes. "I'm guessing some of her sexual behavior patterns stem from that assault as well."

Greg nodded—made sense.

"Lupe tried to talk her into at least getting some counseling. Again, Sofia refused—insisted she was fine."

"Where's Berra now?" Liam asked.

"Prison." Ángela looked grim. "Kidnapping and rape—a year after he allegedly raped Sofia. He was eighteen by then —the victim was fifteen. He's currently serving a twenty-five-year sentence."

"I wonder if Sofia knew about that," Greg said.

"She did," Ángela answered. "Juárez told her."

"Damn." Greg wondered how much that knowledge preyed on Sofia—by not pressing charges, she'd left Berra free to hurt more girls.

There weren't any more questions, so Greg started handing out assignments. He suggested that he and Blake split up so they could cover more ground.

Blake should take Sam and start with Mitchell and Andrews, to find out more about the rumor Mabel spread about her next-door neighbor, Genny Morris.

Greg said he would contact Gail Jones and Frederick Hart. Then he and Ángela would take photo lineups of Jon Zimmerman, Logan Johnson, Frank James, Patrick Weiss, the other two men Olympia and Sofia used to hang out with, and all of Sofia's male coworkers to the hotels she'd stayed at in the past six months, on the off chance any of them were recognized.

~

The Mitchell and Andrews law firm was located in a Queen Anne home built in the late 1800s and converted to offices seventy years later. Blake and Sam climbed the wooden steps, to the wraparound porch.

When they walked in the young receptionist was speaking on her Bluetooth headset. She had multiple piercings in her ears and a silver ring through her right eyebrow. She raised a finger asking them to wait, fed some envelopes into a printer, then completed the call.

"May I help you?" She smiled politely, giving them her full attention. Her name plaque read Amy Meyer.

"Yes. We'd like to speak to Mr. Mitchell or Mr. Andrews if we could," Blake said.

"Well, Mr. Andrews passed away, but Mr. Mark Mitchell, Jr. is in this morning. May I ask what this is concerning?"

"A former employee—Ms. Genny Morris."

"And you are?"

"Sergeant Maddox, Officer Fry, Healdsburg Police."

"Let me check with Mr. Mitchell." She clicked around on

her computer screen for a moment. "Mr. Mitchell? I have a Sergeant Maddox and Officer Fry from the Healdsburg Police here. They'd like to speak with you about a Genny Morris?" There was a short pause. "Yes, sir. That appointment isn't until eleven. Nothing before then." Another pause. "Thank you, sir." She smiled at Blake. "Mr. Mitchell will be right out."

"Thanks, Ms. Meyer."

"Have a seat." She indicated some upholstered chairs behind them in the recess of a bow window, then went back to her work.

Mitchell came out before they had a chance to sit down. He was in his early forties, wearing a suit and tie, his handshake warm.

"Thanks for seeing us, Mr. Mitchell. We have some questions about Genny Morris. She used to work here?"

"Yes, of course. Come into my office."

It looked like Mitchell's office had originally been the home's parlor. There were built-in, dark wood bookcases on either side of a fireplace. A large antique desk filled most of the center of the room. Several robust indoor plants sat in front of the lace-curtained windows.

"What's this all about?"

"We're investigating Mabel Garrity's homicide," Blake said as all three of them took seats in wingback chairs. "Are you familiar with the case?"

"Somewhat," Mitchell confirmed.

"Genny's name came up in the course of the investigation —regarding an incident which occurred sometime in the eighties. Would you have been working here then?"

"No. I didn't join the practice until 'ninety-two, but Genny was still here."

"Do you remember a rumor going around about Genny in reference to the will of a Mr. Luigi Romano?"

"No. But my father might remember something about

that. He's retired, but lives here in town. Would you like his phone number?"

"Yes, sir," Blake replied.

While Mitchell wrote the number on the back of one of his business cards, Blake asked, "Do you know Bud Morris, Genny's husband?"

"Only from our office parties. He's always seemed like a great guy."

"Did Mr. Morris ever express any animosity about Ms. Garrity?"

"Not that I know of." Mitchell's brow furrowed.

"Is there anyone else besides your father I could speak to who worked here at that time?"

"Dad's the only one left. It was always a small office. None of my current staff was working here in the eighties."

"Did your firm ever do any work for Sofia Molina?"

"I don't think so. But let me double-check with Amy." Leading Blake and Sam back out to the reception area, Mitchell asked Amy to look and see if there was a record in their files for Sofia.

She checked her computer. "I'm not finding anything."

"Did either of you know Sofia, personally?" Blake asked Mitchell and Amy.

They both shook their heads no.

Greg and Ángela spoke to the middle-school secretary who told them Frederick Hart had a prep period at ten twenty. They arranged to meet Hart in a small, private conference room next to the principal's office. Hart had a generous smile and the well-defined muscles of a serious weight lifter. Greg guessed that he would be popular with his students but also able to maintain discipline, both necessary qualities in a successful middle-school teacher.

"We want to ask you about an incident in the past involving Mabel Garrity. Do you remember her accusing you of assaulting one of your students?"

"How could I forget? Right after I started teaching. Talk about life-changing moments." Hart gave a wry smile, carefully studying Greg's face. "You were the detective on the case."

Greg nodded.

"How do you defend yourself against an accusation like that?" Hart glanced toward Ángela, as if to gauge her reaction. "Everyone believes you're guilty. Luckily, my principal called the police immediately. It turned out to be a hoax directed at another teacher because of a bad grade." Looking back at Greg, he asked, "Don't you have all this in your files?"

"Yes, but why did Mabel Garrity name you as the perpetrator?" Greg asked. "Did she know you?"

"As far as I know, we never met. She called me and said she'd overheard a couple of girls talking about a sexual assault on one of their friends, purportedly committed by an English teacher at the school. I have no idea why she thought they were talking about me. She said she was going to report me to the principal. I told her she should report it—that the claim had to be investigated."

Greg remembered all that. And he remembered Hart's outwardly calm and cooperative demeanor in his interviews. Hart never expressed any animosity toward Mabel or the kids involved.

"Mabel didn't answer me at first," Hart continued.

It took Greg a moment to figure out what Hart was saying. Ángela was busy scribbling notes.

"I thought she might have hung up, but when I asked if she was still there she said yes. She asked me if I really wanted to risk having my reputation ruined."

Greg sat up. He didn't remember this from the initial investigation.

"I answered that if she was calling me, my reputation was already damaged and only an investigation could clear it. Then she did hang up. I called the principal myself right away, but I didn't know the names of the students involved."

"Why didn't Mabel call the principal or the police directly?" Greg asked. But he knew: blackmail—had to be.

Hart didn't bother to spell it out. "She started spreading the rumor around town right after she talked to me."

"Are you wealthy?"

"No way!" Hart took a breath and lowered his voice. "All the parents were up in arms, asking for my head. My principal put me on administrative leave. I was afraid I'd lose my job and be labeled a sex offender for the rest of my life. It took you guys a week to uncover the student who started the whole thing—she wasn't even in my class—and she admitted she'd invented the whole story—the assault never happened."

This was obviously still a very bad memory. Hart continued to show admirable restraint.

"You must have been pretty angry," Greg said.

"No kidding."

"Why didn't you mention blackmail when we interviewed you ten years ago?"

"Mabel never actually asked for money and I didn't have any proof."

"Did you have anything to do with her homicide?"

"No."

"Did you know Sofia Molina?"

"I read about her in the paper—I didn't know her."

10

T he palatial stucco home on Matheson Street looked like
it had been built in the 1930s. The green lawn and
hydrangea shrubs reminded Blake of Mabel's garden a few
blocks away. But unlike Mabel, he figured these people didn't
do the gardening themselves.

Mark Mitchell, Senior, answered the door.

"You had questions about Genny and Bud Morris?" Mark
asked, after introductions. "Come through here. My wife is
making coffee and will join us shortly."

Blake and Mark sat in two large, upholstered chairs on
either side of a fragrant wood fire. Sam took a seat on the
couch. Several lamps brightened the room. Persian rugs
covered much of the dark oak floor. Behind the sofa, a narrow
table held a large bouquet of autumn flowers.

"Beautiful home you have here, Mr. Mitchell." Blake said,
looking around, impressed.

"Thank you. We were able to buy it right after our son was
born. I couldn't afford it today, but back then, when Healdsburg was just a little farm town, these old places were pretty
reasonable."

Not for my parents, Blake thought, smiling stiffly.

"However, I don't think you're here to discuss real estate. Why don't you tell me specifically what information you're looking for. And please, call me Mark."

Just then a gray-haired woman carrying a laden tray, came into the room.

"Ah, here's Rose, my wife." Mark stood up and took the tray from Rose and placed it on the coffee table. "I've asked her to join us. She may be able to help answer some of your questions. She served as office manager for the firm until we retired."

Rose was lean and tan, with a pleasingly weathered face. As she shook Blake's hand and passed in front of him to take a place on the sofa he smelled a fusion of perfume, cigarette smoke, and alcohol. Considering it was still mid-morning, Blake wondered how reliable her information would be.

"We've been informed Mabel Garrity started a rumor about Genny Morris, saying she leaked information about Luigi Romano's will back in the eighties, before it became public record. I'd really appreciate anything you can tell me about that incident."

"Will you take a cup, Sergeant?" Rose asked while pouring the coffee.

"Thanks, I'd love some. Black, please." Bending forward to accept the cup from Rose, he said, "Specifically, I want to know anything you can add to this story and also get your assessment of Bud Morris."

Mark spoke first, while Rose poured a cup of coffee for Sam. "I've known Bud since we hired Genny. He's a good man."

"I agree." Rose had a slight quaver in her voice. "Bud and Genny were both hurt by the rumor, but we all knew it wasn't true. And, although there was a lot of speculation in the papers, the facts of the will were not leaked. Everyone was shocked when the will was made public and Mr. Romano had left his entire estate to several Catholic schools in the area. His children were furious. Of course, they contested, but they lost their case. Each of them had hoped they would be his primary heir, but they were all cut out completely. They were a sorry bunch of freeloaders, and their father wanted his money and assets put to better use for the good of the community."

"Did he specify that in the will?" Blake asked, surprised the old man would treat his children so callously, no matter how undeserving they were.

"Not in those exact words," Mark answered.

"But the implication was clear," Rose said.

"Do you have any idea why Mabel would start a rumor that wasn't true?"

"You have to understand something about Mabel," Rose said. "She had high social aspirations. I think Mabel was always pressuring Cliff to better himself. Back in the sixties and seventies she joined a number of local clubs, including the Garden Club, which is how I got to know her. It was clear Mabel wanted to move in more elite circles and Cliff didn't. She forced him to attend charity events—balls, that sort of thing. You could see he was uncomfortable. I don't mean to sound like a snob, but it was obvious they were both out of their milieu."

She did sound like a snob, Blake thought with an inward smile. He bet she treated Mabel like a servant in the Garden Club.

"But I don't know why she targeted Genny," Rose went on. "No one believed the rumor for a minute. The whole incident kind of backfired and hurt Mabel's reputation. Her efforts at social climbing started petering out after that."

Rose looked at her husband, a satisfied smile on her face. "Anything you want to add?"

"Rose is correct," Mark said, putting his coffee cup on its saucer. "As soon as we heard about the rumor, we advised Genny to just ignore it and let it blow over. She was an exemplary employee. I never really knew Mabel—not like Rose did. But all this happened so long ago. You don't think her murder is connected, do you?"

"Do either of you know if Mabel had spread any gossip recently?"

"There might have been something about a teacher at the middle school," Rose said. "But that was quite a while ago, also. Mabel dropped out of the Garden Club after Cliff killed himself. I haven't heard anything about her for years."

"I haven't either," Mark confirmed.

"Well, thank you both for your information." Blake stood up, inwardly shuddering at the thought of Sydney locking horns with either Mabel or Rose. That would not be a pretty sight.

During the forty-five-minute drive to Sebastopol, Greg and Ángela discussed their impressions of Hart. Ángela agreed that Hart seemed to have handled the whole business with remarkable restraint. He obviously understood that even an unfounded rumor of sexual assault in a school could ruin his life.

"It's remarkable he has such a tranquil personality."

It's more than that, Greg thought. *The guy doesn't seem to have any guilty skeletons in his closet.* "He's lucky the girl recanted. Or he might have ended up in prison."

When they got to Gail Jones's apartment, only her sad, brown eyes gave any hint of her losses. She wore loose-fitting linen clothes and Birkenstocks. After she invited them in, Greg estimated she had to be at least fifteen years younger than Mabel and Cliff Garrity.

The furnishings didn't match, as if they'd been purchased at different times from different stores. But the overall effect in the tiny apartment struck Greg as cheery and inviting. As he and Ángela took seats, Greg explained why they were there.

"I read about Mabel in the paper," Gail said. "I thought you might want to talk to me at some point."

"Could you tell us about your relationship with the Garritys?"

"Sure." Gail pulled a red throw pillow from behind her back and crossed her legs. "Tristan told me about his interview."

Greg didn't mind that, as long as they both told the truth. So far, he had no reason to doubt either of them.

"Cliff was a regular at the bar. And a gentleman. One night he stayed later than usual because his wife was in Oregon, visiting their daughter. It was a quiet night and we got talking. Before I knew it, it was closing time. Cliff offered to walk me to my car. When we got there he kissed me." Gail paused, smiling wistfully, rubbing her thumb across the edge of the pillow. "I hadn't been expecting that."

"Go on," Greg said.

"Ricky, my son, was up in Ukiah with my ex-husband, so I invited Cliff to come home with me. After that, we got together whenever we could, which wasn't often. Cliff wanted to divorce Mabel, but he felt he was being selfish."

"How do you know he wanted to divorce Mabel?" Greg asked.

"He told me. But he was struggling with the decision." Gail looked down at the pillow. "Of course, we were never going to have a happy ending. Cliff wasn't callous enough to leave her—that's partly what I loved about him."

"When did this all happen?" Greg asked.

"Nineteen ninety-one. It didn't take Mabel long to discover what was going on. She caused so much trouble that I decided to resign from my job. I didn't want to hurt Tristan's business. And Mabel was phoning me all hours of the day and night, telling me to leave Cliff alone. I figured the best amends I could make was to leave town. I found some work down in Tracy, which is where my folks lived." Gail's lower lip trembled.

"We heard things didn't go well for your son after the move," Greg said.

"He died of a heroin overdose ten years ago." Gail's eyes filled with tears. She pulled a tissue out of her pocket and dabbed at them. "Ricky's dad is an addict too. But I can't help wondering, if I hadn't had that affair with Cliff, would things have turned out differently?"

Greg waited, giving her space to reveal more.

"To make everything worse, Cliff's relationship with Mabel never recovered. I think, in the end, he killed himself because he couldn't go on living with her."

"How would you know that?" Greg asked. "Did you keep in touch with Cliff after you moved?"

"No." Gail paused, twisting the pillow in her hands. "I'm just going by what Tristan told me." She paused again, looking thoughtful. "All three of us are partly responsible for what happened—me, Cliff, and Mabel. But I don't think this could have had anything to do with her death."

Gail didn't seem to be sugarcoating the story to make herself sound less culpable, but she certainly had reason to hate Mabel. "What made you move to Sebastopol?" Greg asked.

"Both my parents passed away. I wanted to move back to Sonoma County."

Greg nodded, thinking this was probably the extent of her involvement in the case. "Did you know Sofia Molina?" he asked.

"Who?"

"A similar homicide—just before Mabel's," Greg said.

"Oh, I guess I did hear about that on the news, but I didn't remember her name." Gail looked from Greg to Ángela, a question on her face.

"I take it you didn't know her," Greg said.

"Sorry—no."

"Can you tell us where you were Sunday morning?" Greg asked.

Gail's expression turned a little sad. "Do I need an attorney?"

"No. It's just routine. We're asking everyone with a connection to Mabel or Sofia," Greg explained.

"Here," Gail said. "Alone."

Greg thanked her and they left. On the way to their car, Greg and Ángela discussed Gail's interview. She had a couple of good reasons to be angry with Mabel, but why wait so long to take revenge? And Gail seemed calm and cooperative, not even going on the defensive when Greg asked her where she was Sunday morning. If she did kill Mabel, she was a good actor.

"I don't think either she or Hart had anything to do with Mabel's murder," Greg concluded, frustrated by two more dead ends. "We're not making much progress, are we?"

"Not yet." Ángela grinned, put on her sunglasses, and opened the driver's-side door. "This is all ancient history. We need to find out who Mabel's been tormenting this year."

Greg's cell rang while he was buckling his seat belt. It was Bob Montgomery from the forensic lab. "We found a match for the fingerprints lifted from Mabel Garrity's house shingles —where those hairs were discovered."

"And . . ." Greg said, holding his breath.

"Frank James," Bob said. "We lucked out—his fingerprints are on record for his contractor's license."

"If I remember correctly, Frank said he helped Mabel around the house." Greg looked at Ángela to confirm.

She took out her notebook and leafed through it quickly.

Greg thanked Bob and ended the call.

"You're right," Ángela said. "That could explain his fingerprints."

"That's right where the perpetrator probably hid—so he could sneak up on her." *Damn.* Frank could claim the fingerprints were left when he was doing a home repair. "What are we missing?" Greg ran his hands through his hair. "We need a solid breakthrough."

~

Ángela and Greg interviewed the staff at each of the hotels Sofia had booked in Rohnert Park, Santa Rosa, and Windsor. The bartender at the Eastside Inn said he thought he remembered Sofia having a drink with a man in August, but he couldn't remember what he looked like.

"The only reason I remember her," he smirked, pointing at Sofia's picture, "is that she had a super hot body." Ángela thanked him politely, internally shrugging off his arrogance, wondering what Greg thought about the guy's attitude.

Ángela heard it all the time in her line of work. Sofia probably thought she was taking revenge on these men—didn't see how she was feeding their entitled sexist outlooks.

More to the point, the bartender didn't recognize any of the photos in the lineups.

Ángela tripped on a patch of uneven sidewalk as they walked back to the vehicle.

Greg quickly reached out his hand to keep her from falling. "He's a pig," Greg muttered under his breath.

Ángela shrugged, not sure she'd heard him right. She didn't need any special coddling just because she was a woman, or even worse, because of her personal history. She could handle blatant sexism. It was sympathy that squashed her.

A few staff members at the other hotels remembered checking Sofia in. They said she'd registered alone and without luggage. In each case, she claimed her husband would be joining her later. They didn't recognize any of the photos either.

Ángela drove Greg back to Healdsburg, listening to the police radio. Things had been quiet in town—a few minor traffic violations, a group of truant high school kids smoking marijuana at a picnic table at Memorial Beach, a city maintenance worker discovering the copper wire had been pulled from conduits in Badger Park, probably during the middle of the previous night.

Greg rode shotgun, writing up interview notes on his laptop, engrossed in his work. The dispatcher broke into the radio traffic with an urgent announcement. An apparently deranged man was harassing tourists in the plaza, screaming at them to leave the area.

Ángela heard Sam respond. "Heading south on Healdsburg Avenue at Plaza Street," he said. "ETA thirty seconds."

Ángela took the Center Street exit and turned on her siren and flashers, to give Sam backup. There was a small crowd gathered in the center of the plaza. Ángela and Greg climbed out of the car and approached quickly.

Sam was on the other side of the crowd—walking slowly toward the disturbed man, who was standing near the fountain. His hair was long and greasy and his clothes a dirty olive green color. He waved his arms and shouted at the crowd. Sam motioned for everyone else to move back. Ángela and Greg gently urged the crowd to disperse. Sam took a couple more steps forward, speaking in a low, calm tone. It wasn't long before he had the man sitting in the back of a patrol car, wrapped in a warm blanket, ready for transport to County Mental Health Services in Santa Rosa.

On her way home from work, Ángela replayed the scene in her mind—how respectfully Sam handled the mentally ill man. Ángela was so tired of being alone. But the thought of another relationship made her heart race and her palms sweaty. She just wasn't ready to put herself in the path of danger and heartbreak a second time. Not that she believed for a minute Sam would be anything like Felipe. But you never knew.

Sam was the only guy who'd made even the slightest overture since her divorce. Ángela wasn't like Sofia—she didn't attract men like flies—and she certainly didn't hunt them down the way Sofia had. Ángela considered herself plain and shy. She'd been so quiet in high school and college that she'd largely gone unnoticed by the opposite sex until she met Felipe. Back then it felt like a liability, but now she was grateful—realizing it saved her a lot of hassle.

She'd expected Sam to lose interest as soon as she turned him down the first time, over six months ago, but he hadn't. He never pressured her, or got mad when she said no, just carried on as friendly as ever. But, under the circumstances, she knew she should request a new patrol partner, just to defuse the situation. The problem was, she didn't want to get him in trouble. Besides, she liked working with him better than she did anyone else in the department.

Blake arrived at Vineyard Roasters promptly at 1800. Denise waited for him on a small, vinyl couch. The coffee shop was almost empty. Hawaiian music played softly in the background. He waved to her from the counter and ordered a coffee before sitting down.

Denise wore snug jeans and a long sweater. Her thick, dark hair was pulled back from her face by a white fabric headband. Blake couldn't detect any makeup.

"How's the job search going?" Aaron had told him Denise still hadn't found a job since she'd graduated and moved back home last June.

"I have an interview with Vortex in Petaluma on

Monday," Denise said. "Keep your fingers crossed." She tucked her legs up under her on the couch.

"I will. So, what's up?"

"I'm planning a surprise birthday party for Aaron Saturday night. At my parents' house. Sorry it's such short notice, but I was hoping you could help me."

"Are you sure that's a good idea?" Blake could remember a surprise party during his college days that had backfired miserably. The birthday guy had shown up late and drunk, and his girlfriend was furious. Blake had no desire to go through that again.

"Why not?"

"Not everyone appreciates being surprised. Or they find out about it ahead of time. Then they have to act surprised, and it's obvious they're faking it."

"Okay, I get your point, but I'd still like to try. As far as I know, Aaron's never had a surprise birthday party. My parents are okay with the idea."

"Fine—just don't say I didn't warn you. What do you need me to do?"

"Help with the guest list. I haven't been back long enough to have contacts for all of his friends. Some advice on music would help, too."

"Sure, Denise, I can do that. But why such a big deal for a thirty-first birthday?"

Denise looked down at her coffee. Her face crumpled. Tears ran down her cheeks.

"Denise? What's wrong?" Blake asked, a kernel of dread forming in his chest.

"Don't tell him I told you, but he has leukemia. We're hoping he'll respond to treatment, but this could be his last birthday."

Blake froze. Aaron had been his best friend since they were toddlers. They'd attended the same schools and graduated from high school together. They were more like brothers than friends. "Shit, Denise. Your parents must be devastated. You all must be."

"I think we're still in shock—we just found out on Tuesday. He asked me not to tell anyone yet. I'm sure he'll be telling you soon."

"Damn." Blake felt a familiar stab of horror and sorrow remembering his dad's losing struggle with pancreatic cancer ten years before. "What kind of treatment do they plan?"

"Chemo and radiation, starting Monday, hopefully followed by a stem cell transplant. It's going to be a long, drawn-out process. That's another reason I want this party to be really special. Once the treatments start, he won't be feeling very well."

"Anything I can do for the party, or to help in any way, just let me know."

"Thanks, Blake." Denise smiled and squeezed his hand. "Would you call his friends and invite them? Tell them it's a surprise—not a word to Aaron. And I want them at my parents' house by five thirty. Aaron thinks it's just going to be a family dinner. Do you have any suggestions for the music?"

"I'll bring music. And why don't we make it a potluck? That way you and your parents don't get stuck doing all the work. I'll organize it with the guests. You provide the paper goods, decorations, and the cake."

"Oh, Blake, that would be wonderful. But I hate to dump all that on you."

"It won't be a problem. I want to do it for Aaron and your family. I'll start calling everyone tonight."

"And when Aaron calls you, act like you don't know about the leukemia."

"Sure thing. God, Denise, I just can't believe this. I don't know what to say."

"There isn't much you can say. Just be there for him."

They stood and Blake gave her a hug. They both had tears in their eyes now. Blake walked her out to her car.

After another quick hug and goodbye, Blake went straight home. He would tell Sydney about Aaron's leukemia. For one thing, she never spoke to any of his friends, if she could possibly avoid it. For another, she was a master at keeping secrets.

"I'm sorry, Blake. I know he's your best friend," Sydney said when he told her.

"Will you go to the party with me?" If ever Sydney owed it to him to show up and be nice, it was now.

"We'll see. I'd have to find a babysitter."

"We don't need a babysitter. Let's bring Jeremy. I'm sure there will be other kids there and everyone will want to see him."

"I don't like him being up so late."

"It's Saturday—one late night won't hurt him."

"There will probably be a lot of drinking."

"Who cares? This might be Aaron's last birthday."

"I'll think about it."

Shit, Blake thought. *Couldn't she put her petty dislikes and judgments aside for one lousy night? She'd probably be happy if Aaron died, figuring I'd spend more time with her.* As soon as he thought that, Blake felt guilty—he wasn't being fair.

Sydney turned her attention back to her TV program.

Blake stood there for a moment, wanting to argue. But he realized he was trying to distract himself from his fears for Aaron. Plus, he didn't want Jeremy to overhear Sydney and him fighting. It never did any good anyway. Instead, he went into the kitchen to make his phone calls.

A loud moan woke Charlotte. Briefly disoriented, it took a few moments to remember she was in a hotel and to realize she'd been having a nightmare. She could remember some of it: Genny Morris was questioning her. Charlotte was over at the Morris house, playing with Abby and Cassandra in their bedroom. She'd done something—she didn't remember what —but Mrs. Morris was very upset and asking her a lot of questions. Charlotte didn't know how to answer them, but somehow knew that her answers were very important. She started crying, but Mrs. Morris wouldn't stop badgering her. That's when Charlotte woke. Her face was wet—she must have been crying in her sleep.

Wide awake now, she lay racking her brain, trying to remember why Genny Morris was grilling her so intently, but the memory was too vague. All Charlotte knew was that something bad happened when she was a child and it was important. At the same time, none of it felt real—as if she were imagining the whole thing.

Bud was the only person still alive who might know what actually happened. She was going to have to ask him again. Not being able to remember was driving her nuts. She hated to push the old guy—he'd made it clear that he didn't want to talk about it. But he was her only option.

Giving up on sleep, she dressed, ate breakfast in the hotel dining room, and drove to her mom's house. Charlotte had met with the real estate agents the day before. She'd selected one of them and the ball was rolling. The house wasn't much, but the location and large lot just a few blocks from the plaza made it prime property.

Pulling into the driveway, she smiled at the "For Sale" sign in the front yard. She'd be happy when she'd seen the last of this place. She sat in the car for a minute, wondering how to confront Bud again. In the end, she decided to just ask him outright, one more time. But, to sweeten the pot, she'd do it over lunch at The Fitch Mountain Grill.

The blinds were cracked open, allowing bright stripes of sunlight to stream onto the tabletops and industrial carpet in the conference room Friday morning. Ángela and Greg reported they'd bombed at the hotels. Greg and Blake summarized the previous day's interviews with the Mitchells, Gail Jones, and Frederick Hart.

Ángela checked Gail Jones's criminal record—she didn't have one. Her son Ricky, however, had an extensive history of drug possession, selling, and juvenile hall time prior to his overdose in 2004.

"Mabel Garrity had a negative impact on a lot of people," Ángela said. She sat, twirling a paperclip on the tip of a pencil, shielding her eyes from the sunlight with her other hand.

Sam got up and closed the blinds.

"What if she found out about Zimmerman's record?" Greg mused. "Could she have threatened to blackmail him?"

"Seems like we'd have heard right away if any of the neighbors learned about Zimmerman's past from Mabel," Sam said.

"Not if he killed her before she had a chance to spread it

around." Blake was sitting beside Ángela. "Remember how she called the teacher and tried to blackmail him? Maybe she did the same to Zimmerman."

"We have to consider the possibility," Greg said. "What else have we got?"

Ángela had completed another national crime database search. There were roughly ninety strangulations in the US every year. The details varied, but none of the recent crimes were similar enough, or geographically close enough, to appear related to their two homicides. She'd also confirmed with Logan Johnson's wife that she'd been in San Francisco in the afternoon and evening of October tenth.

"So she has an alibi, but her husband doesn't. He's the one that had sex with Sofia at his daughter's twenty-first birthday party," Greg reminded everyone. "Then Sofia dumped him like a used condom. Would he have been mad enough to murder her?"

Liam spoke up. "Or was he just thrilled to have scored a quickie with a beautiful, sexy young girl?"

"Some guys might get violent—if they feel manipulated." Greg tried to suppress the irritation he felt every time Liam butted in to defend one of Sofia's sex partners. "Johnson said she wouldn't even talk to him anymore."

"Okay." Liam smoothed his mustache. "I have to get back to the budget report. Keep up the good work, everyone." He left the room.

Greg stared after him. Was Liam going out of his way to steer suspicion away from these men Sofia had hooked up with? Why would he do that? Was he having an affair?

"The way Sofia was jerking all those guys around," Blake said, "she must have pissed a lot of people off."

"Just like Mabel," Ángela said.

"You're right." Greg sighed and stood up. "Let's focus on finding the man Sofia met at the Windsor Inn Friday night."

Greg could feel a dull headache starting. Walking back to

his office, he took a deep breath. This was the hardest part of the job—waiting for a break while the case got colder and colder. He knew everyone else was getting frustrated as well. Maybe Liam was regretting he hadn't brought in another department to assist. Maybe that's why he was being so contrary.

After the briefing, Greg reviewed all of the case information once more, trying to find some detail they'd missed or hadn't followed up completely. He wasn't finding anything when Blake interrupted his search.

"Zimmerman's here! He must have gotten Sam's messages."

Greg felt a surge of anticipation. "I'll be right there."

The squad room was quiet—all the desks empty. Greg and Blake paused to check out Zimmerman through the one-way glass before they entered the interview room. He looked to be in his fifties, slight and balding, wearing jeans and a blue nylon windbreaker over a plain T-shirt. He was very still, sitting in the softly lit room, staring at the coffee table as if deep in thought, with a frown on his face.

"He looks pretty calm," Blake said.

"Could be an act. Remember, he's been through all this before."

Blake nodded and they entered the room.

"Mr. Zimmerman, do you know why we asked you to contact us?" Greg asked after they'd seated themselves and turned on the recorder.

Zimmerman wouldn't make eye contact—he stared at some point on the wall between Greg and Blake. "I assume it has to do with Mabel Garrity's murder," he said. "I read about it in the paper. You discovered my record and decided I'm a person of interest."

"Where did you go on your vacation?"

"Palm Springs."

"When did you leave Healdsburg?" Greg asked.

"Sunday, about nine in the morning."

"Did you know Mabel Garrity?"

"No."

"Why didn't you return our calls sooner?"

"I wasn't about to interrupt the first vacation my wife and I've taken since we moved back to California." For the first time, there was some anger in his voice. "I figured whatever you wanted could wait."

"Do you know this woman?" Greg showed him the photo of Sofia Molina.

"No. Am I a suspect for her murder as well?"

"So you know she was murdered." The hell with the kid gloves. This guy was a pain in the butt.

"I read about her in the paper. That's all I know."

"Where were you on Friday, October tenth?"

"At work."

"What time did you get off that night?"

"Seven. My wife didn't get home until nine thirty. There's no one to confirm my whereabouts. If I had realized I'd need an alibi I would have gone over to my son and daughter-in-law's place."

Greg studied Jon for a moment. "These are just standard questions, Mr. Zimmerman. We're not accusing you of anything. We're interviewing all the neighbors and asking them about both victims."

Zimmerman didn't reply. He continued to stare impassively at the art print behind Greg's head.

"You work at the pharmacy here in town?" Greg asked.

"Yes."

"And you don't know anything about either of these murders?"

"I'm sorry, Detective—I don't know anything about either of these women," Jon replied in a plaintive tone. "I don't know any of my neighbors. My wife and I are a little apprehensive about making friends."

"Because of your arrest in San Mateo?" Blake asked.

Zimmerman nodded.

"Please answer verbally for the recording."

"Yes."

"Did Mabel Garrity know about your history?" Blake asked.

"I have no idea." Jon looked sullen again.

"What can you tell us about that case in San Mateo?" Greg asked.

"What do you want to know?"

"Your side of the story."

"It's ancient history. I was innocent and I was acquitted. But it's still a frigging nightmare. I don't see why I should have to defend myself all over again every time someone else gets murdered."

"Mr. Zimmerman, we would love to cross your name off our list," Greg said. "You might help us do that if you'll just tell us what really happened back in San Mateo. That's all we're asking."

Zimmerman must have heard something reassuring in Greg's tone, because he seemed to relax and made eye contact for the first time. He started speaking. In 1997 he and his wife had owned a modest home in San Mateo, had a three-year-old son, and had good jobs in the retail industry. Cecelia Albert was in her seventies, living just down the street. When they first moved in, she had welcomed them with home-baked cookies and offered to babysit anytime.

"There was a bad winter storm and Cecelia's fence fell down. She offered to pay me to replace it."

Talking about Cecelia, Zimmerman's voice softened. Greg thought he could detect genuine affection in his tone.

"There was no way I'd let her pay me, considering all the times she babysat and baked for us. She was like a grand-mother to my son." Jon's face sagged. "My wife and I were devastated when we found out she'd been robbed and strangled to death two doors away and we hadn't been able to help or protect her."

Greg asked him what happened next.

"I was arrested for the murder." Jon's voice rose and he spoke faster. "We couldn't believe what was happening." He shook his head. "My wife held on to her job, but she didn't make enough to pay the defense attorney, the mortgage, day care fees, and the other bills, so she was forced to sell our house and rent a crummy one-bedroom apartment in Burlingame. Even then, she fell behind and our debt soared. It's taken us a long time to get everything paid off."

Greg could understand Zimmerman's pent-up resentment, if his story was true.

"The worse part was that my reputation was trashed, in spite of the acquittal."

Greg knew how that went.

"My wife was guilty by association. We lost our home, our friends, everything. I spent two years in jail. And unless they figure out who actually killed Cecelia, I'll remain under suspicion."

Zimmerman went on to explain that when their son landed a job in Santa Rosa and purchased a house in Healdsburg, he suggested his parents move down as well. Zimmerman and his wife figured enough time had passed since 1997 that no one in California would remember who they were. But they kept their distance from their neighbors and maintained a low profile.

Their life sounded like the witness protection program. The only thing they hadn't done was change their names. Greg studied Zimmerman. His story sounded plausible.

"Do you have any theories about who did kill Mrs. Albert?" Greg asked.

"I think it was one of her kids," Zimmerman said. "They never had any time for her when she was alive. But as soon as she was dead, they were right there with a full list of her assets, complete with insurance appraisals. I thought that was interesting—along with the fact that they had cast-iron alibis. I heard from my attorney that the San Mateo police investigated both of them after my acquittal, but they couldn't make a case. Anyway, it was definitely someone she felt comfortable enough to invite into her house and I know it wasn't me."

After Zimmerman left, Blake leaned back in his chair, lifting the front legs off the floor. Balancing on the back legs, he said, "What're the odds of living in two different neighborhoods where an old woman gets strangled to death?"

"I don't know." Greg stood up and patted Blake's shoulder. "What're the odds we'll ever solve either of these cases?"

"Dry Creek Cellars is one of my accounts." Daphne Knowles glanced around the interview room at the low lighting, comfortable couches, and pastel-colored walls. She'd called the information hotline while Greg and Blake interviewed Jon Zimmerman, saying she might have some information. The dispatcher asked her to come by the station. Daphne arrived shortly before 1100. She was a certified public accountant, in her early fifties.

"I met Sofia there." Daphne adjusted the multicolored scarf around her neck. "I was just sick when I read she'd been killed. She was always so nice and friendly."

"What is it that you wanted to tell us?" Greg asked.

"I don't know if this will be helpful. I don't have any idea who could've killed her." Daphne paused, taking a sip of the tea Blake had brought her. "But the other day I was talking to my friend about Sofia and I remembered something. Zoey said I should tell you, even though it might not be important."

"Just tell us what you remembered, Ms. Knowles," Greg said.

"I saw Sofia in September, on Dry Creek Road. There's a house being remodeled about a quarter-mile in toward town from the winery. She was out front, talking to a man next to a white pickup truck. I wondered what she was doing so far from work."

Greg asked her what the man looked like.

"He was tall—quite a bit taller than Sofia, anyway."

"Race? Hair color? Clothing?"

"Caucasian; his hair was light; jeans, maybe a leather jacket. I drove by pretty fast, so it was just an impression."

"Do you know what date in September you witnessed this encounter?"

"Yes, as a matter of fact. I looked through my calendar. I was at the winery on September ninth."

"Thank you, Ms. Knowles. We'll look into it."

As soon as she left the room, Blake said, "That was Frank James she was describing. Everything matches. He said he's renovating a house out in Dry Creek."

Greg nodded. "It sure sounds like him. Let's drive out there and check it out."

A quarter-mile before the Dry Creek Cellars Winery they drove past a house with a large sign in the front yard advertising the James Construction Company. Blake made a U-turn and drove back to the house, where they parked and took a few minutes to look around.

The large, flat lot was separated from the road by a low stone wall. Beyond the house, the ground sloped gently downward to the edge of the vineyards. These extended across the wide valley to the redwood-covered hills on the west side. The exterior of the home had been completely refurbished with dark stucco, white-framed windows, a slate roof, a deep front porch, and stone pillars. A brick-lined concrete driveway led to an attached, four-car garage filled with large cardboard boxes.

Drilling sounds came from the open doors and windows of the house. Three pickup trucks with toolboxes in their beds were pulled off to the side on the dirt lot. None of the trucks was white. A short Hispanic man in a hard hat and a leather tool belt walked toward them from the front door with a worried look on his face.

"Can I help you?"

"Yes, Detective Davidson and Sergeant Maddox, Healdsburg PD. We're looking for Frank James."

"He's at the lumber store. He'll be back in an hour."

"And you are?" Greg asked.

"Miguel Sánchez." His handshake was dry and firm, the hand rough from manual labor, his accent heavy.

"Are you an employee of Mr. James?"

"Sí. Crew supervisor."

"How many employees does he have?"

"Two here today. And the cabinetmaker."

Greg had noticed an Armstrong Cabinets sign on the door of one of the trucks.

"Do you know who was working here on September ninth?"

"*No sé.*" Miguel seemed to be giving it some serious thought. "We would be doing the roof, windows, stuccoing in September."

"Do you remember last Monday? Mr. James hoisted some supplies with a rope and it slipped through his hands?" Greg asked.

"We worried he might be hurt, but . . ." Miguel seemed to be searching for a word. "Gloves protect his hands." Miguel lifted both hands, to demonstrate what he meant.

"Have you ever seen this woman?"

Blake showed Miguel a photo of Sofia Molina. Miguel took a long time to study it. "No seguro." Not sure.

Miguel didn't look up at Blake, but continued to stare at the photo.

"Please think about it very carefully," Greg said.

Miguel finally looked up with a worried frown on his face, "There is something . . ." Miguel shook his head. "I can't remember."

Greg gave him one of his cards. "Please contact us if you remember anything more. And ask Mr. James to call me when he gets back. Thanks for your time."

Driving back to town, Blake said, "Miguel's hiding something."

"Or he saw Sofia's picture on the news." Greg was silent for a minute, formulating his thoughts. "We need to show Daphne a photo lineup of Frank James and all the men who were here on September ninth."

"I bet Miguel saw Sofia here, talking to Frank, but he's trying to him. He doesn't want to lose this job."

"Maybe. But she could have been talking to one of the subcontractors. Let's make sure." Greg tried to control his excitement. His gut told him they were on the right track. Frank lived across the street from Mabel. He matched the description Daphne had given them. If Frank knew Sofia, especially after denying he knew her, he would definitely become a suspect.

∼

While Greg and Blake were out in Dry Creek Valley, Ángela and Sam were checking Frank's other work site on Sunrise Avenue. Three guys in construction gear were removing siding from a house high on the hill. Ignoring them, Ángela and Sam went to the other homes on the block, all of which had views of town and the westside hills. They asked if anyone remembered seeing Frank's truck on the street Sunday morning. They were trying to confirm his alibi for the time Mabel was killed.

Most of the neighbors remembered seeing the truck at one time or another, but none was able to confirm he was actually there on the twelfth. Too much going on in their busy lives to remember exactly what days the white truck was parked on their street.

Back in the patrol car, Sam called the dispatcher and said they were headed for lunch at the pizza parlor. When they were seated, Sam looked at Ángela with a quizzical expression on his face.

"What?" she asked, laughing.

"Just wondering what made you go into law enforcement."

"When I was nine," she said, "my family got into a car accident."

"Was anyone hurt?" Sam asked with concern.

"Not seriously, thank God. But it was pretty awful anyway. It was the other driver's fault. Eighty-nine-year-old woman, driving without a license, and half blind. Ran a stop sign and broadsided our car. Luckily, she was only going about twenty-five miles per hour. The impact broke my mother's arm and leg and our car was totaled. The old woman's forehead was split open and she broke a number of ribs."

"And that made you want to be a police officer because…" Sam asked, taking a bite of pizza.

"A woman was the first responder. She was reassuring and kind to all of us, including the old lady, who was pretty hysterical and in a great deal of pain. She took command—called the ambulance, called for backup to handle the traffic, called the tow truck—did everything smoothly and efficiently, like it was all routine."

"That's cool," Sam said.

"You remind me a lot of her—"

"The hysterical broad?" Sam grinned.

"The policewoman, you idiot." Ángela had second thoughts about saying this, but what the heck—it was true. "You have that same professional, calming manner." Ángela shrugged, embarrassed. "It makes you a good officer."

"Thanks," Sam said, obviously surprised and pleased. "You're pretty good yourself."

Ángela nodded. He was right. They made a good team.

Charlotte took her neighbor, Bud, to the Fitch Mountain Grill for lunch. While they were waiting for their food on the sunny patio, she asked about his kids. He caught her up on their marriages and the grandchildren. After the table was cleared and they were waiting for the check, she finally worked up the courage to ask him about the past.

"Bud, I know I asked you about this before, but I'm still trying to figure out what happened when I was six years old. I had a dream about it last night. I was over at your house, playing with Abby and Cassandra, in their bedroom. Then Genny was questioning me. I was scared, and I was crying, but she wouldn't let up. After I woke, I realized it was related to that scene in my kitchen that I described to you on Wednesday. Are you sure you don't remember?"

"I've been trying, ever since you asked me, but nothing comes to mind. Are you certain it really happened? You know how dreams are."

"I'm not certain about anything. But it's driving me crazy."

"I'm sorry, honey, but I don't remember anything like what you're describing," Bud said, looking concerned and taking her hand. He rubbed it a little and suggested, "Maybe your subconscious is playing tricks on you. Your mother's murder has been a terrible shock."

"Maybe you're right," Charlotte said, pulling her hand back in irritation, "but I hate having this feeling that something dreadful happened and I don't know what it was."

Bud's face seemed to close up, and Charlotte felt guilty about badgering him. Poor old guy.

After lunch, she returned to her mom's house. She put her purse in the hall closet before flopping down on the couch and calling her sister.

"All this sorting and packing is killing my back."

"I'm sorry you have to do it all by yourself," Isobel said.

"Not to worry. It'll help just to see you tomorrow." Isobel and Ben were going to drive down early on Saturday, pick up their mother's cats from the animal shelter, collect the boxes Charlotte had packed for them with Mabel's china and silverware, and return home on Sunday. They couldn't afford to be away from the farm any longer.

"The strange part is," Charlotte continued, "it's forcing me to sift back through our childhood . . . Oh! Before I forget, the real estate agent is planning an open house a week from Sunday."

"Wow! Fast work."

"Listen, Izzy. There's something I wanted to run by you." Charlotte told her about her flashback and dream and her conversations with Bud. She asked if Isobel remembered anything about those events.

"Nothing. Of course, if you were six, I would have been four, so it's not surprising I don't remember. Do you think Bud's lying to you?"

"I honestly don't know. If he is, why won't he just tell me what happened? What harm could it do, after all this time?"

"Maybe he or Genny did something he's ashamed of."

"All I can say is that it's the strangest feeling, having these memories at the tip of my brain. It really makes me doubt my sanity."

"Well, let me assure you that you are one of the sanest people I know."

"Thanks." Charlotte didn't know how to soften her next question. "Would you say we had a happy childhood?"

"What do you mean?"

"It seems like there was a pall over our family. Maybe whatever happened when I was six caused it."

"Well . . . Mom never seemed particularly happy. But I thought the rest of us were. At least until I started fighting with her about marrying Ben and moving to Oregon."

"Do you remember Mom and Dad arguing about Genny Morris?"

"No."

"Bud said Mom made up a rumor about Genny. I think Genny stopped talking to Mom after that."

"That sounds vaguely familiar. The part about Genny not talking to her. I'd forgotten all about that. We stopped playing with the Morris kids as we got older—was it because Genny wasn't speaking to Mom?"

"Maybe. There's one more thing. I also heard Dad might have had an affair with another woman."

"Where was I when that was happening?"

"Oregon. Detective Davidson asked me about it. I didn't know either. I was in San Francisco. But it makes a lot of sense. Maybe that's why Dad killed himself."

Isobel was quiet for a few moments. "Mom would've made his life miserable."

"Exactly."

"Poor Dad."

"Or could Dad's suicide be related to whatever happened to me when I was six?" Charlotte asked.

"In what way?"

"I have no idea—but what if it was something really nasty?"

"Do you think this is why Mom was murdered?"

"I don't know. I guess it's a possibility. Right now I just want to get these disturbing memories out of my head."

"Damn, Charlie, this makes our family sound horrible. Things weren't that bad, were they? I always thought we were pretty normal."

"We were. These are the kinds of problems normal families have—I see it in my work every day." Charlotte thought about the messy divorces she handled as a paralegal, with accusations of abuse, neglect, cruelty, and unfaithfulness flying around. "I just wish Bud would talk to me and tell me exactly what happened in ours."

"Have you considered hypnosis?"

"I don't know. That sounds kind of like hocus-pocus—even creepy."

"Well, promise me that if you get to the bottom of this, you'll let me know what you find out, no matter what."

After Charlotte got off the phone and resumed packing, she thought about being hypnotized. The idea of losing control made her uncomfortable. All she could picture was grown men acting like chickens and other stage tricks used in nightclubs for entertainment.

12

Greg showed Frank James and his attorney, William Richards, into the interrogation room with the hard chairs and bright lighting. Blake examined Richards's well-cut suit and expensive haircut, then turned toward Greg and raised his eyebrows a tiny bit. Greg thought Blake must be thinking the same thing he was: if Frank pulled in the big guns for this interview, he must be worried. Frank didn't pull his chair all the way to the table—he seemed to be distancing himself from the proceedings. There was dirt and sawdust on the knees of his jeans.

Blake started the recording and pulled out his notebook.

"We need information about your job on Dry Creek Road," Greg began.

"What's that have to do with the Garrity murder?" Richards asked.

"We think that case might relate to another murder we're investigating," Greg answered, then looked directly at Frank. "We discussed it at your last interview—Sofia Molina."

"I need a few minutes alone with my client," Richards said.

Blake turned off the recording. He and Greg left the room and waited in the hallway.

"What do you think this means?" Blake asked.

"Doesn't necessarily mean anything. My guess is Frank didn't tell Richards about the Molina case. Richards will want the background so he can properly advise him during the interrogation."

Richards called them back five minutes later. "Thanks, Detectives—you may proceed."

Blake turned the video recorder back on and Greg restated the time, date, and names of those present.

"First," Greg said, "we need the names and contact information for the employees and subcontractors working at the Dry Creek site on September ninth and again on October tenth of this year. We also need to know where you were on those dates."

"I'd have to look most of that up," Frank said.

"My client will supply that information," Richards answered, looking down at his notepad, writing.

"You stated in your previous interview that you went to Creek Brewing last Friday evening, October tenth?"

Frank didn't answer right away. Greg waited, hoping Frank would incriminate himself by lying. "I stopped there for a few beers and dinner."

"Alone?"

"Noreen said she was going to a PTA board meeting and the kids were both off at parties."

"Can anyone verify you were at Creek Brewing?"

"I don't know."

"Who was the bartender?"

"I don't remember."

"Was it a man? A woman? Can you describe the bartender?"

"I don't remember who it was that night."

"What time did you get home?"

"I don't know . . . a little after nine?"

"What type and color vehicle do you drive?"

"White Ford F-250."

"Do you know this woman?" Greg turned to Blake, who handed Frank a copy of Sofia's photo.

Frank swallowed, staring down at the picture. "That's Sofia Molina."

"How do you know her?"

"From the TV and the paper."

"Are you sure that you didn't know her personally?"

"Yes, I'm sure."

"Did you know that she worked in Dry Creek Valley? Not too far from where you're remodeling that house?"

"I may have read that, I'm not sure."

Greg was stern. "Mr. James, you're going to be signing a sworn statement at the end of this interview. This testimony can be used at trial. If you're lying and we find out about it, it's perjury. If you did know her, it would be wise to tell us now."

Richards broke in, asking for time alone with Frank again. A few minutes later, the interview resumed. Richards was stone-faced. Frank wouldn't make eye contact with any of them.

"My client states he did not know Sofia Molina, Detective. Is there anything else we can do for you?"

"Have you remembered anything else about Mabel Garrity that you want to tell us?"

"No."

"What were you doing on her porch?" Greg took a chance —they hadn't proved the hairs they found there were Frank's, but they could have been—the color matched. "Around the corner from the front door."

Frank's jaw dropped. "I replaced some of those shingles a few months ago . . ."

"We need your photo, fingerprints, and a DNA sample."

"Do I have to allow that?" Frank's eyes flashed toward Richards; a look of panic washed over his face.

"We can arrest you if you don't submit voluntarily," Greg answered.

"On what charge?" Richards asked.

"The murders of Sofia Molina and Mabel Garrity."

"You don't have any evidence—if you had, you would have arrested him already."

"We have enough evidence to arrest and hold him for forty-eight hours. That would get us fingerprints, a booking photo, and a DNA sample. If your client is innocent, this will help us to clear him faster."

"When you arrest him, you can collect your data—not before," Richards said, calling their bluff.

Frank's eyes widened and he looked from Richards to Greg and back again.

Greg watched him for a moment, then decided to back off for the moment. "We're probably going to need to speak with you again after we get your employee records."

As soon as Frank and Richards left, Blake turned to Greg. "Frank's lying."

"Maybe," Greg said. "Let's not get ahead of ourselves. Innocent people lie too. We need to do this by the book. Send Ángela and Sam to Creek Brewing to check his alibi. And as soon as Frank gets those employee names to us, look up their DMV photos and have six-packs made that include Frank and all the others. Show them to Daphne Knowles. Let's see if she can recognize him."

Jeremy, Blake's five-year-old son, talked nonstop about T-ball throughout Friday's dinner. One of the boys in the neighborhood was on a team. In a rare display of graciousness, Sydney had invited the boy to come over and play with Jeremy for a couple of hours that afternoon. Now Jeremy wanted to join the league.

Blake was happy Jeremy was showing an interest in sports, but he already knew that Sydney wouldn't get along with the coach or the other team parents. That is, if she allowed Jeremy to play at all. Knowing her, Blake thought, she was going to come up with plenty of reasons why T-ball was too dangerous for Jeremy. Blake could force the issue—T-ball was about the safest sport he could think of—but if Jeremy got hurt, Blake would never hear the end of it.

After Jeremy was in bed, Sydney turned on *The Bachelorette*. Blake couldn't stand the show, but Sydney loved it, recorded it, and was always asking him to watch it with her. His phone rang.

"It's Aaron. I have to take this." Blake got up and walked out to the kitchen. "Thank God. You saved me from *The Bachelorette*. Did you see the game last night?"

"Go Giants! Didn't I predict they were going to win the Series again this year?"

"It's not over yet. They still have to win four more games."

"Have faith, man." Aaron paused. "Listen, I don't want to bum you out, but there's something I need to tell you."

Blake braced himself, praying against all reason that Denise had got it wrong. "What's up?"

"I have leukemia."

"Shit, Aaron." Blake felt like a fraud, pretending he didn't already know. His best friend was facing a possible death sentence and Blake couldn't even have an honest discussion with him. And he couldn't say anything about the party, either. Why did women insist on all these damn secrets?

"Yeah . . . I know . . ."

"When did you find out?"

"Tuesday."

"That really sucks."

"Yeah. Anyway, I just wanted you to know."

"What kind of leukemia is it?" Blake asked, stupidly. He wouldn't know one type from another—if there even were different types. But he wanted to keep Aaron talking.

"Acute myeloid," Aaron answered. "It's bad. But, if I'm lucky, curable." He briefly described the chemo, radiation, and stem cell transplant options available.

"What can I do to help?"

"Nothing right now. Mom's going to drive me to my chemo appointments. At this point I don't think I need anything else, but I promise to let you know."

"Anything—just call or text."

After they ended the call, Blake walked back out to the living room. Sydney paused the replay and lifted her eyebrows in question.

"Damn," Blake said. "I wish there was something I could do to help him."

"Well, you're helping with his birthday party—that's something."

"Have you decided if you'll bring Jeremy?"

"I will. But we might have to leave early. I don't want to keep him out too late."

"No problem. And, thanks. It will mean a lot to Aaron's family to have you and Jeremy there."

"What about Denise?"

"What about her?"

"Will it mean a lot to her if Jeremy and I come?"

"I'm sure it will, Sydney. They'd all like to see more of you."

"I bet." Sydney hit the play button on the control and Blake let the subject drop. He wasn't sure what she was getting at, but the last thing he wanted to do was stand here and argue about whether or not Denise wanted to see Sydney. He sat down next to her on the couch. Denise probably didn't give a damn either way, but she'd definitely want to see Jeremy.

Greg woke, stretched, and looked at the clock. Julia was still sleeping, curled away from him and the light coming in through a crack in the curtains. He got up quietly and padded to his kitchen to start coffee. He was skimming through the Saturday paper and drinking his second cup when Julia stumbled in, looking ravishing in one of his T-shirts, her hair rumpled.

"I can't believe I slept so late. I have a hair appointment in forty-five minutes. What are you planning to do today?"

"Go for a run this morning. Sounds like you won't be able to join me."

"Sorry. No time." Julia was pouring a cup of coffee, her back to him. "Can't see you tonight, either—I'm meeting some of my girlfriends for dinner."

"What about tomorrow?"

"Want to go into the city? I've been craving dim sum."

Greg stood and pulled her toward him. "I'd love to." He kissed her. "How about I pick you up at nine?"

"I'll be ready." Julia smiled, then went back upstairs to dress, while Greg washed up.

It was a little before nine o'clock by the time he arrived at the Joe Rodota trail. Built on an old railroad line, the trail skimmed the backside of housing developments, farms, vineyards, and the Laguna de Santa Rosa Wetland. Greg jogged past several groups of walkers taking advantage of the cool air and sunshine. The farther he ran from Santa Rosa, the fewer people he encountered.

He wished Julia could have spent the day with him. She was always so busy, which was ironic, because in his previous relationships, his partners had the same complaint about him.

He was beginning to see how they felt. When he first got together with Julia he couldn't believe his luck—no strings, no probing into his past, no drama. Plus, she was gorgeous, smart, and financially secure. Everything he wanted in a woman.

So why do I feel let down? Greg wondered. *Do I really want it both ways—a woman who'll drop everything for me, but places no demands on my time?*

About three miles out he was tired and sweaty. He found a bench shaded by an oak tree and sat, drinking from his water bottle. He watched a few red-winged blackbirds flying around the hay field on the other side of the path. The wind shifted slightly and picked up the faint, acrid odor from a distant dairy farm.

His thought about the murders. Frank James was looking guilty, even though he was denying a connection to Sofia. If they could establish a link to her, Frank would become their prime suspect. Especially now that Jon Zimmerman was looking like a dead end.

He couldn't help but see the parallel between Frank's refusal to admit he knew Sofia and his own refusal to tell anyone about Colleen. He was no more honest than Frank. Of course, he hadn't killed Colleen. But she might have died. It would have been his fault. Greg remembered his mother's pale and tear-streaked face as she climbed into the ambulance to ride to the ER with Colleen that day. And then her sad, worried look when he asked her not to tell Hana about Colleen's accident.

Did Colleen still hate his guts? Would she demand restitution? What could he possibly do to make up for the damage he'd caused?

Was that why he'd wanted Julia with him today? So he wouldn't have to think about Colleen? What if Julia found out about her? Would she still want to be with him?

A woman was walking along the trail from the Sebastopol

direction, wearing a short skirt and a long-sleeved shirt, with a camera on a strap around her neck. She held a leash attached to a small brown-and-white spaniel. Greg thought she looked familiar, but it wasn't until she was close that he realized who she was.

"Dr. Bransen?"

"Yes?" Mary paused, looking at him in confusion.

"Detective Davidson. Healdsburg PD."

"Oh, of course. Sorry I didn't recognize you." She surprised Greg by sitting next to him on the bench. The dog immediately jumped into her lap. "Hope you don't mind if I join you for a moment."

"Make yourself comfortable. I didn't recognize you at first either—different context. Are you doing okay? Finding Ms. Garrity last weekend must have been pretty upsetting."

"Mostly because I'd just lost my husband and brother," Mary agreed, staring out into the field.

"Did you walk all this way from Santa Rosa?"

Mary laughed. "Yes. I may live to regret it, but I'm committed now."

"Do you mind if I walk back with you?"

"I'd enjoy the company. I have to warn you, though—Lily stops a lot, so we may go slower than you'd like."

"I'm not in a hurry." They both stood up and started back toward the city. "You mentioned your husband on Sunday—but you lost your brother as well?"

"He was killed shortly after my husband died."

"I'm sorry." No wonder she was so tearful when he interviewed her.

"A drunk driver ran a red light and and plowed right into him. He died in the ambulance on the way to the hospital. Internal bleeding."

"Was Jacob Arnold your brother?"

"Yeah."

"I remember that accident." The other driver had multiple

DUIs and was driving without a license when he killed Jake.

They walked in silence for a few minutes. Greg searched for a subject to cheer her up. The only thing he could come up with seemed lame, but he went with it anyway. "How did you and your husband meet?"

"Japanese Tea Garden—Golden Gate Park—I was there with two other interns from UCSF."

It worked—she had a big smile on her face. Greg couldn't believe how much it changed her appearance and how good it made him feel.

"He walked up and started chatting. We all ended up at an Indonesian restaurant on Clement Street." Mary was breathing a little heavier. In spite of her warning about Lily, both dog and owner kept up a brisk pace.

"Children?"

"Couldn't figure out how to juggle parenthood with two full-time careers, so we eventually decided not to have any."

Greg worried he was asking too many personal questions. "Don't mean to pry. Bad habit—carries over from work."

"I don't mind. I like talking about Enzo. Most people are afraid to ask because they think it will make me sad. But then it starts to feel like he never even existed."

She's so open, Greg thought. And so easy to talk to. She must have had a great bedside manner when she was practicing. "Why Healdsburg?" he asked.

"We used to visit my brother and his wife. We fell in love with the place."

"You seem a little young to be retired," Greg said, thinking she was about his age. He'd never seen the attraction of retirement himself—what would he do? "Was that hard?"

"Everything happened at once—retirement, a new town, widowhood, losing my brother—that's what made it so hard." Mary was quiet for a few steps. "I loved my work, my colleagues, my patients. I miss a lot of it."

Mary paused to let Lily sniff around and pee. "But I don't

miss the long hours, the stress, the constant push-back from insurance companies, the meetings, the politics."

Greg could relate. That's why he never wanted to be chief of the department: budgets, public relations, management.

Mary was speaking again. "I figured it was time to step aside and let one of my younger colleagues have a go. I had a beautiful new home, Enzo was retiring, there was so much we wanted to do. I never dreamed I'd end up alone like this." Mary was looking down at the gravel path. "That's the worst part."

Greg understood loneliness. He'd isolated himself because of guilt. But Mary wasn't like him. She could talk about her feelings—even to someone she hardly knew. Women—it seemed like they could talk about anything. Then they moved on. Greg realized he never had. By trying to hide the central tragedy of his life, it had grown to monstrous proportions. And now he was being forced to confront it against his will.

They were back within the city limits, walking beside a condominium complex. Greg could see upstairs balconies with barbecues, patio furniture, and potted plants. He wondered about the lives of the people living there. What heaven or hell were they experiencing right this moment? Or was this just a routine Saturday—trip to Costco, kids' soccer game, college football on the tube, and beer?

Mary's voice brought him back to the present. "Enzo got up early to go running. He was making coffee and I heard glass break. I ran into the kitchen and he was lying on the floor—dead. One day everything was fine. The next day, life as I knew it was over, without any warning. I saw so many of my patients go through tragedies like this. But you're never prepared when it happens to you."

"I know what you mean," Greg said with feeling.

Mary turned to look up at him, a question on her face. He longed to explain—to tell her how his sister's accident had completely altered his life. Even though he'd never shared it with another human being, he thought he could tell her. But he held back—not while she was a witness in his investigation.

A group of women pushing strollers, in leggings and workout tops, jogged past them, heading west. They were all young, pretty, laughing, and chattering like a flock of birds. The bundled babies were either fast asleep or gazing straight ahead, absorbing the sights and sounds of the trail. Mary and Greg had to walk single-file to allow them enough room to pass.

"There's almost nothing left to hold me here, except Lily," Mary said when they were side by side again. "Sometimes I feel like I could just drift off into the atmosphere. Sometimes I wish I would."

Greg had no idea what to say to make her feel better. He thought about his own life—how few and shallow his connections were. For him, it was work that kept him tethered—that provided purpose and, hopefully, some kind of redemption. Mary didn't even have that anymore.

"I don't mean to sound so melodramatic," Mary said with a little laugh. "I'm sure you don't want to hear all this."

"No. I mean I do. It makes sense."

"I know it sounds like I'm feeling sorry for myself, but, actually, I was very lucky."

He assumed Mary meant lucky in marriage, or life in general. He envied the degree of love and support she must have shared with her husband—something he'd never been able to give or receive from a woman.

After they'd walked in silence a few minutes, he asked, "So what do you do to fill your time now—besides walk?"

"Paint—watercolor." Mary paused to allow Lily to sniff again. "And I foolishly agreed to teach a watercolor class at the Boys and Girls Club starting Monday."

"Good for you."

Her laugh was infectious, making Greg feel lighter inside. "I must have been crazy to say I'd do it."

"You're getting on with your life. I admire you."

"Believe me . . ." Mary didn't finish her thought.

Greg glanced at her. Her eyes brimmed with tears. He found himself drawn to her pervasive sadness, her air of vulnerability.

"Sorry. I just start crying at anything now." She wiped at her eyes with the hand that wasn't holding the dog leash. "Come on, Lily, let's keep moving." Mary picked up the pace again.

Greg soon felt sweat running down his temples—the morning chill was gone. He was impressed by Mary's stamina.

"How long have you lived in Sonoma County, Detective?"

"Please, call me Greg. All my adult life."

"And call me Mary. Where'd you grow up?"

"San Rafael."

"Did you always want to be a policeman?"

"Pretty much." Greg didn't exactly know when he'd decided that would be the way he could make up for Colleen's accident. He just remembered believing that's what he needed to do.

"Children?"

"Two. And two granddaughters."

Mary smiled. "Nice."

They made it back to Santa Rosa shortly after noon. Greg walked her to her car. "Thanks for the company," he said. "I really enjoyed it."

"Same here."

Mary's smile was very pretty. Greg noticed how white and straight her teeth were. On impulse he asked, "Would you like to do it again sometime?"

Mary hesitated. Greg immediately regretted asking her. Running into Mary by chance and walking with her was one thing. But to arrange a second walk, no matter how platonic, felt wrong somehow, not to mention completely unprofessional.

But then she said, "As long as you don't mind Lily coming along."

"It probably wouldn't be until after this case ends," he said, backpedaling. "It's not a good idea to fraternize with the witnesses." Greg smiled to soften his words and held out his hand. He wondered what in the hell he was doing, hoping she'd just forget he'd asked.

What he really needed was to have the kind of honest, open conversation with Julia that Mary had just had with him. Encouraged by that thought, he vowed to make more of an effort when they went to San Francisco.

Mary took his hand, but her brow scrunched up a little and she looked off to the side. "That reminds me . . ."

Greg waited, wondering what it could be.

Mary shook her head and pulled her hand away. "It's probably nothing."

Greg raised his eyebrows to encourage her.

"I saw Mabel Saturday afternoon—the day before she was killed." Mary stopped again. "She was walking across the street—as if she'd been over at the Jameses' house. She was smiling." Mary looked up at him, a question in her eyes. "She never smiled. I remember thinking it made her look so much more attractive."

Blake called as Greg was walking to his car. Frank James had faxed all his employee and subcontractor records that morning. Greg hadn't expected Frank to act so quickly. Which meant there must not be anything incriminating in those records. He told Blake he'd meet him at the station in thirty minutes.

Miguel Sánchez and Frank had both been working on the Dry Creek site all day on September ninth, along with several sub-contractors. Frank and Miguel were the only two there on October tenth and Frank indicated they both left at six that night.

Greg and Blake assembled photo lineups before calling Daphne Knowles in. Besides Frank, there were pictures of Miguel, each subcontractor working for the James Construction Company in Dry Creek on September ninth, and similar-looking men pulled from police computer files.

Daphne carefully examined each six-pack.

Greg and Blake waited, keeping their expressions and body language patient and neutral, not saying a word.

She took her time, spending over ten minutes. She kept going back to the page with Frank's photo. "I only saw him for a second, as I was driving by. I was going fifty-five, so I can't be sure. But it might have been this man." She was pointing at Frank James.

13

Ángela and Sam had been unable to confirm Frank's alibi for the evening Sofia Molina was murdered. They'd driven to Creek Brewing on Friday. None of the employees remembered Frank from the week before, although they said he was a regular customer. Frank had told Greg and Blake that he sat alone that night, paid cash, and threw away the receipt, which was his normal practice.

"So he doesn't have an alibi for the period when Sofia was killed," Greg reported to Liam on the phone Saturday afternoon. "Plus, he doesn't have an alibi for the period when Mabel was killed. There's no one to verify he was at the Sunrise Avenue house last Sunday morning. Daphne Knowles tentatively ID'd him speaking to Sofia at his work site on September ninth. Mary Bransen thinks Mabel was over at his house last Saturday afternoon, after we notified the media about Sofia's body. I want a warrant to search his house, his truck, and that house on Dry Creek he's remodeling." Greg waited through the silence on the other end of the line as he looked out his window, wishing the liquid amber trees lining the station parking lot contained the missing pieces of information in their leafy branches.

"Just because he knew Sofia and might have spoken to Mabel the day before she died, it doesn't mean he killed them," Liam said slowly.

"But why lie about it?" Greg asked. "Do you think we're jumping the gun here?"

"Not necessarily," Liam said with a big sigh. "I agree, it looks suspicious. But Sofia was involved with a lot of men."

Greg turned his office chair so he could show Blake by his pursed lips and wrinkled brow that he was frustrated with Liam's response.

"Go ahead and request the warrants," Liam finally said, sounding resigned. "It'll probably be Monday before they're approved, if the judge even signs them. Meantime, keep investigating. I'm not convinced he's our man."

Blake walked Sydney and Jeremy up the path to the Kings' front door. He'd wanted to get there early to help Aaron's sister, Denise, set up for the surprise party. But showing the six-packs to Daphne Knowles and waiting to hear Liam's decision about the warrants had kept him at work until 1710. He'd barely made it home in time to shower, change, and load everything into the car.

Denise had decorated with crepe paper streamers and about a hundred helium balloons. "Wow, this looks fantastic," Blake exclaimed. He left Denise and the Kings gushing over how much Jeremy had grown. He hurried to get the rest of the stuff from the car, hoping Sydney wouldn't make any snide comments while he was gone.

Coming back in, he asked Denise where he should set up the speaker and she took him into the living room. She wore a burnt-orange, off-the-shoulder minidress with a figure-hugging silhouette and brown stiletto heels. Her dark hair was up. She looked and smelled wonderful.

"Do you think Aaron'll be surprised?" Denise asked with a doubtful frown.

Too late for second-guessing now, Blake thought. "Who knows. You did everything you could." He gave her what he hoped was a reassuring smile and went back to join Sydney, who was spreading cheese on a cracker for Jeremy.

She looked gorgeous herself, with her long, red hair flowing freely over a tailored white silk blouse, a black skirt, lace stockings, and heels. He put one arm around her and kissed her on the temple.

"How are you two doing?" he whispered in her ear.

"Just fine. But what are we going to do for a half hour until Aaron gets here?"

Can't she just enjoy herself instead of complaining about every little thing? he wondered.

"The least you could do is help me watch Jeremy," Sydney continued, in her customary sarcastic tone of voice.

Blake inwardly rolled his eyes. If she wouldn't hover over Jeremy like a hawk it wouldn't be such a chore. But he forced himself to smile at her and made a point of keeping Jeremy engaged while everyone else showed up.

When Aaron opened the door just before six and called, "Mom, Dad, I'm here." There was a moment of total silence before everyone shouted, "Surprise!"

Aaron looked shocked and Blake's stomach lurched. We shouldn't have done this, he thought. But then Aaron spotted Denise in her party clothes and gave her a big grin.

"Happy birthday!" Denise walked up and hugged him, followed by their parents.

Aaron then made his way around the house, greeting everyone who had come. He looked happy—not at all uncomfortable at being surprised. He didn't show any signs of worry or depression, either, which made Blake feel a lot better.

Three hours later, after dinner and cake, some of the guests started collecting their coats, preparing to leave. Sydney came up to Blake and said she was ready to take Jeremy home.

"Take the car," Blake said. "I'll catch a ride with someone later. I want to stay and help the Kings clean up."

"Haven't you done enough already? Anyway, I've had some wine and don't think I should be driving."

He stared at her, hating her in that moment. "Fine. I'll drive you home and then come back."

"Whatever." Sydney turned away to fetch their coats from the guest bedroom. Blake found Denise to tell her he'd be back.

"You don't have to come back. Go home and be with your family."

"No, I really want to help. Besides, I didn't get to talk much with Aaron tonight." No one had mentioned the topic of Aaron's leukemia all evening. It had to be looming in everyone's mind. Blake wanted to give Aaron a chance to open up, if he was ready. "Maybe I can visit with him while we clean up."

"Okay, you can hang out as long as you like, but don't feel like you have to do any work."

On the drive home, Sydney took the opportunity to criticize the Kings' shabby furniture and stained carpet.

Blake wanted to defend them. With Aaron's treatment looming, they had more important things on their minds than interior decorating. But he knew better than to set Sydney off. He momentarily wondered why he'd ever married her. But he knew—she was the first pretty girl who ever took a serious interest in him and he'd been crazy about her back then.

Jeremy was sound asleep in the backseat. Blake carried him into the house and directly to bed. Sydney said she'd undress him, so Blake left her to it and drove back to the party.

A half dozen people were still sitting in the living room, shooting the breeze when Blake returned. He grabbed a beer and joined them, feeling himself relax for the first time all night.

Mr. and Mrs. King came into the room and said good-night. "We're going to bed. Don't worry about cleaning up." This was directed to Denise and Aaron. "We'll take care of it in the morning."

"Okay, Mom. We'll just put away some of the food," Denise called over her shoulder.

Blake stayed two hours, first talking with his friends, then picking up trash and washing dishes. By the time the house was back in order, everyone was gone except Denise and Aaron. Aaron asked for a ride to his apartment because he'd had too much to drink. "Have to live it up now—chemo starts Monday."

When Aaron excused himself to go to the bathroom, Denise gave Blake a big hug. "Thanks again. It was a huge success."

"Even the surprise worked out. I'm glad we did it."

"Me, too. You're the best." Denise turned her face up to his, smiling, her arms still around his neck.

Blake smiled down at her, reluctant to let go. Denise had grown up while she was away at college. She fit seamlessly into Aaron and Blake's crowd now—the four-year age differ-ence no longer mattered. Blake relished the easy camaraderie he felt with her, something he never felt at home.

He wanted to kiss her. The longer they stood there, the less preposterous the impulse seemed. And Denise wasn't pulling away either, just gazing up at him without guile or censure, pupils dilated, possibly a little drunk.

When his lips brushed hers lightly, she momentarily froze, then tightened her arms and kissed him back. He could feel her breasts pressing against his chest. Her lips were soft and her tongue brushed against his lips. Blake's friendly intentions evaporated in an erection. He pushed thoughts of Sydney and Jeremy out of his mind.

He later wondered what would have happened if Aaron hadn't suddenly cleared his throat behind them, causing Denise to drop her arms and push herself away. Blake sheepishly reached over to grab his slow cooker. Denise, flushed, eyes downcast, opened the front door for them.

"Drive carefully," she admonished, giving Blake a quick smile behind Aaron's back. Blake had no idea what to say, so he silently followed Aaron out. He heard the door close softly behind them.

Aaron didn't mention the kiss on the drive home. Blake, relieved that Aaron had finally broached the subject of his leukemia for the first time that night, repeated his offer to help in any way he could.

"Could you meet me for coffee tomorrow morning?" Aaron asked.

"Sure." Blake thought the look Aaron gave him as he got out of the car was a little dubious. He wasn't sure if it was because Aaron was dreading chemo or if it was because of the illicit kiss.

Fortunately, Sydney was asleep when he got home. He pulled off his clothes and climbed into bed. Then he tossed and turned for two hours, excited and remorseful, thinking about the way Denise had felt in his arms, the softness of her lips, and all of the reasons why he shouldn't have kissed her.

∾

Charlotte gave Isobel and Ben a big hug, reluctant to let them go, wishing they could stay more than one night. They'd driven down the day before, loaded Isobel's boxes in the car, then taken one last look through the house and yard before checking into the Healdsburg Avenue Inn.

After breakfast, Isobel and Charlotte stood at the curb with the luggage while Ben collected their car. He and Isobel were driving down to the animal shelter in Santa Rosa to pick up Mabel's cats before heading back to Oregon.

"Any more dreams or flashbacks?" Izzy asked.

"Nothing. And Bud won't tell me anything," Charlotte said with resignation.

"Won't or can't?" Izzy asked.

"I don't know."

"I still think you should try hypnosis," Izzy said with a glint in her eye.

～

When Blake woke Sunday morning, he could hear Sydney in the kitchen, talking to Jeremy. Blake joined them, feeling guilty.

"Did you have a good time when you went back to the party?" Sydney was cooking pancakes, flipping them, a frown on her face.

"It gave me a chance to sit down and talk to Aaron for the first time all evening," Blake said defensively.

"I know you'd much rather be with your friends than with me and Jeremy."

Blake wondered why he'd never noticed how grating and high-pitched her voice sounded when they first met. Fantasies of divorce floated tantalizingly through his mind. Then he immediately felt horrible for even considering inflicting that much heartache on Sydney and Jeremy.

"You could have stayed with us. Jeremy could have fallen asleep on one of the spare beds." Blake rubbed the back of his neck, knowing he was being dishonest. He wouldn't have had such a relaxed, easy conversation with his buddies if Sydney had stayed at the party. Of course, if she had, he wouldn't have kissed Denise, and then he wouldn't feel so shitty this morning.

"Jeremy doesn't sleep well in a strange bed. Besides, none of your friends like me. They only tolerate me for your sake."

"Sydney, you never give them a chance. And it wouldn't have hurt Jeremy to miss a little sleep. It's not like he has to perform brain surgery this morning. I don't know why you always want to keep him to yourself."

"I'm not trying to keep him to myself. And you don't notice the mean remarks your friends are always dropping. Mrs. King implied that I don't let your mother see Jeremy very often. Can you believe that? Your mom doesn't want him around."

"That's crazy! Mom would love to spend more time with Jeremy." There was no way Blake was going to let Sydney get away with this crap.

"See, that proves my point. They're all poisoning your mind against me."

"Well, prove them wrong. Let's call Mom and ask her to babysit Jeremy this afternoon. We'll see what she says. You and I can drive out to the beach or even work around the house if you want."

"I'm not going to leave Jeremy over there alone. What if your uncle and his partner come over?"

"Sydney, they're gay, not pedophiles." Blake stood up and spread his arms, palms up. "You complain that Mom doesn't want to spend time with Jeremy, but you never give her a chance. And Uncle Ken would never do anything to hurt him."

"I'm not comfortable leaving him at your mom's house, where he isn't even wanted. And I don't trust your uncle."

"That's bullshit!" With that, Blake stormed out of the

house. Before he closed the door he could hear her in the kitchen, talking to Jeremy as if nothing had happened.

~

Blake drove to Vineyard Roasters and waited for Aaron, angrily rehashing the fight with Sydney in his mind.

What did Aaron want to talk about anyway? Blake hoped it wasn't the kiss, because he had no idea how to explain it, even to himself. God knows what Sydney would do if she found out. He almost wished she would, he was so pissed. But he cared more about Aaron's and even Denise's feelings than Sydney's at the moment. He probably owed Denise an apology. He didn't owe Sydney a damn thing.

God damnit, he thought. *Why do I stay married to such a mean-spirited bitch?*

When Aaron walked in, Blake blurted out, "I'm beginning to wonder why the fuck I married Sydney."

"Whoa." Aaron held up a hand to stop him, then dropped into a chair. "Does this have something to do with that kiss last night?"

"I don't know . . ." Blake trailed off, realizing he'd never discussed his marital problems with Aaron before. He was bad-mouthing Sydney behind her back for the first time and he didn't feel the least bit guilty.

"I was beginning to wonder if you'd ever come to your senses." Aaron smiled.

Blake let out a sigh—at least Aaron didn't seem to be judging him. The last thing in the world he wanted was a rift between him and his best friend.

"What about marriage counseling?" Aaron asked.

"I don't know. I'm not sure she'd even agree to go. She has such a big chip on her shoulder."

Aaron studied him for a moment. "I can't tell you what to do, Blake. I can see there are problems. But I suggest you consider this very carefully. Once you start down this road, there may not be any turning back. And, it's none of my business, but please don't mess around with my sister. I don't want her caught in the middle and I don't want her hurt."

"Sorry." Blake held up his hands as if in surrender. "Is that why you wanted to meet today?"

"No. I wanted to say thanks. The party really meant a lot —Denise told me how much you helped her."

"You're welcome. But it was all Denise's idea. I just helped out a little."

Dark green oaks dotted the hillsides of Marin, the pillars of the Golden Gate Bridge were free of fog, and the brilliant blue bay was dotted with white sails as Greg and Julia drove to San Francisco.

Strangely, it was Mary he was thinking about. Greg found himself envying the obvious affinity she'd shared with her husband and her ability to talk about her feelings—things he had avoided all his life. He'd been relieved more than anything else when his divorce from Hana was complete— never again wanting to be in a position where someone could pressure him to open up and expose himself the way she had.

But fuck if he wasn't realizing how emotionally constipated he was. Not that he had the foggiest idea how to change. Here he was, fifty-nine years old, and as clueless as an interplanetary alien about human intimacy.

While they stood in line at the tiny dim sum restaurant on Clement Street, Julia pointed toward another couple who had just finished eating and were vacating their table. She quickly grabbed it, leaving Greg in line to place their order at the counter.

When he joined her, he was carrying a tray heaped with bite-size buns, dumplings, and tarts. Julia ate quickly for a few minutes in silence. Greg toyed with his food, brooding over what he wanted to say.

"What's wrong, hon?" She picked up another dumpling.

"What would you think about taking our relationship to the next level?" Greg blurted out, feeling his heart begin to race.

Julia's chewing slowed and she rested the hand holding her chopsticks on the edge of the table. "What, exactly, do you have in mind?"

"I'm not really sure." Greg's palms were sweaty. He wiped them on his paper napkin. Now that he'd brought it up, he really didn't know what he wanted, but felt he had to propose something. "I'd like to spend more time with you. What about living together?"

"Greg, what is this? We agreed we didn't want a live-in relationship."

"I know—it's crazy," he said, but it wasn't, not really. "I feel like I've been keeping everyone I love at arm's length my entire life. I don't want to do that anymore. Especially not you." Greg felt terrified and excited at the same time. "I don't even know how to do this. I've been on my own for almost twenty years. I guess what I'm asking is, would you like to try?"

"No!" Julia looked straight into his eyes. "I'm sorry, but that's not what I want. I like our relationship just the way it is. I love having my own place, making my own choices without having to compromise. I told you when we met—I've been married and it didn't work for me. I don't want to go back there. I'm only with you because you assured me you didn't want that either."

"I hope there's a little more reason than just that."

"Of course there is. You know what I mean."

"I'm sorry, you're right." Greg fought to swallow his disappointment. "Forget I brought it up."

"Are you sure?" Julia took Greg's hand. "Because I want you to be as happy as I am."

"You're right—we shouldn't mess up a good thing." Greg pulled his sweaty hand out of her grasp and popped a dumpling into his mouth, but he couldn't taste it.

"Okay, good. How's the case going?"

"I don't know . . ." Greg shrugged. "I'm waiting on a search warrant."

They spent the rest of the day exploring the renovated California Academy of Sciences museum in Golden Gate Park. Greg tried to appear upbeat and interested in the displays, but he could tell from Julia's worried glances and the increasingly long silences that he wasn't succeeding.

Lying awake beside Julia that night, Greg wondered what was happening to him. Julia was gorgeous. They had a lot of fun together. He didn't want to fuck things up. But deep down he wanted more. He needed more.

Maybe his age was making him question some of the choices he'd made in the past. Maybe he was afraid of Colleen and wanted someone to stand by him when he confronted her. That was a humiliating thought. Was he that much of a coward? Maybe he was just an idiot and should get some sleep.

Returning from her health club Monday morning, Frank's wife, Noreen, saw three police vehicles crowding the street near her home. Not again, she thought, pulling into the driveway and hurrying toward Detective Davidson standing on her front porch.

"What's happened? Is someone hurt?"

"No, Ms. James," Greg said. "Sorry to frighten you. Where's Frank?"

"At work." She looked around, confused. Officers began

climbing out of vehicles and unloading equipment—she recognized Sergeant Maddox and Officer Fry from previous interviews during the past nightmare week. "He left at six thirty, heading to the hardware store. I'm not sure which job site he's at right now. I could call him, if you like."

"Don't call him," Greg said grimly, handing her some folded papers. "We have a warrant to search your house. I'd like you to unlock the door and let us begin. If we need to take any evidence with us, we'll give you a receipt."

Noreen was stunned. Had it come to this already? *God damn Frank!* She looked around at the evidence techs and officers gathering in the driveway, shook her head in despair, and silently unlocked the door, holding it open for them to enter.

When Frank had called her Friday to say he was being summoned for a second interview at the police station, she'd panicked.

"Why do they want to talk to you again?" she'd asked, her voice rising to a whiny level she hated, but couldn't control.

"Calm down, I'm sure it's routine," Frank had answered.

She'd wanted to believe him.

"They obviously don't have any leads and are just fishing. Bill's going to be there with me, so it should be fine." Thank God Frank had called his business attorney, she'd thought. Bill Richards would take care of everything.

But when Frank had arrived home that night he seemed agitated, telling her they'd requested a DNA sample. He'd refused to give it. But now the police were at her house, looking for something—she wasn't sure what.

Noreen watched as Davidson spoke quietly to Maddox, in the front yard. After about a minute, Davidson left with one of the police cars. Maddox motioned Noreen inside and asked her to sit down, instructed her to not make any calls, other than to her attorney if she desired, and left a uniformed officer to watch her. Noreen didn't know what to do—

couldn't think straight. Everything was going wrong and she didn't know how to fix it.

Greg turned onto the driveway of Frank's Dry Creek construction site and pulled off to the side to make room for the police vehicle coming in behind him. Frank James was in the front yard, looking over blueprints spread on a piece of plywood set on two sawhorses. Greg watched Frank's eyes narrow in puzzlement or annoyance—he wasn't sure which.

"What's going on?" Frank asked as Greg stepped out of his car.

"We have a warrant to search this house and property and to impound your truck for a forensic examination."

"You've got to be kidding."

"I'm afraid not." Greg held out the warrants. "We'll need the keys to your truck and the keys to this house."

Ignoring the warrants, Frank pulled two sets of keys out of his pocket.

"Truck," he said, handing a set to Greg. "House," dropping the second set into Greg's palm.

"All of your workers will have to leave until we're done searching. We'll let you know when they can come back."

Frank called Miguel over, instructing him to vacate the house and to postpone the painters who were due later that day. Miguel glanced quickly at Greg, worry lines between his brows, before hurrying over to his truck and pulling out his cell phone.

One of the patrol officers called for a tow truck to transport Frank's vehicle to the forensic garage. Greg and the evidence technicians began searching the house.

The first thing that drew Greg's eyes as he walked through the front door was the view of vineyards framed in the huge windows across from the entry. He turned to the left, where shiny stainless-steel appliances, cherrywood cabinets, and granite countertops had been installed in the kitchen. While one of the techs began shining an ultraviolet light around, Greg walked through the house, careful not to touch anything, hoping to find scuffed flooring, a broken fingernail, maybe even drops of blood.

~

Blake and his two evidence technicians struck out in the Jameses' house. Feeling discouraged, Blake led them to the garage. He opened a storage cupboard and slowly removed the contents. At the very back, shoved behind a bag of rose fertilizer, he found a pair of black leather gloves. The leather between the thumb and first finger of each glove was a little shredded. He carefully bagged and labeled them, filled out a receipt, and took it into the house for Noreen to sign. He wasn't sure, but her face seemed to pale when she saw what he had in the bag. She was very still for a few moments and when she signed the receipt, her hand left a damp mark on the paper.

Blake called Greg as soon as he reached his car. "They were stuffed behind a bag of fertilizer in the garage. You should have seen Noreen's face when I showed them to her. She knows Frank's guilty. How's it going out there?"

"The techs are still checking, but they aren't finding much. If the Dry Creek house is a crime scene, somebody did a good job of cleaning up. I followed Frank's truck to Richmond. We found a coil of rope in there that looks like a match for the one around Mabel's neck. Great work finding the gloves— between them and the rope, I'm sure we've got enough for an arrest warrant."

14

Greg sat with Blake on one side of the table while an officer led Frank and his attorney, William Richards, in from the holding cell at the station.

Frank looked around nervously at the windowless walls, plain white table, and straight-backed chairs, waiting while his handcuffs were removed, then sat next to Richards.

"We have a witness who saw you speaking to Sofia Molina outside your Dry Creek job in September," Greg said. "The rope in your truck matches the one used to strangle both Sofia and Mabel Garrity. We have a pubic hair found on Sofia's corpse. When we get your DNA test results, we'll be able to prove you had sex with her."

"My client and I had an opportunity to consult before this interview," Richards said. "He's prepared to make a statement about Sofia Molina." Richards nodded at Frank.

Frank leaned forward, resting his forearms on the table, hands clasped. "Sofia and I were having an affair. It began in August."

"How did you get involved with her?" Greg asked.

"She walked by the Dry Creek job and stopped to ask me about it. She wanted to look through the house. I wouldn't normally let a stranger walk around a job site, but there was something about her—I couldn't say no."

Couldn't any of these jerks resist her? Greg wondered. He was glad he'd never met Sofia. He already had too many regrets—Colleen, his failed marriage, his distant relationship with his kids.

Frank leaned back, looking downward. "Right before she left, as if it were an afterthought, she asked if I was married. God help me—I wanted to see her again. Before I could even decide how to answer, she smiled and suggested I meet her at the Eastside Inn in Santa Rosa, in the bar, on Saturday night." Frank looked at Richards as if hoping for corroboration. "Nothing like this ever happened to me before."

Greg raised his eyebrows. There was no way a good-looking construction guy like Frank wouldn't have at least the occasional woman coming on to him. Greg had certainly had his share of propositions, and he wasn't nearly as attractive.

"I was never tempted before," Frank clarified, as if reading Greg's mind. "Noreen just happened to be taking the kids to Sacramento for the weekend, so it was perfect timing." He grimaced. "Perfect timing to ruin my life."

"So you met Sofia at the Inn?"

Frank nodded. "She didn't have much to say when I joined her. I tried to ask about her job and where she lived—but she seemed wary, like she didn't want me to know anything about her. I was starting to get a weird vibe and I was about to tell her I was leaving, when she pushed a key card across the table. She told me to wait ten minutes, then follow her up to the room. She left before I could reply. The whole thing was bizarre—kind of like a horror film. I didn't want to follow her—but it was like I didn't have a choice."

"What happened then?" Greg asked.

"We had sex. After that first time, we never even had a drink first. She'd just meet me in the parking lot of a hotel and give me a room key, and I would follow her up five or ten minutes later. She never seemed to want anything else."

There was a long pause. Greg let it draw out, watching Frank's expression. Frank didn't try to fill the silence, so Greg asked, "Was she a prostitute?"

"No."

"Did she ask you to leave your wife?"

"Never."

"Did she try to blackmail you?"

"Nope."

"Were you with her on October tenth?"

"Yes."

"Where?"

"The Windsor Inn."

"What happened that night?"

"The usual. We had sex and I left about ninety minutes later. She was alive the last time I saw her. When I heard that her body had been discovered the next day, I threw up. Had to tell Noreen I had a twenty-four-hour flu. That's the entire story. I didn't kill her or Mabel, and I don't know who did."

"Who booked the hotel rooms?"

"Sofia."

"Who paid for them?"

"Sofia." Frank's eyes darted around the room, as if trying to find the right answers printed on the walls. "I offered to pay. She refused."

"Were you with her when she registered?"

"Never. She always checked in by herself, then brought a key out to my truck and told me to meet her in the room ten minutes later."

The information Frank was giving them confirmed what they knew from Sofia's credit card records and the hotel staff reports. But that didn't mean everything he said was true.

"I thought it was strange that she went to so much trouble to avoid being seen with me," Frank volunteered. "She wouldn't even call me or let me call her—said she didn't want a phone record."

"What was she trying to hide?"

"Hell if I know. I was beginning to think she must be married."

"Did she try to break up with you?"

"She never said anything about breaking up, although I did have a feeling that I wasn't going to see her again after that last night."

"So she did break up with you?"

"No. She didn't say it was the last time—nothing like that. But I got the impression she was bored with me. When I left, she didn't give me instructions for our next meeting, like she normally did. Frankly, it was a relief—I didn't want to see her again, either."

"And when you left, she was still in the hotel room?"

Frank nodded.

"Please give a verbal response for the recording."

"Yes. But I was still sitting in my truck when she came outside around ten minutes later. I watched her get into her car and then I drove home. That's the last time I saw her."

"Did you actually see her get into her car?"

"Yes."

"What was she driving?"

Frank looked off to the side for a moment. "Blue . . . Honda Fit, I think."

"What was she wearing?"

Frank had to think again before answering. "I think it was a red dress. High heels—not sure what color."

Greg consulted his notes. That matched the outfit Sofia was wearing when they found her body.

"Did she see you watching her in the parking lot?"

"If she did, she ignored me."

"Did she drive off before you did?"

"No."

"Did you go to the Creekside Brewery, like you claimed at your last interview?"

"No."

"Why did you lie about your whereabouts?"

Frank's lawyer, Richards, shot out an arm in front of Frank. "Don't answer that," he said.

"How did her car get to the market in Healdsburg?"

"I have no idea."

"Did you follow her to the market?"

"No."

"He said he didn't see her again after he left the hotel parking lot," Richards said.

Greg acknowledged the attorney with a nod. "Why didn't you come forward when we were trying to identify her?"

"I didn't want anyone knowing about our affair."

"Didn't you want us to find her killer?"

"Yes."

"Didn't you think we'd discover your connection to her? And that you would be our prime suspect, since you were the last person to see her alive?"

Richards's arm shot out again. "Don't answer that." He looked at Greg. "That's two questions, Detective."

Frank gently pushed Richards's arm away. "I obviously wasn't the last person to see her alive."

"Do you think her death was related to your affair?"

"Don't answer," Richards said again before looking at Greg. "You're asking my client to speculate."

Frank ignored Richards. "I don't know what to think. I just don't want Noreen and the kids hurt."

"Then why did you kill Sofia?"

"I didn't!" Frank's expression changed. Frustration seemed to drain from his face and he looked thoughtful. "She was probably seeing other men besides me. She seemed to know what she was doing, with the hotel rooms and such..."

Frank was right about that, but it looked like he was the

last one she had sex with. "Any idea who any of these other men were?" Greg asked.

"No."

"How many times did you meet her in hotels?"

"Five. Twice in August, twice in September, then October tenth."

"We have a witness who saw Sofia speaking to you at your Dry Creek job on September ninth. Do you remember that incident?"

"Yes. We'd planned to meet at a motel in Rohnert Park on the tenth. She had to postpone to the next night—the eleventh. She walked down to tell me. Miguel was working inside the house. I didn't think he saw her."

So Frank thought Miguel was their witness. Greg didn't correct him. He consulted his notes again, then looked at Blake to see if he had any further questions about Sofia's murder.

Blake shook his head no.

"I'd like to switch gears now to Mabel Garrity. We found some hair on the siding above her porch. We're running a DNA test. Will we find a match?"

"I told you last time." Frank sounded tired. He leaned back again, rubbing his face. "Mabel asked me to fix those shingles a few months ago."

"Was she blackmailing you?"

"Why would she?"

"Did she know about your affair with Sofia?"

"If she did, she never said a word. And, I don't see how she could possibly have known."

"Mr. James, you'll be formally charged with the murders of Sofia Molina and Mabel Garrity at your hearing on Thursday. Until that time, you'll be held in custody at the Sonoma County jail. Is there anything more you'd like to add?"

Frank stood up and gripped the edge of the table tightly, his fingertips white. "I didn't do it."

Richards stood up and took Frank's arm. "Don't say anything else." Turning to Greg, he said, "Are you finished, Detective?"

"One more question," Greg said, standing up as well. "We found the gloves you wore when you strangled Sofia and Mabel in your garage. Why did you keep them?"

"What gloves? I have no idea what you're talking about. I keep my work gloves in my truck."

Mary schlepped a heavy box of supplies into the Boys and Girls Club Monday afternoon. She had doubts about teaching this class in the first place, and being in the club made her sad, probably because Enzo had been so enthusiastic about volunteering here himself.

She paused in the dim foyer to get her bearings. To the left was a large gymnasium with bleachers along one wall. Kids in scrimmage vests ran up and down the court. The bounce of the basketball and referee whistles almost completely blocked the loud laughter from three preteen girls sitting halfway up the bleachers. Mary walked up to the office window straight ahead of her to check in.

The receptionist, a young woman named Gemma, offered to show her the classroom. Mary followed her down a hallway, watching Gemma's long, blond braid bounce from side to side.

"I'm really sorry about your husband," Gemma said. "All the kids in the homework program loved him."

"Thanks." Mary struggled to keep her voice from breaking. "He loved tutoring here."

"Here we are." Gemma opened a door to a room filled with natural light. A counter with several sinks and cupboards lined one wall. "Eleven kids signed up for your class."

"This is perfect." In fact, it was much nicer than Mary had expected.

Gemma left Mary to unpack. It wasn't long before she returned with a small girl. "This is Amelia."

"Hi, Amelia." Mary squatted down to be on eye level with her. "I'm Mary. How old are you?"

"Six." Amelia smiled shyly, looking down at the floor. A blue headband held her long, thick black hair from her face.

"Would you like to help me set up?"

Amelia nodded shyly. Mary instructed her to place paint tubes, brushes, and plastic plates on each table. While Amelia did that, Mary filled plastic cups with water.

Gemma gradually ushered the other students into the classroom. The last three were the girls from the bleachers, sauntering in behind Gemma as slowly as possible. After introducing herself and asking the students their names, Mary told them to choose seats.

"Okay, everyone, let's get started. Welcome to Beginning Watercolor." Mary took a deep breath, her eyes darting nervously, like a pinball, between the eight girls and three boys, ranging in age from six to twelve. "The paint in the tubes is very concentrated, so just squeeze a tiny dab onto one of these plates." She took her eyes off the kids to demonstrate. That calmed her down. *Just focus on the technique,* she reminded herself. *You may not know the kids, but you do know how to paint.* "Dip your brush in the water and then in the paint, like this." Mary painted a swirling curve onto the tablet propped on an easel beside her.

"You can always use more water to thin out the color, blend it, or spread it around. Go ahead and try that. Call out if you have any questions."

Mary walked over to Amelia, who grinned up at her. "This is pretty!"

"It's almost the same color as your sweater. Now try using

the yellow. That's right. Paint that yellow next to the blue and let them blend together. See how that makes green?"

Mary moved on to the girl sitting by Amelia. "Very good, Jennifer. Remember to rinse your brush in the water and just use a tiny bit of the paint."

The bleacher girls were talking and laughing about the boys they'd been watching in the gym. They were messing around with the paint, but Mary got the impression they weren't taking it very seriously. They were too old for this class and were probably bored.

After twenty minutes, she called the class to attention. "Okay, everyone—you're doing great with the watercolor technique. Now grab a fresh sheet of paper, and this time, I want you to try to copy this simple picture."

Mary placed an example of her own work—a sailboat on Bodega Bay—on the easel before going around the room, pulling used practice sheets out of the way, refreshing water cups, and wiping spilled water and paint off the tables.

Mary checked on each student, giving them a few tips on how to accomplish what they wanted. Most showed no inhibition and were clearly having a good time. At one point, Mary sensed the bleacher girls were mimicking her instructions, which she found humiliating. But everyone else seemed engaged. Glancing back at Amelia's painting, Mary was impressed. The proportions and perspective appeared very realistic, and Amelia was having some success at mixing a number of colors to recreate the different tones and light reflections off the bay—something that was very difficult to do.

Mary was gratified to hear some groans when she announced it was time to stop for the day.

"Before you go, empty your water and throw away the cups and plates." Mary started collecting the paint tubes and leftover paper to store in the cupboard when she noticed the three bleacher girls getting ready to leave the room without cleaning up.

"What did you think of the class?"

"It was okay," the tallest of the group said with a smirk on her face.

"I know it was pretty basic, but I plan to introduce more technique next week."

"Whatever. I'm not coming back—I'm starting a babysitting job."

"Well, I hope you two will give it another chance." Mary looked at the other two girls, who had been silent.

"Sure," one of them mumbled before all three turned to leave, bursting into loud guffaws before they were out the door.

Mary's enthusiasm and confidence slipped away. What was she doing here, anyway, so soon after Enzo's death? She didn't know how to teach—not like he did. These kids didn't even appreciate her efforts.

She was alone in the room, putting away supplies, when Gemma came back.

"That was a huge success," Gemma beamed.

"The three oldest girls didn't seem too impressed," Mary said.

"Don't worry about them," Gemma said. "They hang around the club because the boys play basketball here. That's all they really care about."

Mary's eyes landed on Amelia's painting. It was the best in the class. "I'm kind of excited to see what Amelia could do with a little training."

She suddenly realized she hadn't thought about Enzo, Jake, or even Mabel the whole time she'd been teaching. She'd been totally focused on the kids and the painting.

"Wow," Gemma said, looking over Mary's shoulder. "It's really sad—her mom died of cancer three years ago. Her dad's raising her. She's here as part of the after-school program."

Another good reason to stick this out.

The police had given Noreen a receipt for the gloves they found in the garage. As soon as they were gone she'd called Frank's cell, but he didn't answer. Voice mail kicked in when she tried to call their lawyer, Bill Richards. Not knowing what else to do, Noreen carried on with her routine, including Josh's football practice that afternoon.

Bill finally returned her call while she was sitting in the bleachers. "Sorry, Noreen. I couldn't get back to you sooner. I have some bad news. Frank's been arrested."

"Just a minute, Bill. I'm at Josh's practice." Noreen quickly made her way down the bleacher steps and out into the parking lot. "Arrested for what?"

"It's pretty bad. Murder. Sophia Molina and Mabel Garrity."

"Oh, my God." Noreen squatted down against the side of her car, holding the phone to one ear and pressing her other hand against her mouth.

"Are you okay, Noreen?"

"Where is he?" she asked, when she could speak again.

"In the county jail. He has a hearing on Thursday. He'll plead not guilty. You'll have to contact a bail bondsman." Bill paused, and Noreen sensed he was going to drop another bombshell on her. "Noreen, what do you know about Sofia Molina?"

"The police keep asking—but we didn't know her."

"Frank has admitted to having an affair with her."

"Oh, no," Noreen moaned.

"Apparently he was with her the evening she was killed. He says she was alive when he left. The police don't believe him. Do you know what time he got home on Friday, the tenth?"

Noreen had to think back for a moment. "I was at a PTA meeting. He was home when I got back around ten . . ."

"Okay, that's what he said." Bill sounded grim. "I know this is all a horrible shock. But with any luck, Frank will be home Thursday afternoon. Also, he's going to need a criminal defense attorney—I've got some recommendations for you. Do you have any questions at this point?"

Tears flooded her eyes. She struggled not to sob. "What do I tell the kids?"

"The truth—right away. It's going to be on the news tonight and all their friends will hear about it."

Noreen slid down until she was sitting on the pavement, leaning against her car. Her mind raced, trying to think of everything she needed to do, what she should say to the kids, and how this was going to impact all of their lives. She suppressed another rush of tears and pulled herself up, using the door handle. She forced herself to walk back into the bleacher enclosure and return to her seat. Her friend Yvette asked her if everything was okay.

"No." She felt a little nauseated and leaned forward, her head between her knees. She couldn't bring herself to tell Yvette about Frank's arrest. She wanted a few more hours before it was public knowledge. It wouldn't be real until everyone knew. Then there would probably be months of humiliation and anxiety before it was all over. If it ever could be over.

"Is there anything I can do?" Yvette rubbed Noreen's back.

"Not right now," Noreen said, sitting back up.

"Okay, hon'. Let me know . . ."

Noreen sat through the rest of practice, stone-faced, without registering anything that happened on the field. She didn't cheer when Josh caught a long pass and ran for the goal line. Yvette gave her a worried look before she hugged her goodbye in the parking lot.

Noreen sat in the car waiting for Josh, thinking about the set of drums he'd been requesting for Christmas. Then she thought about Madeline, her beautiful daughter, joking around with her volleyball teammates, speculating on who would be offered athletic scholarships and to which colleges. These were the kinds of concerns that kids their age should have.

They weren't the kinds of problems Noreen had struggled with, growing up in a broken home, with an alcoholic mother and absent father. Noreen thought back to their broken-down mobile home just outside Forestville. She remembered the time she was alone with her younger siblings for four days, without transportation, money, or food while their mother was on a bender. All of them hungry, cold, and scared.

When their mother did come home, Noreen had to scurry around, cleaning up vomit and urine, making sure her mom didn't burn down the trailer with an untended cigarette. As scared as she felt when she didn't know where her mother was, or even if she were alive, the extra work when her mother was home was just as bad. There were times Noreen almost wished her mother would die.

Now, Noreen had to tell Josh and Madeline about Frank's arrest. How would it affect their lives? How could Frank do this to them? Would the kids be able to keep up with their sports and their schoolwork if there was a lengthy trial? Could they even get accepted to college if Frank was convicted? Would they lose all their friends?

She jumped, startled, when Josh opened the passenger door. She hadn't seen him walk up to the car. He talked the whole way home, describing in detail the play he successfully executed at the end of practice. When they got home, she told him to go upstairs, put away his gear, and get Madeline.

Several minutes later, the kids trooped into the kitchen

talking about a TV series on Netflix they'd been watching. Noreen stopped her dinner preparations and sat with them at the kitchen table. They both gradually wound down their conversation and looked at her questioningly.

"I have to tell you something," she started out. The kids just sat there, waiting for her to go on. "Your dad's been arrested . . ." Noreen stopped, sick that her next words would change their lives irreparably. "For murder." Seeing the horrified expressions on their faces, she hastened to add, "He didn't do it."

They didn't respond. Probably couldn't believe it. Josh was only twelve and Madeline sixteen.

"It's probably going to be on the news." They had to be confused and overwhelmed—she wasn't explaining this very well. Should she tell them the rest or not? "He knew the woman he's accused of murdering. He was with her shortly before she died. That's why the police suspect him."

"Why was he with her?" Madeline was crying.

Noreen hesitated again, furious with Frank, desperately trying to figure out a way to soften this, but she couldn't. "They were having an affair."

Madeline looked stricken.

"Are you going to get a divorce?" Josh asked.

Noreen hadn't thought of that. Should she divorce Frank? God knows he'd betrayed her and everything they'd worked for. What would be the best thing for the kids? Especially if he was convicted? Would it make Frank look guilty if she filed for divorce right away? Would it make her look like a sucker if she stayed by his side?

"No," Noreen answered as firmly as she could. Whatever she decided in the future, she needed to reassure the kids now. "We're going to work this out together."

"Is Dad going to be okay?" Madeline asked.

"Yes." She didn't want them to worry needlessly.

"Is Dad coming home?" Josh asked.

"He has a hearing on Thursday morning. If all goes well, he'll be home that day."

Noreen explained how bail worked and tried to answer their questions about jail as best she could. She wanted to give them a little respite before she was forced to continue. "He didn't do it, but Dad's been accused of murdering Mabel Garrity from across the street as well."

Josh started crying at that point.

Noreen gave them more time to absorb everything. "Your friends will be probably be talking about it. I don't want you caught off guard."

Josh got out of his seat and walked toward her. Noreen pulled him into her lap, bracing her leg muscles against his weight. She wrapped her arms around him and rested her chin on the top of his head. In another year, he would be too tall for her to do that. Josh smelled of sweat and his hair was still damp.

"This is important." She waited until she was sure they were both listening. "Don't talk about the case with anyone, even your closest friends."

The kids were clearly devastated. Noreen grabbed Madeline's hand and pulled her into a group hug. Noreen lost control for a minute. "Just remember," she said through her own tears, "your dad and I love you very much. We'll get through this."

Later, the three of them sat in silence, pushing food aimlessly around their plates. Noreen wondered if she should keep the kids out of school. She didn't know what would be best. Facing all their friends' questions would be hell, but hiding at home, with fewer distractions, might be worse.

It was all too much—just like when her younger brothers and sisters were hungry and cold and there wasn't anything Noreen could do but try to comfort them. *God damn you, Frank,* she thought. *How could you do this to us? How can our lives ever be normal again?*

15

F rank's arrest put everyone at the station in a celebratory mood. Ángela joined Greg, Liam, Blake, and Sam for a drink at Tristan's Bar. In the dimly lit interior, they pulled an extra chair to a table for four. Ángela ordered a glass of red wine. In the midst of the good-natured banter and congratulations, she glanced toward Sam and smiled. His tender look caught her off guard.

Watch it, she thought. *Don't send him mixed signals.* It would be cruel to get Sam's hopes up, just to turn him down again. Was a smile too much encouragement? Would he take it the wrong way?

This was ridiculous—she hated being in this position. Ángela glanced at Greg. He wasn't saying much and he didn't look that happy. While Blake was regaling the others about the arrest, she asked Greg if anything was wrong.

"I wish Frank would have confessed," he answered softly. "I don't think we have enough evidence to convict him. And I'm at a total loss for an alternative suspect."

Ángela gave him an encouraging pat on the arm and decided to call it a night. She was too tired to deal with Sam's devotion or Greg's doubts right now. They'd all worked a lot of overtime since the murder. It sounded like they really didn't have good cause for a celebration yet. Besides, the house wine wasn't that good. She put down her half-full glass and stood up. "I have to go. See you all tomorrow."

She was walking back to her car at the station when she heard Sam call out, "Ángela. Is something wrong?" He hurried up beside her.

"No. Yes. I don't know."

"Okay, thanks for clearing that up." Sam smiled.

Sam needed stronger discouragement so he'd stop seeing her as a romantic interest and they could just be work colleagues. She stopped walking and studied his face, uncertain what to do.

He waited, meeting her gaze.

"I can't have any children." Ángela looked away, immediately regretting she'd blurted it out like that. She struggled to fight back tears. She didn't know if she was crying because her unborn daughter was killed so brutally by her husband or because she was burning a bridge between herself and the nicest man she knew. Maybe both.

Sam stood quietly. She was afraid to look at his expression.

"I know," he said softly, taking her hand. "I'm so sorry."

"Does everyone at the station know?" Ángela's eyes jerked up in alarm, imagining them all talking about it behind her back.

Sam's face showed concern, not disgust or disappointment as she'd feared. "Probably," he answered gently. "It was in the report."

Ángela could feel her shoulders and neck tensing up. She tried to relax. Of course they knew the details. Her assault, the trial, the whole sorry nightmare had been in the media. Everyone in the department had chipped in for flowers and cards. What was she thinking?

"It's been a long day, Sam. I'd better go." She turned to walk away.

"Ángela, wait. For what it's worth, it doesn't change the way I feel about you."

She turned back to face him. "I think most men would regret it if they couldn't have kids of their own." She hated the petulant sound of her voice.

"That's life," Sam said, looking directly into her eyes. "We can't always have everything we want."

Ángela searched his face, wondering what he meant, unsure what she wanted other than the impossible—to undo her marriage to that bastard Felipe in the first place.

"So," Sam asked, "are we good—still friends?"

Ángela nodded, confused. Did Sam really want to be friends—or something more? At least he knew the worst. She couldn't have kids, and it didn't seem to matter. That was reassuring, although she wasn't sure why.

Mary couldn't believe how upbeat she felt. She called her sister-in-law, Zoey, to tell her all about the watercolor class and Amelia, the cute six-year-old art prodigy.

"Eventually she'll need a real teacher. I just have to be careful not to stifle any of her creativity."

"That's really great," Zoey said. "There's something else I've been meaning to suggest."

"What's that?"

"Do you know Leah Rogers—owner of the Plaza Art Gallery? I could mention your work when I see her at the Downtown Business Association meeting."

"Don't do that, Zoey," Mary said, panicking. "I'd rather approach her on my own, when I'm ready."

"Nonsense. You are ready. Besides, all I'd be doing is

getting you an audience. What's the worst that could happen?"

"She might tell me my work's no good, crush all my hopes, discouraging me from ever painting again," Mary said, half joking, half serious.

"On the other hand, she might say she'd like to represent your work in her gallery. You might actually sell some stuff. You might be discovered by a famous art critic."

Mary laughed—that wasn't going to happen. But what the heck? Why not take another risk?

"I guess I could use an objective opinion." Mary couldn't believe she was saying this. "Okay, ask her. Thanks."

"You're welcome. Oh, before I forget, you remember Daphne Knowles, the woman who does my accounting? Turns out she also does the books at Dry Creek Cellars."

"Yeah?"

"Well, we had lunch last Thursday and I asked her if she knew Sofia Molina, that young woman that was killed."

"Why did you think she would?"

"Sofia worked at Dry Creek Cellars and I happen to know Daphne does their accounting, too," Zoey declared, clearly pleased she'd made the connection.

"Good work, Nancy Drew," Mary laughed.

"Anyway, Daphne remembered she saw Sofia talking with a man out in Dry Creek Valley not too long ago, so I told her to call the police. She was reluctant to report it because it didn't seem important, and she didn't know who the man was. But I said they're desperate for information and she should step forward."

"Did she?"

"Yes. I'm glad I brought it up, because she'd forgotten all about seeing Sofia that day until I asked her. And guess what?"

"What?"

"They arrested Frank James today for the murders."

"No!" Mary's hand flew to her mouth. She looked nervously around her kitchen. "It couldn't be him. He remodeled my house."

～

"Do you want the good news or the bad news first?"

Greg sat in his office talking to Bob Montgomery from the Forensic Services Lab on Tuesday morning. Greg straightened a couple of folders in his in-box and took a sip of coffee. "Let's start with the bad news."

"There's no evidence that Molina was ever in James's truck or in that house in Dry Creek."

Greg digested that for a moment. Not a surprise. "What's the good news?"

"The rope in James's truck's a definite match for the rope that was used in the Garrity murder and the fragments found on Molina's neck."

Greg felt his hopes rising.

"But, it's a common brand, available at almost any home improvement store in the county."

That was the good news?

"However," Bob continued.

Greg rolled his eyes and turned to face his window.

"The gloves recovered from the Jameses' garage match the leather traces we found on the rope. The leather is scraped off the palm and thumbs exactly where we expected it to be."

That was more like it.

"We got a full set of Garrity's fingerprints off the outside of the gloves and one of Molina's."

"Now we're getting somewhere."

Then Bob had to throw in another spoiler.

"Most of the other fingerprints are so smudged we haven't been able to identify them, and we weren't able to recover any DNA from the inside of the gloves."

"That's progress, anyway." Greg stood up. "Thanks."

Greg drove to the DA's office, located in the jail and courthouse complex in Santa Rosa. Janet Flores was serving her third elected term and the scuttlebutt was she planned to run for state office in the next election. Greg knew her for a no-nonsense prosecutor with an enviable conviction rate. He'd faxed a report over the night before, and he knew, walking in, that she was going to have doubts about the evidence against Frank James. Hopefully the forensic report this morning would bolster the case somewhat.

Greg took a moment to check out the latest photographs decorating her bulletin board. Jagged, snow-covered peaks rising above stands of pine and cedar, deep blue lakes surrounded by meadows of wildflowers—all taken in the High Sierra, where he knew she backpacked every summer.

"I read your report," Flores said, leaning back in her chair and motioning Greg to a seat.

Greg quickly summarized the new forensic data.

Flores frowned. "He looks good as the perp, but I don't think the case is strong enough to go to court."

Greg nodded, reluctantly agreeing with her.

"Now, if you had a witness who saw Frank speaking to Sofia in the market parking lot— or a witness who saw his truck near the spot where her body was recovered—something that can't be explained by the affair alone . . ."

Greg wished to God he knew where to look for that hypothetical witness.

"And it would really help if you had a witness who saw him going to or coming from Mabel's porch the day she was killed—or at least heard him threaten her."

Flores was right. The evidence was all circumstantial. That didn't mean Frank couldn't be convicted, but most juries these days were conditioned by forensic TV shows—they wanted concrete scientific evidence. They actually expected proof without a shadow of a doubt.

"The judge will probably grant bail," Flores said thoughtfully. "James is a longtime resident of the area, has no previous record, and owns his own business. He's not going to be considered a flight risk."

But if Frank was the perpetrator, he was far too dangerous to be out on bail. Greg frowned, worried.

"I'll see what I can do Thursday," Flores said. "But do you have any other suspects?"

The woman coming out of the psychologist's office looked pretty normal. Charlotte couldn't see any signs of bizarre, hypnosis-induced behavior. That, along with the good sleep Charlotte had enjoyed in her own bed the night before, went a long way to reduce her anxiety.

Dr. Schroeder looked about fifty. She wore a soft rose-colored silk tunic, loose-fitting pants, and a wool pashmina shawl that managed to look both comfortable and sophisticated. She asked Charlotte to call her Randi, offered her something to drink, and indicated she was welcome to sit anywhere she liked. Charlotte sat at one end of the couch, feeling reassured by Randi's demeanor and the inviting elegance of her consultation room.

Randi looked over Charlotte's answers on the intake form, clarified a few items, and then clipped the form into her chart. "Now that's out of the way, why don't you tell me what brings you here."

Charlotte related the story of her mother's murder and the two flashbacks she'd recently experienced.

Randi explained that flashbacks from childhood were often associated with traumatic events. "Are you ready to face whatever might be revealed?"

Charlotte assured Randi that she would rather know what happened than be haunted by vague and unpleasant memories for the rest of her life. Randi carefully explained the hypnosis process and the follow-up appointments that would be necessary. Charlotte agreed to proceed.

Randi asked her to lie down on the couch and close her eyes. She asked Charlotte to describe the most peaceful place she could imagine.

Charlotte described a mountain meadow, full of wildflowers, the buzz of insects, birdsong, and the trickling sound of a small brook running down the center. "I'm lying in the grass, soaking up the warm sunshine after a long hike, tired and happy."

Randi started talking in a slow, calm voice. Charlotte found she was able to answer her questions, but she felt like she was dreaming.

"You are standing up and walking into the forest bordering the meadow," Randi said softly. "You walk down a dirt path, spongy with pine needles. Sunlight filters through the trees. You approach a rock face and see a dark opening." She asked Charlotte to enter the cave, where she would find a stone stairway, descending into a subterranean realm filled with mist and the sound of dripping water. She told Charlotte to take each step slowly, counting as she went. "Each step is taking you back a year in your life." After thirty-six steps, Randi asked her where she was.

Charlotte looked around, recognizing Abby and Cassandra's bedroom in the Morris house. Charlotte described yellow organza curtains, white furniture, and dozens of stuffed animals, surprised at how young her voice sounded.

"How old are you?"

"Six."

"What are you doing?"

"We're playing make-believe." Charlotte felt a wave of dread. "I think Mrs. Morris is mad."

"Why would she be mad?" Randi asked gently.

"I don't know." Charlotte didn't want to know. Something really bad happened.

"Tell me about the make-believe," Randi urged.

Charlotte described a game in which she chased the Morris sisters around the room. She was holding a plastic, glitter-filled magic wand in front of her pelvis and pointing it at them. They were giggling, screaming, and running into the furniture. One of the girls bumped into a chair, causing it to bang against the wall. Their mother barged in.

"What's going on in here?" she demanded.

"Charlotte is trying to make us touch her wiener," Abby cried out with delight. "She's chasing us and we're trying to get away."

Charlotte's voice trailed off—that's what was bad. But she didn't really understand why. The memory seemed to freeze right there. She couldn't see anything else.

Randi asked her to imagine walking through another opening in the cave, to another mist-filled chamber. "Where are you now?"

"I'm in the Morrises' kitchen. Cassandra and Abby aren't there. I'm in trouble, but I don't know why." Mrs. Morris was asking her questions about the game and Charlotte was starting to feel afraid. Mrs. Morris was upset. Charlotte didn't want to say the wrong thing. Mrs. Morris kept asking her where she got the idea for the game. Charlotte didn't know how to answer and she started crying.

"Mrs. Morris wants to know if my daddy asked me to touch his wiener. I say yes."

"Did your daddy do that?"

"No."

"Why do you lie?"

"If it's Daddy's idea, maybe Mrs. Morris won't be mad anymore."

"Does that work?" Randi asked.

"No. She's even madder. She never wants to see or hear

me playing that game again. And she's going to tell Mommy and Daddy I was bad."

After a few minutes of quiet, in which Charlotte wrestled with overwhelming sensations of shame, Randi again led her gently into another section of the cave. "Where are you now?"

"My backyard. Playing with Izzy. It's hot. Mommy's begonias are blooming. It must be summer." She heard voices in the house and saw that the Morrises were in the kitchen with both of her parents. She went over to the glass door and stood there watching them.

"They don't see me standing there," Charlotte continued. She couldn't make out all their words through the glass, but she heard enough and read enough from their expressions to know that everyone was upset. Charlotte didn't understand what was going on, but felt it was related to the previous episode at the Morris house. She heard her father say, "I absolutely did not do that, ever, to Charlotte or Izzy any other little girl." Her mother was saying, "How dare you . . ." Charlotte couldn't remember ever seeing her look so angry.

Mr. Morris, who had been silent through most of the discussion, seemed to be trying to persuade all of them to calm down. Suddenly, he started to smile. Charlotte could make out a few words as he talked: *Giorgio Park, Charlie, bathrooms, a man.*

Charlotte understood enough to see that Mr. Morris was making everyone feel better. The next thing she knew, there was a policewoman at their house talking to the Morrises and her parents, and then Charlotte was called in to answer questions. She was asked repeatedly if the man in the park had shown her his wiener. She was afraid to answer because she didn't want everyone to start yelling again. She didn't want to say the only man in the park had been Mr. Morris, and that she'd been afraid of his wiener because it was surrounded by dark hair and seemed so big.

He had coaxed her away from the other kids and parents

on the playground and over behind the bathrooms. She'd wanted to be a good girl because she liked him and trusted him, but she stood there, paralyzed, afraid to touch his wiener as he requested. Finally, the tension became too great for her to handle, so she ran back to join the other kids, not understanding what had just happened.

But after Mrs. Morris got so mad when Charlotte agreed it was Daddy who taught her the game, she didn't want to tell them it was actually Mr. Morris. All the adults seemed to think it was a different man—a stranger—and she decided that she would just let them go on thinking that, because it seemed to make everybody feel better.

Randi slowly led her out of the hypnosis, walking her back through the chambers of the cave and up the stairs, counting back to the present year. When Charlotte was fully awake, Randi asked her if she remembered what she'd said while she was under.

"Yes, I think I do." Charlotte shuddered and stared wide-eyed at Randi. "How will I ever face Bud again?"

"Is Bud Mr. Morris?"

"Yes."

≈

"My God!" Isobel exclaimed, the outrage palpable in her voice. "Do you think that's why Dad killed himself?"

Charlotte had returned to her condo Tuesday evening, sick with what she'd learned. Before she even removed her coat, she poured a large glass of wine. She drank the first glass and poured a second before she took off her coat and called Izzy.

"I don't know. I hope to God not."

"How did Bud get away with it? The bastard!"

"The way most pedophiles avoid detection—the kids are too scared or confused or ashamed to tell anyone." Charlotte lay down on the couch, feeling disgusted and drained, like the time she had the stomach flu when she was ten. "I've felt haunted from the moment I started clearing out Mom's home. I wonder if this was the reason. Or did I make it up? It still doesn't feel real."

"Could you have made it up?"

"Randi said it's possible. It's been such a long time, and the memories could be very distorted. She has to file a police report anyway, in case there are other victims. You're sure Bud never did anything to you?"

"Not that I remember . . ." Isobel's voice drifted off. "I hope not. What's going to happen now?"

"She told me to tell Detective Davidson—but I'm dreading the conversation."

"Why? You're the victim here."

"I don't want him feeling sorry for me," Charlotte said. "Or worse, not believing me."

"That's why so many bastards get away with this shit. Think of the other kids he might have abused."

"Calm down, Izzy. I'm going to do it. I'm just saying it makes me uncomfortable."

"Sorry. I'm just so upset. I hate that creep for what he did to you."

"God only knows what would have happened if I hadn't run away from him." Charlotte felt a surge of nausea. "And then he lied about it. That almost seems like the worst thing." Charlotte paused, not sure Isobel would want to hear this, but needing to reinforce her decision. "I'm going to talk to Bud one more time."

"What? Are you crazy?"

≈

Charlotte Garrity stopped by the station early Wednesday morning before Greg could call her. She had dark rings under her eyes and her hair was pulled back sloppily in a ponytail.

She looked vulnerable and upset—not the composed paralegal he'd met the night of her mother's murder.

"Before we start," he said, "I need to tell you we arrested Frank James for the murder of your mother."

"Oh . . ."

Why did her face drop like that? He thought she'd be pleased.

"Okay. Maybe this isn't related to Mom's murder, but there's something . . ." Charlotte stopped, seeming reluctant to continue. She looked away. "It's difficult to talk about—I'm not sure how to begin."

"What is it?" Greg asked, wondering what could possibly be upsetting her this much.

She took a deep breath. "When I was packing my mother's stuff and getting the house ready to sell, I started having these flashbacks. I couldn't make any sense out of them, but they bothered me. So I made an appointment with a psychologist to try hypnotherapy."

Charlotte's lips trembled slightly and her eyes darted around the room for a second before she looked back at Greg.

He waited, wondering what in the heck she was talking about.

"I remembered . . . I'm sorry. This is really hard." Charlotte's eyes welled with tears.

Greg handed her a box of tissues. "Take your time."

"When I was six, Bud Morris took me and my sister and his kids to Giorgio Park to play." Charlotte's lips trembled. After several deep breaths, she blurted out, "He coaxed me over behind the bathrooms and exposed himself to me. He asked me to touch his penis."

Greg felt himself grow cold. Bud Morris? Could this be true?

"A few days later I was playing with Bud's two daughters in their house, and I pretended I had a penis and was trying to get them to touch it."

She never would have done that if some bastard hadn't exposed himself to her, Greg thought with dismay.

Charlotte looked around the interview room again, as if seeking support from the decor. Greg did everything he could to appear patient and supportive.

"The psychologist said that's a normal reaction—that children reenact a disturbing event to try to make sense of it."

Could Bud have murdered Mabel over this incident? Greg wondered. Had they arrested the wrong man? Wouldn't Mabel have been more likely to murder Bud? And how would it relate to Sofia's murder?

"Bud's wife, Genny, overheard us and asked me what I was doing."

Wait—didn't she say hypnotherapy? Could they trust a story derived from hypnosis about an event that occurred decades ago? Greg's mind was darting all over the place. Something obviously happened when Charlotte was a kid, but after all this time, how could she be sure it was Bud who exposed himself? On the other hand, if she was right, what would Mabel have done if she found out? Did Bud kill her to keep her quiet? But if Bud killed Mabel, how did the gloves end up in Frank's garage?

"Next thing I remember, the Morrises and my parents were talking in our kitchen. I think Genny accused my father of molesting me. Bud made up a story about a stranger speaking to me at the park. That seemed to calm everyone down."

Greg pulled his attention back to Charlotte—to what she was telling him. "Can you be absolutely certain it was Bud Morris who exposed himself to you and not some stranger?"

"My psychologist says there's no way to be certain after repressing the memory for thirty-six years."

"Did Bud ever exhibit any other inappropriate behavior that you remember?"

"I haven't remembered anything else so far. We're going to

try hypnosis again. Also, I checked with my sister—she doesn't think he ever molested her." Charlotte sat back in her chair, looking less anxious than when she'd arrived.

Greg considered her story. In his limited experience and training on these issues, he knew these types of memories were often unreliable. Children got confused easily. And Charlotte had been only six. He had no reason to doubt her honesty. Plus, as far as he knew, she had no reason to accuse Bud maliciously. But her accuracy—that was the question.

"Thanks," he said. "I know that wasn't easy to talk about, but it's important we know. For one thing, Bud may still be molesting children. Do you have any reason to believe this is related to your mother's murder?"

"No. But I want to talk to Bud again," Charlotte said with calm determination.

"That's not a good idea," Greg said. "It could be dangerous."

"I need to ask him some questions." Charlotte seemed desperate. "I need to know what happened to my family."

"You can't talk to him alone. And you have to wait until I give you the go-ahead. I don't want you tipping him off."

16

"If Mabel discovered that Bud exposed himself to Charlotte all those years ago, she probably would have confronted him." Greg was in the conference room with the rest of the investigation team, looking at the schematic of North Street where Mabel's murder took place. "Would Bud have killed her to keep it quiet?"

"Maybe she threatened to blackmail him," Sam said. He and Ángela were standing in the back of the room—ready to head out on patrol.

"That fits Mabel's character—but how would she find out, if Charlotte didn't even remember what happened until now?" Ángela asked.

"More important, can we believe Charlotte's statement? And if she's right, does that necessarily mean Frank didn't kill Mabel?" Liam frowned, absentmindedly smoothing his mustache. "Either way, Frank's defense lawyer could use this information to provide an alternative explanation for Mabel's murder. Especially since the evidence against Frank is so circumstantial."

"What do you think, Ángela? How reliable is this memory of Charlotte's?" Greg asked.

"You'd have to consult with a psychologist, but I think we have to take it with a grain of salt. It's been a long time and our brains play all kinds of tricks on us. Just the fact that she forgot all about it until now—who knows what her brain might do to protect her."

"If Bud did kill Mabel," Blake said, " then who killed Sofia?"

"It's got to be the same person," Greg said. "Both victims' fingerprints were on the same pair of gloves. Could there be a connection between Sofia and Bud?"

"And if Bud's the perpetrator, what were the gloves doing in Frank's garage?" Blake asked.

"Bud could've planted them there," Sam said. "It would be pretty easy to do."

"Have forensics double-check for Bud's prints on the gloves," Greg told Ángela. "And check with her LA relatives to see if they've ever heard of Bud."

"Liam," Blake asked, "how about using Charlotte's statement to get a search warrant for Bud's home? During a child pornography search, we might turn up evidence that he's our strangler."

"Let me make some calls."

"I'll call her psychologist," Greg said, looking through his notes. "Randi Schroeder. Charlotte already signed a release form. We can include her report in the warrant request."

After the fax arrived from Randi Schroeder, Greg took it down to Liam's office.

Liam shuffled some papers from his desk into a folder and looked over the report.

"This should be plenty for a warrant to search for child pornography, but without further evidence, we don't have a case for murder," he said with a frown.

"I know," Greg said. He had a sinking feeling that the case against Frank was slowly dissolving and that Bud was going to slip through their grasp as well.

Bracha Pacanowski blew into the interview room at the county jail, interrupting Frank and Noreen's silent vigil. They'd sat—not making eye contact—until she arrived. It took everything Noreen had just to sit there waiting, not knowing what would happen next, feeling her life disintegrate. Neither she nor Frank had mentioned his affair. She could only imagine what was going through Frank's mind right now, and didn't particularly want to know.

Pacanowski carried a large briefcase and a leather coat in her arms. Her blond hair hung straight past her shoulders. She looked too young to be a member of the Bar. Why did Bill recommend her? Frank had left the decision entirely to Bill Richards when Noreen said she wouldn't have any idea who to hire. Bill said she was the best—but he hadn't warned Noreen that she looked like a teenager.

The young woman dispelled Noreen's doubts as soon as she began speaking.

"Let's get started. I want to go over the entire case with you today to prepare for tomorrow's arraignment. From what Richards told me, there's a good chance we can get bail. We might be able to get the whole case dismissed, but that's a long shot. Right now, I need you to fill me in on the background."

"I didn't kill either of them," Frank said.

"That's a good thing." Pacanowski didn't even look up from the items she was pulling out of her briefcase. "Tell me all about your relationship with Sofia Molina," she instructed, "then we'll get to Mabel Garrity."

Noreen sat back, mortified, while the sordid details of Frank's affair poured out. She clarified points only when specifically asked. The one saving grace was Pacanowski's nonemotional attitude toward the facts. Noreen studied the strained planes of Frank's face, read the remorse in his eyes.

She wasn't completely indifferent to his suffering, but he was the one that got them into this mess. The kids were her priority.

Toward the end of the interview, Pacanowski suggested the kids attend the hearing the next day. "A family presence looks good—helps sway a judge to grant bail." Noreen swallowed a hard rush of animosity toward the attorney for wanting to use her kids in that way. "I think it would be better for them to go to school."

Pacanowski stood up abruptly, her lips pressed together. She stuffed her notepads and digital recorder into her briefcase. "Okay then. I'll see both of you in court tomorrow morning."

Frank kept his mouth shut, but he gave Noreen a worried look.

Noreen wasn't about to defend herself to either that young lawyer or Frank—they could think whatever they wanted. She wasn't going to expose the kids to any more of this nightmare than she had to.

~

Fox News blared from the TV when Bud opened his front door. Greg took in the torn upholstery on the couch and yellowed walls. A large photograph of a middle-aged woman dominated the mantel. Greg assumed that was Genny, Bud's late wife. From her generous smile and twinkling eyes, she looked like a nice woman.

Greg asked Bud to turn off the TV. Then he presented the warrants to search Bud's house and computer, and asked Sam to keep an eye on him. Bud didn't resist. He politely offered coffee to the police officers and evidence technicians, then showed them where he kept his computer, in a back bedroom.

A few minutes later the forensic computer specialist called

Blake into the room. "You need to see this." The specialist, a thin man with thick magnifying lenses in his glasses, sat down and began manipulating the mouse over a frayed black pad.

Greg noticed chips in the walnut veneer along the edge of the desk—particle board showed through.

"He didn't even have passwords," the tech shook his head, "and this is what he's been viewing."

He stood up to allow Greg to sit on the frayed upholstery of the ergonomic chair. The tech showed him how to navigate through the site. Greg spent thirty horrifying minutes scrolling through photos of naked children in various poses with adult men and women. Some of the children were crying, some looked frightened, and the eyes of the rest looked empty, like they'd lost their minds. Thinking of his granddaughters, Greg felt sick to his stomach.

Bud was old enough to have molested Sofia as a child. Greg focused on the girls' faces, mentally comparing them to the photo of Sofia at age six, the one they saw in her apartment. Blake and the two other officers turned away in disgust and resumed their search of the house.

They found a handful of child porn prints stuffed in Bud's bedside table, the glossies covered with greasy fingerprints. Dozens of ancient, moldy child porn magazines were discovered in the garage—in two large, damp boxes labeled "Tools."

"This asshole's going down," Greg muttered under his breath, disappointed he hadn't seen any kid looking like Sofia. He turned to the tech. "Take everything into evidence." Just because they hadn't found a link to Sofia so far didn't mean one didn't exist. The techs would comb through every picture again with facial recognition software.

Greg walked out to the kitchen, where Sam was sitting with Bud. Bud wouldn't meet his eyes. Greg arrested him, read him his rights, and asked the officers to take him to the station for questioning. He advised Bud to call a lawyer. Before he left the house, he took one more look at Genny's photograph on the mantel, wondering if she had known about her husband's perversions. And if she did, how could she stand living with the man?

Back at the station, Greg and Blake met with Liam in his office. After telling him what they'd found, there was silence for a full minute.

"Any evidence that he knew Sofia?" Liam finally asked.

"Not so far. She's too old for him now—judging from the pictures he's been jerking off to." Greg's anger was rapidly dissolving into sorrow. The images he'd seen that morning would haunt him for the rest of his life.

Liam shook his head, frowning. "Better go talk to him."

Greg's phone rang before they left Liam's office. It was the fingerprint technician—Bud's prints, which were taken when he arrived at the station, did not match any on the gloves taken from the Jameses' garage.

~

Bud sat hunched in the interrogation room. Humiliation seemed to have caused him to shrink and curl up upon himself.

Greg nodded hello to the well-known attorney, Imran Malik, sitting next to Bud. Bud must have great connections to have summoned him so quickly.

Malik's grandfatherly white hair, corduroy pants, and tweed jacket didn't fool Greg. Previous courtroom experience had taught him that Malik was a master at disarming witnesses and twisting their testimony.

"You're being charged with felony possession of child pornography," Greg began.

Bud gazed at the table, not reacting. Malik remained stoic, jotting notes on a legal pad.

"You've also been accused of child molestation based on a report made by Charlotte Garrity and her psychologist, Dr. Randi Schroeder," Greg continued. "Would you like to comment on that?"

"My client is invoking his Fifth Amendment rights," Malik said calmly, not even looking up from his notes.

Bud started crying. "I never meant to hurt her. I loved her. I made one terrible mistake, but I never did it again."

Malik put his hand on Bud's arm. "Don't say anything more."

Greg waited, hoping Bud would ignore his attorney and confess further, but the only sound in the room was his quiet sobbing. Greg couldn't feel any empathy for the man—he'd seen those kids' faces.

"Can you explain the child pornography we found in your computer and in your house?"

"No comment," Malik answered, expressionless.

Bud continued to cry, covering his face with his hands.

"Is that why you killed Mabel Garrity?" Greg asked, hoping to get a reaction. "Did she find out you exposed yourself to Charlotte when she was six? Or did she somehow find out about the other kids? Did she try to blackmail you?"

Bud sucked in some air.

Malik turned to his client, a stern look on his face. "Don't answer that."

"I didn't kill Mabel," Bud insisted. "She didn't know about Charlotte or the other stuff."

"Don't respond to these leading questions." There was a faint tone of exasperation in Malik's voice.

Greg suppressed a grin. "Mabel spread that rumor about your wife. Was that to get even with her because she accused Cliff of molesting his own daughter?"

Bud stopped sobbing and looked up. "That might have been the reason."

Malik threw up his palms toward Bud in a stop sign.

Bud just ignored him. "I tried to stop Genny from going over there and accusing Cliff. I had to think fast to come up with the stranger in the park. I was terrified Charlotte would tell them it was me. I just wanted everyone to forget all about it."

Mucus and tears ran unchecked down Bud's face. Malik pulled a white handkerchief from an inside pocket of his jacket and passed it to Bud. Greg thought he could detect a subtle look of revulsion on the attorney's face. Greg wasn't sure if it was due to Bud's pedophilia, his inability to follow sound legal advice, or the disgusting fluids dripping off the pedophile's jaw.

~

Frank and Noreen were finally home, sitting in the kitchen where they'd collapsed after his arraignment and bail hearing on Thursday morning. Frank had pleaded not guilty to both charges of first-degree murder. His attorney had worked a miracle to get him out on bail. Noreen hadn't slept much over the past few nights and she guessed Frank was as exhausted as she was. She glanced aimlessly around her spotless kitchen and out the windows to her backyard before forcing herself to get up and start lunch.

Frank broke the silence, following her with his eyes. "What time will the kids be home from school?"

"Josh won't be home 'til six. He has football practice. Madeline'll probably be home around three thirty."

"God, I hate what this is doing to them."

"You should have thought of that before you started screwing that woman. Our lives have been a living hell since your arrest." Noreen slammed a plate on the table in front of him. The tuna sandwich and sliced apple jumped. She walked back to the refrigerator and pulled out two sodas, placing them on the table.

"Christ, Noreen, I'm sorry," Frank pleaded. "Having that affair with Sofia was the biggest mistake of my life."

Noreen walked back to the counter to grab her plate. Standing there, with her back to him, she said, "How could you do this to us?"

"I was insane," Frank said. "I know that sounds lame, but it's the truth."

She didn't know if "insane" was the right term, but it sure as hell was fucking stupid and selfish.

"Anything I can do to make it up to you and the kids, I will. Anything."

"You can't make it up to us!" Noreen yelled. She tried to get herself under control, using every ounce of strength to lower her voice. "All either of us can do now is damage control. I want this to be over. I want the kids' lives to get back to normal." Noreen knew things would never be normal again, but she hoped the kids could recover and move on with their lives.

"You don't believe I killed Sofia and Mabel, do you?"

Noreen sighed, wondering how to answer. "Of course not. And if you had told the truth about the affair from the beginning, you probably wouldn't have been arrested. You made things a thousand times worse by lying." She left her untouched plate of food on the counter—she was sick of talking about Frank's mess. "I can't take any more of this right now. I'll be upstairs."

Lying wide awake on their bed, Noreen let her eyes wander to the wood fireplace mantel Frank had installed. It was painted white to match the walls and wainscoting. Sheer lace curtains were filling and falling gently in the intermittent breeze coming through the open windows. The sound of a lawn mower and the smell of cut grass drifted into the room from somewhere down the street.

Frank had virtually rescued Noreen from the rusted mobile home she'd grown up in. He'd married her, started his own business, purchased and lovingly restored every inch of this beautiful home. He'd been her prince.

Her eyes rested on the framed blue ribbon she'd won in high school for her 4-H lamb. She'd kept it all these years. One of her mother's serial boyfriends, a grizzled, tough man named Diego, introduced Noreen to 4-H. He'd invited Noreen and her siblings out to his West County ranch. While they were watching the new lambs on a green hillside dotted with poppies, Diego offered to let Noreen raise one of them. He signed her up for 4-H, built a shed next to their trailer, bought feed and hay, and helped her enter the lamb in the judging. He promised each of the younger kids they could have one when they turned sixteen.

Diego was the nicest man her mother ever hooked up with. The only one who'd made an effort to improve their lives. He fixed the leaky toilet, patched the trailer roof. But he stopped coming around soon after the fair. Noreen suspected he couldn't tolerate her mother's drinking binges anymore. Whatever the reason he left, Noreen and the younger kids had missed him much more than their mother did.

The best thing that came out of that relationship was Frank—Noreen met him at the county fair, with all the other kids showing their livestock. Frank had been tall and cute. But his hardworking, sober parents attracted Noreen more than Frank himself. When Diego disappeared from their lives, so did her 4-H membership. But she had continued to see Frank, even though they lived in different towns.

When she married Frank, Noreen believed that as long as she did her part—didn't drink, was a good wife and home-maker—Frank would love and protect them. Her children would never have to experience the uncertainty and depriva-tion that Noreen grew up with. Up until now, everything had gone according to plan.

Frank's construction company thrived. Noreen kept house and raised a beautiful daughter and a beloved son. She did volunteer work and discovered a talent for fund-raising and nonprofit organization. The kids excelled in school. Frank had never so much as flirted with another woman, to Noreen's knowledge, before that evil Sofia showed up.

Now Noreen had completely lost her faith in Frank. And she didn't know if she could ever get it back. She could never trust that he wouldn't walk out on her and the kids someday —like her father, Diego, and every other man her mother ever slept with did.

∾

Mary stood in the Rogers Gallery on Thursday afternoon, nervously watching the owner, Leah Rogers, look through her portfolio of watercolors. Leah scrutinized each painting carefully. Then she offered to put two pieces on consignment. Mary called Zoey as soon as she got home.

"Oh my gosh! That is so fabulous! Which ones?"

"The view of the river from Healdsburg Ridge and the old railroad station with the tracks and the wildflowers in the foreground. She wants the originals framed, but before that she wants me to order limited-edition prints and notecards. I'm so excited I can't think straight."

But even as she spoke, Mary's sprits plummeted. Enzo would never know about any of this—never see her work hanging in the gallery. He wouldn't be there to help her celebrate if she actually sold a piece. He wouldn't have any part of her new, artist life.

Zoey must have sensed something of her mood, because she abruptly changed the subject. "Did you hear they released Frank James on bail?"

"No, but I don't believe for a minute he's a murderer. That has to be a mistake." Mary felt sorry for the whole family. She should do something to reach out, but she didn't know what.

~

"I didn't kill your mom." Bud hadn't even sat all the way down.

Charlotte was in the visiting room of the county jail. Greg had told her she was free to speak with Bud there, with a guard in attendance, if she still insisted on doing so.

It wasn't Charlotte's first time in a jail. It was a rare event in her work as a paralegal—mostly handling separations, divorces, wills and trusts. But she'd had the occasional incarcerated client that still needed to take care of business. The room was small and crowded with tables, prisoners, families, and despair. The guards stood watchful and impassive against the walls. Bud finished sitting, leaned forward, and looked at her imploringly.

Charlotte tried to ignore her revulsion and focus on her questions. She found she couldn't look him in the eye—she kept her gaze on his mouth.

"Why did you let Genny accuse my dad of molesting me?"

Bud sat back—his mouth open in surprise.

What did he expect? That she'd coddle him, play along with his lies? Well, he had another thought coming. She waited, stone-faced, until he began speaking.

"I didn't know what else to do. I hated myself—your dad was my best friend."

Shit, he was starting to cry. Charlotte felt a burning, queasy pain in her stomach. *How could she ever have loved this sleazebag?* "Some best friend you turned out to be. How could you do that to me? To my dad? To all of us?"

"I don't know, honey." Bud looked around furtively, as if he were afraid someone in the room was listening. "Nothing was the same after that."

"What in the fuck did you expect, you pervert?" Charlotte was shaking with anger.

Bud seemed oblivious, caught up in feeling sorry for himself.

"Your parents stopped speaking to us. Then your mom started that rumor about Genny and the Romano will."

"Don't make this about my mom," Charlotte warned.

"I'm just trying to answer your questions, honey." Bud's lips trembled. "Genny was devastated by that rumor. It broke my heart to see her so unhappy."

Charlotte remembered the cold silence in her own house back then. Her dad furious with her mom—arguments Charlotte couldn't understand.

She looked away from Bud, toward a black woman at the next table, speaking rapidly to a young man in prison clothes. The woman must be his mother—there seemed to be a resemblance. The son looked sullen. What was she telling him that could possibly help matters now?

Charlotte took a deep breath. "I think that was the beginning of the end for my parents' marriage."

Bud's head seemed to droop, as if it were too heavy to hold upright any longer. "They never seemed happy after that," he agreed. "Then you and Isobel moved away. Eventually I heard rumors about your dad having an affair, and Mabel driving his mistress out of town. Next thing I knew, your dad killed himself."

"Did he kill himself because of the affair?" Charlotte needed to know why her dad shot himself. She needed to feel less guilty about not being there when her dad obviously needed her help.

"I have no idea. He wasn't talking to me at all by then."

She was wasting her time. Either Bud didn't know or wouldn't tell her. She couldn't bear to be in the same room with him any longer. She stood and signaled the guard that she was finished. Drained and sad, she walked out without saying goodbye.

Later, she called Greg to thank him for the opportunity.

"Are you going to be okay?"

"I'll be fine." In saying so, she knew it was true. "We already got an offer on the house—over the asking price. I've accepted it. I hope I never have to set foot in this damn town again."

17

"The Molina chick checked in by herself, around seven in the evening, asked for two keys, and didn't have any luggage. She left the building after she registered. I thought she might be a high-class hooker." Brent Hunter gave a sheepish grin. "She sure looked like one."

Greg and Blake were interviewing Hunter at the Railroad Square Hotel in Santa Rosa. They were seated in his supervisor's office—a small, utilitarian space with metal furniture, no windows, and no decoration other than a few family photos thumb-tacked to the walls. Hunter was slight, probably in his early twenties, with acne-pitted skin and scraggly dark hair hanging over his uniform shirt collar. He seemed twitchy—Greg wasn't sure if it was excitement, nervousness, or drugs.

"What do you mean?" Greg asked, trying not to show how much this sleazy kid was irritating him.

"Short, low-cut dress, stiletto heels—you know." Hunter waved his hands in the air, as if outlining a curvaceous figure. "She came back in, nine thirty, or a little after. Still no luggage, and she walked directly to the elevators. About three minutes later, a man came in, took a quick look around, and followed her up. He looked shifty—tried to keep his face turned away from me. Most people, they come in the front door and look over toward the desk. If we're not busy, they smile or say hi or something on their way to the elevators. I figured he was a john for sure."

"What did he look like?"

"Medium-tall, husky, mustache, bald."

"Caucasian?" Greg asked.

"Yeah."

Greg tried to picture the lobby. The distance from the front entrance to reception was about one hundred feet. From the elevators to reception about forty feet. That was close enough to get a pretty good look at someone.

Hunter jiggled his leg up and down. His smile had turned smug.

"Did you recognize him?" Greg fought to keep the impatience out of his voice and body language. The kid obviously knew something. Why wouldn't he just tell them what it was?

"Not at the time." Hunter's smile got bigger. "But when I heard you were asking about Ms. Molina, I looked up the story online. There was a picture of him in the article."

"What story are you referring to?"

"About her murder."

"Well, who was it?"

"Healdsburg chief of police—Liam Friedman."

Sick at heart, Greg continued to question Hunter. He showed him a photo lineup that Ángela had quickly assembled and faxed to the hotel. Hunter picked out Liam's picture immediately. Greg thanked him and asked him to complete a written statement.

Back at the station, the dispatcher said Liam was in his

office. Greg left Blake in the deserted squad room and slowly walked down the hall. Liam's door was open.

Greg stood in the doorway looking at the framed picture of Liam's wife, Karen, sitting on the windowsill. He wanted to protect both of them from the tsunami of trouble that was going to hit, but didn't see how he could. They were his closest friends and he was probably going to lose them both over this mess. Greg was having trouble believing that Liam would have fallen for Sofia's obvious wiles, let alone that he might be a murderer.

Liam looked up from the report he was reading on his computer screen and raised his eyebrows in question.

"Can I have a word?" At Liam's nod, Greg walked in, closed the door, shoved his hands in his pockets, and leaned back against the wall. "We have a new witness in the Molina case."

Liam put his elbows on the desk and rubbed his face and the back of his neck before gesturing toward one of the chairs.

Greg ignored the gesture, preferring to stand. "He's a clerk at the Railroad Square Hotel in Santa Rosa."

Liam sat there, staring up at him for several long seconds. His eyes looked resigned, as if he'd known this would surface eventually. Greg lost all hope of a simple misunderstanding. He remembered Liam's reaction when he first saw Sofia's body near the railroad tracks and the way Liam cautioned them to look beyond her sexual partners for the murderer.

Thank God Liam had been shocked by the sight of her body. He wouldn't have been caught off guard if he'd been the one to kill her. Then again, what if he killed her but someone else moved her body?

"I should have told you when we found her." Liam shook his head slowly, as if he couldn't believe his own stupidity. "I'm just like all the other suckers—ashamed I hooked up with her and not wanting anyone to find out about it."

Liam's eyes darted toward Karen's picture. A wave of anger and hurt swept through Greg, catching him off guard. Liam had betrayed all of them.

"What took him so long to come forward?" Liam asked.

"What the fuck difference does that make?" Greg said in a cold, controlled voice.

Liam just looked at him with a defeated expression, which made Greg feel even worse. He pulled his eyes away to get a handle on his emotions. "He was on vacation."

Greg looked back at Liam and added, "You understand this makes you a suspect, right?"

Greg and Blake seated themselves across the interview table from Liam and his attorney, Walter Brown, at 1700 on Friday evening. Liam's mouth was in a straight line, his brown eyes resolute. Greg nodded at Brown, who sat next to Liam, fidgeting with his pen. *Thank God he's got an experienced criminal lawyer,* Greg thought, before gesturing to Blake, who turned on the video recorder and opened his notepad. None of them wanted to be here, doing this, but it was important that they did it right.

After the formal introductions and statements of the date and time were completed, Greg asked Liam to tell them about his relationship with Sofia Molina.

Liam looked at his attorney, who gave a curt nod.

"I met Sofia on May fourteenth, after the city council meeting."

"May fourteenth of this year?" Greg asked.

"Yes."

"Where did you meet her?"

"The Redwood Bar," Liam said, naming the bar and restaurant in the new Healdsburg Avenue Inn Sofia had been known to frequent.

"I noticed her when we walked in, but I didn't know who she was. The rest of the council members left about forty-five minutes after we got there. I was just finishing my drink and getting ready to head home, when Sofia sat next to me and struck up a conversation. A bit later she asked if I'd walk her to her car." Liam paused for a drink of water. "She said her friends had all gone home. I figured she just wanted protection."

Yeah, right, Greg thought, trying to picture the sexy young woman coming on to the chief of police. Could Liam, tired after a long day and tedious meeting, be oblivious to her flirting? Unlikely, Greg decided. "Did you think she was a prostitute?" he asked.

"No . . . not at first. But when we got outside she asked me if I'd like to join her in Santa Rosa, that she had a room at the inn. I couldn't believe she'd proposition a policeman." Liam grimaced. "I was thinking, 'Fuck, I'm too tired to arrest her. Maybe I should just give her a warning.'"

Greg felt anger and anxiety burning a hole in his stomach.

"She must have read my mind. Assured me she wasn't a prostitute. She was so matter-of-fact about the whole thing—didn't even seem offended by my suspicions."

How could Liam be so fucking stupid? Greg wondered. *Why didn't he just say no?*

"I called Karen, my wife," Liam added for the recording, saving Greg the trouble of clarifying, "and told her I might be out a few more hours, so she shouldn't worry. Then I drove to Santa Rosa, met Sofia in her room at the hotel."

"Why?"

"I don't know. Maybe I was curious."

"About what?"

Liam shrugged. "What she wanted—what it would be like with a different woman."

Greg sat, studying Liam, trying to decide if he knew this man at all. "Were you in the habit of using prostitutes?"

"No," Liam said. "Never."

"Did she ask you for money at any time?"

"No."

"Any conversation at the hotel? Plans to meet again?"

"Minimal conversation. No plans made that night."

Liam's attorney hadn't said a word, just scribbled vigorously on his legal pad.

"How long were you there?"

"About an hour."

It was maybe a twenty-minute drive between Healdsburg and Santa Rosa at that time of night, Greg thought. Then another fifteen minutes back to Windsor. Liam would've been home in less than two hours from the time he'd called Karen. She wouldn't have been worried. "Did Sofia give you her real name?" Greg asked.

"Yes."

"Did you see her again?"

"She managed to run into me two more times," Liam answered. "Asked me to meet her once in Rohnert Park and once in Windsor. I really had no idea what she was up to, but just like all the other idiots, I couldn't resist. Then I didn't hear anything from her for about a month."

Greg waited, dreading what Liam might reveal next. Things were bad enough already.

Sweat was beading up on Liam's forehead. He pulled a neatly folded handkerchief from his pants pocket and wiped it up. His normally ruddy complexion had taken on a sickly gray cast, just like the day they found Sofia's body. Greg didn't like it—there was something wrong.

"Do you need a break, Chief Friedman?" Greg asked, glancing toward the attorney for guidance. "You look ill."

"No," Liam said firmly. "I want to get this over with."

"Are you sure, Chief?" the attorney asked, looking equally concerned.

"I'm fine," Liam insisted.

Greg wasn't so sure. He looked at Blake, who shrugged slightly. The attorney looked doubtful, but he waved at Greg to continue. Liam's color started to return, so Greg asked him what happened next.

"I saw her jogging one morning in mid-June along the bike path. I pulled over and asked her when we were getting together again. She told me she'd lost interest and just jogged off, cool as could be. That was it. Never spoke to me again. I saw her a few times around town with her friends, the ones you've already interviewed. She ignored me. I felt like a total schmuck."

"Did Sofia know you'd be at the Redwood Bar on May fourteenth?"

"I don't think so. I figure she was trolling for any guy and I just happened to be the unlucky one to catch her eye that night."

"Did she know who you were?" Greg asked.

"I don't think so—not until I introduced myself. Then she seemed impressed, but that could have been an act."

"Did she know you were married?"

"I told her I was."

Damn, Greg thought, glancing at the ring Liam always wore on his left hand. She knew he was married before she sat next to him. "Why do you think she was doing this—if it wasn't for money—with you and all these other guys?"

"Objection," the attorney said. "Requires speculation."

"We're not in court, Walt," Liam said, patting his attorney on the arm gently, before answering. "I don't know. Ángela's theory of sex addiction might be right. I mean," Liam looked down at himself, "why would a woman like that be interested in a middle-aged guy like me?"

"Why didn't you tell us who she was when we first discovered her body?"

The attorney opened his mouth to say something, but Liam forestalled him with another touch.

"I was ashamed and I didn't want Karen hurt. It was a clear dereliction of duty."

"It was obstruction." Greg couldn't believe Liam had put him in this position. He wondered briefly if Liam had agreed to keep the investigation in-house because he believed Greg would protect him. Greg cautioned himself not to take any of this personally. "Other than the friends we've identified, you never saw her with another man?"

"Never."

"Where were you the evening of Friday, October tenth?" Greg asked.

"Working late—finishing some reports. Karen was back in Denver, visiting our kids, so I got some take-out and ate at my desk. I didn't get home until 2130."

"Shit, Liam," Greg said, "that leaves you a perfect window of opportunity to swing by the market, kill Sofia, and dump her body before you went home. That puts you right up there on our suspect list with Frank and Bud."

"What is the estimated time of death?" Liam's attorney asked.

"She was seen on CCTV leaving the market at 2059 Friday night," Greg answered after checking his notes. "But she might have been alive as late as 0200 Saturday morning."

"I didn't go to the market that night," Liam said. "And I didn't kill her."

"Where did you get the take-out?"

"El Cactus," he said, indicating the Mexican restaurant across the street from the station. "I paid with a credit card. I can prove I was there."

"What time?"

"About 2000." Liam sat calmly, his hands clasped in front of him on the table. His gaze was steady and he relaxed against the back of his chair, as if a burden had been lifted from his shoulders.

The El Cactus credit card receipt wouldn't exonerate him, Greg thought. They still needed a witness who saw what happened later that night when Sofia came out of the market. Her purse and keys had been locked inside her car in the parking lot, implying that's where she had been attacked.

"Did you know Mabel Garrity?" Greg asked, switching tactics.

"No."

"Did you have any dealings with her at all?"

"Not that I'm aware of."

"Did you kill her?"

"No."

"Where were you the morning of Sunday, October twelfth?"

"Home with Karen. She came back on Saturday and we were celebrating our twenty-first wedding anniversary."

Greg and Blake spent another half hour with Liam confirming the dates and hotels in which he and Sofia had met. May fourteenth, May twenty-second, and June second all corresponded with booking dates already collected from her credit card accounts.

Later, Greg stood at his desk, packing up his briefcase. He thought Liam had left with his attorney. Someone knocked on the open door. It was Liam.

"Just wanted to let you know I'm heading home now," he said. "I'll tell Karen everything. Don't worry. It's all going to be okay."

Greg nodded stiffly and waited for Liam to leave. Things were definitely not going to be okay, he thought. Far from it. Greg didn't think that Liam had killed Sofia. But he would have to be investigated just like all the other suspects.

Liam would have to resign, or take a leave of absence until the case was solved. He'd be lucky if he didn't end up doing jail time for withholding evidence in a criminal case. And now that Liam was a suspect, Greg knew they'd have to bring in an outside agency.

The fallout from Liam's revelations was going to ruin Karen's life. Greg figured she'd experience even more disbelief and anger than he was going through. He didn't know if he could consider Liam a friend anymore, even if he didn't kill anyone. Greg picked up his in-box, which was full of files, and threw it as hard as he could, scattering papers everywhere and leaving a big dent in the drywall.

~

"Denise?" Blake sat in his car in the parking lot behind the station, where no one could overhear him. Reeling from the interrogation he'd just witnessed, Blake considered himself no better than Liam. Hadn't he kissed Denise Saturday night? And how much further would it have gone if Aaron hadn't been there? Here it was almost a week later and Blake still hadn't apologized. If he were going to be completely honest with himself, he'd admit he'd been dragging his feet—not wanting to own his mistake, unsure how Denise would respond.

"Oh, Blake. I'm glad you called. I got that job in Petaluma."

Blake hesitated—finding it hard to switch gears, but glad for a momentary reprieve from having to make his apology. Denise probably didn't want to talk about Saturday night either. "Hey, congratulations."

"I'm so stoked. I thought both interviews went really well, but you never know. They offered me the job this morning."

"When do you start?" he asked, making an effort to sound upbeat.

"Monday. I can't believe it. I've been looking for months—most of my classmates haven't found anything yet. And this is exactly what I was looking for. I'm going to Petaluma tomorrow to look for an apartment."

She was moving away. Blake felt relief and regret at the same time. Which was dumb—Petaluma was only forty minutes down the highway.

"That's really good news." He searched quickly for a transition from her announcement to his apology. "How did Aaron's chemo go this week?" He really should have called Aaron to check on him before this.

"Not bad—he's been pretty tired, but other than that he feels okay. Mom's over at his apartment right now, helping him with dinner and stuff."

"That's good. Let me know if there's anything I can do to help her out. She might need a break."

"I promise we'll let you know. Thanks."

Blake couldn't stall any longer. "The reason I called was to apologize for kissing you."

There was a brief pause. What was she thinking at this moment? Was she angry? Embarrassed? Had she forgotten all about it?

"Apology accepted," she said. "And I'm sorry I kissed you back."

"Sydney and I are having some difficulties, but I'm trying to work through them."

"Understood—don't worry about it. I'll be moving down to Petaluma. We probably won't see much of each other after this. Nothing more needs to be said."

Was she hurt? Or was she relieved? Or both? He felt disappointed by her breezy dismissal. But wasn't that for the best? He'd done what he set out to do. If he was going to have any integrity at all, he had to leave it there.

∼

"How's the case going?" Sydney asked after Blake put Jeremy to bed and joined her in the living room later that evening.

"Bad." Blake hadn't wanted to bring it up in front of Jeremy, who adored Liam, but now he could speak freely. "Turns out Liam had an affair with Sofia Molina." Blake paused, wondering if he should go on. He wasn't supposed to discuss active cases with Sydney, but this was going to be in the paper soon and she could keep a secret better than anyone else he knew.

Sydney turned away from the TV, her eyes wide. "Oh, my God! How stupid is that?"

"Not only that, he failed to identify her when we had no idea who she was—it's a mess."

A wicked grin slowly replaced the surprised look on Sydney's face. "Maybe you'll get a promotion—if Liam gets fired, I mean."

Blake felt a horrible sinking sensation. Liam assuredly would lose his job at the very least. Sydney didn't give a damn about the man. She didn't like Liam or Karen. She didn't like anyone except herself and her immediate family.

Hold on, he thought, *you just told Denise you were going to work out your problems with Sydney.* He had to let this go—focus on the decision he'd made on the drive home.

"Sweetie?" he asked.

"What?"

"Remember our discussion after Aaron's party?"

She nodded.

"I was angry and said some things I shouldn't have. I'm sorry."

Sydney relaxed and leaned against the back of the couch.

Encouraged, Blake reached for her hand. "But Aaron's leukemia has made me realize how short life is. I want us to start spending more time with our family and friends. We never know how much time we have left—with any of them."

Her eyes narrowed.

"Jeremy's five years old. He needs some friends." Blake stroked her hand. "You're trying to keep him in a bubble. You're smothering him."

Sydney pulled her hand away. "I'm protecting him. And teaching him solid Christian values."

Blake didn't remember religion being that important to Sydney before they got married—but after Jeremy was old enough to go to Sunday school she'd become evangelical. Blake had tried attending church with them a couple of times, but he couldn't get into it. He really didn't know why she was so gung-ho about it either. She criticized most of the church members behind their backs and didn't seem to have any friends there.

"I know. But I want him to have a normal life." Blake tried to clear his voice of exasperation. "I think we should consider getting some family counseling."

Sydney's features pinched in displeasure. "What are you saying?"

"I'm saying something has to change."

She got up, walked to their bedroom, and slammed the door.

Damn, Blake thought, *you handled that well.* He turned off the TV and lights. He wanted to make this marriage work, for Jeremy's sake, if nothing else, but he was reaching the end of his rope. Sydney could make an effort to compromise or not, but from now on, Blake was going to have some say in his kid's life.

He walked down the hall and tapped lightly on the bedroom door before opening it. They weren't done talking and she was going to hear the rest of it tonight, whether she liked it or not.

"My mom's going to babysit Jeremy tomorrow night," Blake said. "I already spoke to her. We can go out to dinner."

Sydney stood, wearing a ribbed tank top and underpants,

next to her side of the bed, pulling back the covers. "I don't think . . ."

"It's not negotiable, Sydney." Blake tried to ignore how sexy she looked. "He needs both his grandmothers. He'll be fine in her hands."

Sydney glared at him for a brief moment, climbed into bed, and turned away from him, pulling the covers up over her head.

~

The phone woke Greg at 0500 Saturday morning. He was sure it would be his sister, Colleen, but it was Karen Friedman's voice on the phone.

"Sorry to call so early, Greg."

"Karen . . ." Greg struggled to emerge from sleep. "Is something wrong?"

"Yes."

Greg heard a sob.

"Liam had a stroke last night. I'm calling from Memorial Hospital."

"Give me thirty minutes."

When Greg arrived, Karen came out of Liam's room and guided him down the hall to an empty waiting area. "He's not conscious. Only family is allowed inside."

"How bad is it?" Greg asked, rubbing her shoulder.

"Bad . . . He may not survive." She started crying.

"Oh, Karen." Greg felt sick. "This is all my fault."

"No . . . It's not. Liam told me everything last night." Karen's crying intensified.

Greg waited, furious at Liam and himself.

After a short time, she took a deep breath and continued. "He was proud of the way you handled the interrogation. He said he hoped you wouldn't beat yourself up too much. He knows you have a powerful guilt complex. Those were his exact words." Karen pulled a tissue from her pocket and blew her nose.

Greg hugged her. "This is so fucked up. I was so angry with him last night."

"Me too."

~

Late Saturday morning Greg sat in his office, staring, unseeing, out the window. Visions of Liam turning gray and Karen crying unconsolably alternated in his mind. He replayed the interrogation over and over, only this time forcing Liam to stop—insisting he see a doctor immediately.

Liam's stroke would be life-shattering for Karen, even if he lived. And she'd been like a sister to Greg ever since they moved to Sonoma County—inviting him over, ever so gradually tunneling through his reticence and finding a way into his personal life. Certainly more than Julia. Karen didn't know the whole truth about Colleen, but she knew Colleen had a disfiguring accident as a child and it had been his fault. Now Greg had let Karen down big time.

Mayor Howard had gone ballistic when Greg called her about Liam's involvement in the case. She'd immediately ordered Greg to contact the California Department of Justice —the DOJ. The city would have to do everything possible to avoid the appearance of a conflict of interest. No matter the expense, a neutral third party would have to assume control of the cases, wresting the investigation out of Greg's hands.

To give the mayor credit, she'd seemed much more concerned about public safety and the integrity of the police department than about any effect the case might have on her own political career. Still, it hadn't been a fun telephone call.

Greg did have the presence of mind to ask Mayor Howard if she'd been at the May city council meeting and if she'd gone to the Redwood Bar with Liam and the others afterward. She said she'd gone for a short time but hadn't noticed Sofia, and hadn't seen her with Liam.

The mayor informed Greg she was appointing him acting chief of police, causing his spirits to drop even lower. The paperwork, the media—especially now with Chief Friedman's incrimination—the petty politics of personnel management—*shit*. He briefly considered suggesting Blake instead.

"I probably don't need to warn you," the mayor said, "but the publicity on this development is going to be daunting."

Greg sighed—no kidding. Blake was motivated, and as sergeant, he'd demonstrated his administrative skills, but he lacked the maturity for the position. If Greg failed in the assignment, it wouldn't matter. His career was almost over. "I'll do it until you can hire someone."

"I'd like you to consider applying for the position permanently."

"No, thank you, ma'am—I don't have the personality for the job. Liam was perfect. You need to find someone like him."

"Don't be hasty. At least give it some thought. And I appreciate your willingness to step up until we can hire someone."

Greg sat there, staring out the window, planning exactly what he needed to tell the DOJ. Retirement looked tempting now—after they found a new chief. He appreciated the mayor's confidence in him. But he hadn't wanted the chief's job when they started the search for Liam and he sure as hell didn't want it now. He had more than enough years in to receive full retirement pay. The phone broke his chain of thought.

Bob at the forensics lab had some DNA results.

Greg sat forward, pulling a notepad closer.

"The skin cells on the rope from Mabel Garrity's neck— some match her DNA, some of them match Sofia Molina's."

"So the same piece of rope was definitely used to strangle both victims—that helps."

"The pubic hair found on Sofia's body and hairs found on Mabel's porch both match Frank James's DNA."

"Okay, good. That confirms what we thought." Greg could hear papers rustling in the background.

"One interesting thing: there was a long, dark brown hair found on Mabel's porch. The DNA matches a hair we found on Sofia's clothing that doesn't belong to Sofia. And it doesn't match James or Morris."

18

B lake was tired—if he hadn't insisted Sydney leave Jeremy with his mom tonight, and if his mom hadn't been eagerly awaiting Jeremy's visit, he'd have canceled their dinner out. He'd spent all afternoon investigating a huge wine theft from a warehouse on Grove Street because Greg had to deal with the mayor and the DOJ. Between his fatigue and his worries about Liam, he didn't feel up to tackling a disgruntled wife tonight.

Sydney was in the kitchen watching Jeremy eat an apple when Blake got home. She looked up at him and smiled. "How'd it go?"

"Tell you about it over dinner. You guys ready?" Blake asked, picking Jeremy up in a hug.

"Where are we going, Daddy?" Jeremy asked.

"You get to go to Granny's. Mommy and I are going out to dinner." He put Jeremy down. "I'll just run and change—give me ten minutes."

Coming back into the kitchen, wearing jeans and a sweat-shirt he said, "How's La Flor sound?"

Sydney shrugged. "Fine."

"I want to go to floor," Jeremy said.

"You're going to Granny's. She's fixing your favorite dinner—macaroni and cheese."

"You don't have to go to Granny's if you're scared, honey," Sydney said.

"Actually, you do," Blake countered, frowning at Sydney. "Mommy's joking—there's nothing to be afraid of at Granny's. Grab your coat and let's get in the car."

Sydney didn't say a word on the drive to his mother's house. She sat in the car, apparently fuming, while Blake delivered Jeremy into his grandmother's eager arms.

Climbing back into the car, Blake looked over at Sydney. "I thought you agreed to this."

"I don't like you forcing him to do something he doesn't want to do."

"How can he know? He's five years old and this is the first time he's been alone with my mom. And you're purposely planting seeds of fear and doubt about her."

"That's not true."

"I've never heard you so much as a hint that he might be afraid to stay with your parents."

"Why should he be?"

"He has no reason to be afraid of either of our parents." Blake forced himself to lower his voice. "Just give it a chance, Sydney."

"I don't need all this drama, Blake."

Blake took a deep breath and looked straight ahead. "Let's go have dinner. I really want to make this work." As soon as the words were out of his mouth he wondered if they were even true anymore. He was too tired to figure that out tonight. "I'm going to need you to meet me halfway."

"Hurry up, then. The sooner we eat, the sooner we can get back here to pick him up."

"It doesn't work that way. I promised Mom two hours and that's what she's gonna get. We're not picking him up until seven thirty."

"Whatever."

~

Greg was late getting home Saturday evening. After he put in the call to the DOJ, he'd spent a couple of hours with the city manager, who'd graciously offered to come in on Saturday afternoon and show him how to submit budgets, payroll, and other administrative reports. Afterward, Greg worked on the spreadsheets and records to make sure everything was up to date for the coming week. It was a much bigger job than he had imagined.

Ángela volunteered to come in on her day off to work the phones—trying to contact the rest of Sofia Molina's family and friends. After she finished the entire list, she reported that not one of them had heard of Bud Morris or knew anything about him. She went home, clearly discouraged by another dead end in the search for a link between the two murdered women.

Now Greg was exhausted, hungry, frustrated with the cases, and worried about Liam. He'd called Karen before he left the station. She said Liam's condition was unchanged. On top of everything else, he still had Colleen's visit looming over him like judgment day.

Greg opened his refrigerator and looked without interest at a loaf of bread—at least a month old—some spoiled milk, and two beers. He'd used up all the eggs. He would have to settle for toast—or drive to the store. Impulsively, he slammed the refrigerator door and grabbed his coat. What he desperately needed right now was a sympathetic ear.

Driving over to Julia's, he wondered if he could coax her into fixing him something to eat while he unburdened himself of the whole sorry mess.

Julia's house was dark when he pulled up—no lights in any

of the windows. Was she working? Greg couldn't remember what she'd told him about her schedule this weekend. He decided to try the doorbell anyway. He stood there, thinking about driving to the store, when the porch light suddenly came on. Julia opened the door a moment later, wrapped in a silk robe, hair tousled, face creased on one side. Greg realized she must have been asleep. It was only eight thirty.

"I'm sorry," Greg said. "I didn't mean to wake you."

"What's going on?" Julia asked tiredly, opening the door wider and gesturing him in. He followed her into the kitchen, where she grabbed a glass and filled it with water from the tap.

He sat on a barstool on the other side of the counter and gave her an abbreviated summary of recent events—Liam's stroke, his acting as chief until they hired someone, the case being pushed up to the DOJ because no one in the Healdsburg PD could be considered impartial anymore.

Julia stood there, sipping from her glass, not saying a word. She looked half asleep—and she wasn't making any encouraging sounds. Greg lost all hope of getting a meal. He'd have to pick something up when he left.

"I hope you're not blaming yourself for Liam's stroke," Julia said with a hint of impatience. "He brought this trouble on himself and, God knows, he probably would have had the stroke regardless. He's probably had high blood pressure for years."

"But the stress of the interrogation could have precipitated the stroke, couldn't it?" Greg asked. "I should have stopped him when I had the chance."

Julia looked impassive. He wasn't going to get any empathy there. Greg glanced down at the hardwood floor. He hadn't planned to tell her about Colleen tonight, but now he felt he had to—just dump the whole thing on her, now, before he lost his nerve. "There's more."

Her forehead wrinkled and she put her glass down in the sink. "What?"

"My sister, Colleen, who I haven't seen for almost forty years, is coming to visit me."

Julia walked around to the kitchen table, pulled out a chair, and sat, facing Greg. Her robe gapped open and Greg could see the cotton camisole and panties she slept in. She rested her elbow on the table, head on her hand. "That's a problem?"

"Probably."

"What am I missing here?" Julia pushed some stray hairs away from her eyes. "I'm sorry, but I had to work twelve hours today and I have to go back at seven tomorrow morning. I'm tired and I don't have time to play guessing games."

Shit, Greg thought—*this was a mistake.* "It's kind of a long story. Maybe I should save it for another time." He stood up. He should have called before he came over. He couldn't take anything for granted in this relationship.

"No." Julia sat up straighter. "I won't be able to sleep now, wondering what it is you haven't told me."

This isn't how I wanted to tell her, Greg thought. But he decided to just get it over with.

"When we were kids, a dog attacked my sister and tore up her face. It was all my fault."

"How was that your fault?" Julia asked, her foot tapping on the floor.

I rushed over here like a baby, Greg thought, *needing reassurance. But, I'm sick and tired of protecting this big fucking secret. I'm going to get it out in the open once and for all.*

"I was eight and she was six. We were both playing in the backyard. I was bored. I climbed our tree and started throwing tennis balls over the fence at our neighbor's dog. Colleen was playing with her dolls, but when she heard the dog bark, she asked what I was doing. I told her I was throwing balls for Gus."

Julia's face looked stony with impatience. Greg blurted out the rest.

"Colleen told me to stop and walked over to the fence and called the Rottweiler to her. I watched the old dog struggle to get up from the spot where he'd been lying and make his way toward Colleen. I took aim and hit the dog right on the nose. Gus gave a loud yelp and lunged at the fence. The boards just gave way and he plowed right through into Colleen. Before I knew it, he had his jaws clamped on her head and he was trying to shake her—it's a miracle he didn't break her neck."

"Oh my God."

"By the time Gus released Colleen, her face was partially torn off and there was blood gushing everywhere."

Julia sat frozen, her mouth parted, a look of horror in her eyes.

"She needed multiple surgeries—and she never looked right. By the time she was in junior high she was cutting herself, overeating, and in and out of psychiatric clinics."

"Your poor sister." Julia covered her face with her hands, as if she was trying to block out the picture Greg's story had painted.

"When I was away at college, she went to work at a mission school in Alaska. She made it clear she hated me and didn't want anything to do with me. Now, forty years later, I get a letter saying she wants to see me."

Greg could hear the kitchen clock ticking. He watched Julia, wondering what she thought about him now. She might not like him anymore, but the truth was finally out and Greg actually felt better. He wondered if Liam had felt this same sense of relief after his confession—it would explain why he looked so relaxed when he stopped by Greg's office to say goodbye.

Julia rubbed her eyes and yawned. "That's quite a story. And I really do want to be supportive, Greg, but I'm exhausted. We'll talk about this some other time."

"You don't understand—I ruined her fucking life and I ruined my parents' lives." He was raising his voice.

Julia enunciated every word slowly: "I can't do this right now."

Greg felt his shoulders slump. He wasn't going to get anything from her tonight.

"Thanks for listening," he mumbled, trying, unsuccessfully, to keep the sarcasm out of his voice.

Julia didn't move or say a word as Greg left.

He closed the front door, checked it was locked, and made his way to his car. He'd broken the rules. Julia wasn't interested in sharing his problems and probably never would be. The more he thought about it, the more he realized he didn't much care.

Driving off, he couldn't help but imagine how Mary Bransen would have reacted if he'd told her. He was sure she would have been compassionate, comforting—but what did he know? Women were a mystery. Anyway, telling Mary wasn't an option. She was a witness. Greg had to maintain a professional distance until the case was over.

His phone rang. Unknown number.

"Greg?"

"Yes?" His stomach dropped. There was only one person this could be.

"Colleen." She gave her name simply. "I'm taking Golden Gate Transit up to Santa Rosa tomorrow. Can you pick me up at eleven?"

"Yes," Greg said, desperately wishing for an excuse to avoid this confrontation—but knowing there was no escape. "How will I recognize you?" As soon as the words were out of his mouth, he slapped his forehead—what had he just said?

Amazingly, she laughed. It was a good laugh—bursting with humor.

Greg couldn't remember ever hearing her laugh after the accident. He felt his mood instantly lighten.

"I'll be the middle-aged woman in a red down vest."

"Okay. See you then." Greg hung up, mystified—she hadn't referred to her scarred face at all.

Greg didn't have any problem recognizing Colleen on Sunday —she looked like their mom, only a little more robust. She was standing beside the bus stop in the shade, next to a large, battered suitcase. Her hair was light brown, with a little gray mixed in. Short and blunt, it wasn't particularly stylish, but it suited her small features. There were some lines at the corners of her eyes and mouth. Her clothes were plain—chinos, long-sleeved oxford shirt, thin cotton sweater, and the down vest. When she spotted him walking toward her, she smiled.

"Greg?"

She didn't look angry or depressed, just a little cautious.

"Colleen." He didn't know if he should hug her or shake her hand, so he just reached out to take her bag. "Let me get this for you." He turned back toward his car. Colleen fell into step beside him. "How was your trip?"

"Overwhelming. It's the first time in almost forty years that I've been outside of Alaska. Most of that time was spent in a tiny village. I'm not used to all the hustle and bustle."

She was direct—not whiny or bitchy. Her voice sounded like their mother's, too.

"I bet it's a huge adjustment." He lifted the suitcase into the cargo area and hurried over to open her door.

"Thanks." She smiled again and he was transfixed. The scars had faded. One still ran from the outer corner of her left eye, down to the jaw. The left eye was lower than the right, her nose crooked. Parts of her right ear and the skin in front of it were a slightly different color and texture, because they were grafts. But the overall effect wasn't as horrific as he remembered. Just a little different. And offsetting the scars was her friendly smile and overall air of confidence. He closed the door carefully and walked around to get in on the driver's side.

"How long are you here for?"

"Permanently."

At his startled look, she laughed. "Don't worry, I'm not planning to move in with you. I've lined up a room with a retired teacher in Napa." Colleen looked over at him. "I just needed to see you first."

Where was the overweight and bitter teenager that wouldn't even speak to him forty years ago? "I'm glad you did, but it's been so long . . ." What the hell—he didn't want to pussyfoot around the elephant in the room anymore. "Why break the silence now?"

Colleen rested her fingers, light as a feather, on his forearm. "I'll explain when we get home."

The rest of the drive, Colleen asked questions about Santa Rosa, Healdsburg, and his job on the police force. Greg struggled to concentrate on his answers and suppress the anxiety he felt building inside. He had no idea what to expect, and he felt worse than ever over the part he'd played in her disfigurement. He carried her suitcase into the condo, showed her around, and left her in the guest bedroom while he went downstairs to start lunch.

When she came down, he couldn't contain his discomfort any longer. "Colleen, that dog should have attacked me instead of you. I've never forgiven myself for what happened."

"I know that, Greg," she sighed as she took a seat at the kitchen counter. "I've always known it. But, when I was a kid, I was hurting too much to help myself, let alone you. I had to get away from everyone who knew me and pitied me and start a whole new life where my scars might not matter. The mission saved me. We're supposed to be helping the Iñupiat people, but it works both ways. Most of us who go up there are running away from something. We bury ourselves in the work and our wounds start to heal. Not that we don't provide desperately needed services. And not that they don't have major problems of their own up there. It's just that their problems are so much different than ours. That's why it helps."

"Did your scars matter in the village?" Greg asked, putting half a sandwich and a small bowl of tomato soup on each plate. They certainly made her existence intolerable back home, he knew.

"Not once they got used to me." Colleen lifted her lunch over to her placemat. "There was some curiosity at first, mostly from the little kids. The adults are too polite to show their reactions. But in a small village, I didn't have to face a lot of strangers. And there are plenty of scars up there among the locals. Accidents are common and medical services are primitive. So, in some ways, I fit in pretty well." Colleen lifted her sandwich and took a bite.

Greg had been expecting an emotional wreck, but damn if his sister wasn't sounding like one of the most well-adjusted people he'd ever met. He sat on the barstool next to her.

"What sort of problems do they have up there?"

"Massive unemployment, climate change, incest, alcoholism." Colleen put her sandwich back on her plate. "Most of the teachers and aides quit after a year, if they last that long. The social problems are bad enough; add in endless winters, a complete absence of any fresh produce—most people from the lower forty-eight can't take it."

"I don't think I could."

"You really have to be motivated," she said with a grin. "I learned the language and the social customs. I was a good teacher. I made some friends. I was useful and busy and, ultimately, happy. I learned how to be more interested in what I could do to improve their world and less focused on all the things I couldn't change about mine."

Greg motioned toward her food, to encourage her to eat before the soup got cold. "Mom and Dad said you were doing well up there. But I found it hard to believe. You were having such a rough time when I left for college."

They both ate in silence for a minute. Greg felt himself relax—finally free to speak candidly about her accident and life after all these years of secrecy.

"I know. I wanted to make it all your fault. I monopolized all of Mom and Dad's time and energy. You got left out. I wanted you to be left out—figured you deserved it." Colleen smiled ruefully. "It took me decades to admit that it was an accident, to stop blaming anyone, and just get on with my life. By the time I was able to do that, Mom and Dad had died and you and I hadn't spoken for so long, I didn't know where to begin. I should have contacted you sooner, but I was afraid of your reaction. After everything I'd done to make you feel guilty, I figured you must hate me as much as you thought I hated you."

That was ironic, Greg thought. Her being afraid of him.

"When I decided to retire, I realized I had to come home, stop hiding, and, most important, get to know you again. You're my brother and the only family I have left."

"But . . . I ruined your life."

"You were eight years old. You threw tennis balls at an old dog. How many kids do you think do things like that?"

Greg shrugged, wishing tennis balls had never been invented.

"From what I've observed in Alaska, I'd say just about every single kid does things like that."

Greg noticed with interest that Colleen had picked up what he could only assume was a very faint Iñupiat accent.

"We were just horribly unlucky," Colleen continued. "We

all—me, you, Mom, and Dad—had to face a lifetime of consequences."

Because of me, he thought.

As if she had read his mind, Colleen said, "Our neighbor chose a Rottweiler for a pet, then left him alone and unexercised in a yard that didn't have a sturdy fence. I chipped away at those fence boards for months, trying to make a hole so I could pet Gus."

Greg wondered if that were true—it would explain why Gus broke through so easily.

"On top of that, my life wasn't ruined. It just turned out differently than any of us would have dreamed." Colleen's eyes followed Greg, who was at the refrigerator, getting more water. "You've had to carry a heavy burden of guilt all these years. That's why I wanted to come see you. To say that I'm sorry for letting you suffer so long and I never should have blamed you to begin with."

Greg leaned against the counter and took a deep breath. "I didn't know what to expect when you said you wanted to visit. I figured you still hated me. And I deserved it." He felt himself tearing up. "Up until last night, I couldn't even tell anyone what I did to you. I was so ashamed." Greg impatiently wiped his face.

Colleen stayed seated. "We've both punished ourselves way too long. I want to be part of a family again, if it's not too late."

"It isn't." He walked around the counter and gave her a big hug. "Welcome home."

Mary and Lily set out for the dog park. Mary saw Noreen James was in the street, near the curb, pulling mail from her box. Mary hesitated. It was the first chance she'd had to speak with Noreen since Frank's arrest. She wanted to say something encouraging, but it felt awkward. What do you say to someone whose husband's been arrested for murder?

She decided to keep it general. "I'm so sorry about Frank. Is there anything I can do?"

Noreen stopped looking through the envelopes. "Just give him the benefit of the doubt. Everyone looks at all of us so warily, as if the whole family's guilty of murder. It's really been hard on the kids."

Mary couldn't imagine what that must be like. She looked around, trying to think of something else to say that didn't sound like another standard cliché. Her eyes fell on Noreen's SUV, with her HBGMOM license plate. Something about the vehicle triggered a memory. Mary racked her brain. All she could come up with was her sister-in-law, Zoey, mentioning one of her customers who lived on Plaza Street. That was it!

"Didn't I see your car parked on Plaza Street the other day?"

Noreen froze. Then she shook her head hard. "It couldn't have been me. Why would I park over there?"

"Oh . . . sorry." Mary tried to remember what day it was—maybe that would jog Noreen's memory. "It might have been the morning Mabel was killed." Had she confused Noreen's car with a similar SUV?

Noreen's face scrunched up in a scowl. She turned and walked back toward her house without another word.

Good job, Mary thought. *Now you've upset her even more.* She called to Noreen's retreating back, "I know Frank didn't do it. Hang in there."

Noreen ignored her.

∼

Colleen wanted to answer some emails, so Greg went out for a run. Heading down the street, he thought about everything Colleen had said. After all this time, the idea that he wasn't solely responsible for her mauling was difficult to accept. So was the fact that his sister had ended up so normal—happy even. Their parents had tried to tell him, but he'd never believed them. He thought they were making it up to spare his feelings.

After lunch, Colleen had shared absorbing stories about high-stakes basketball games in dilapidated village gymnasiums. He told her she should consider writing a book about her experiences in Alaska. She admitted the thought had crossed her mind.

What bothered Greg now was a budding sense of resentment. All this time, Colleen had been healing and maturing, while Greg had stayed home, hiding his guilt and hating himself. He was practically estranged from his children and immersed in an emotionally choked relationship, because that's what he believed he deserved.

A soft knock interrupted Mary's lesson preparation for her art class the next day. She glanced at her watch. Who could be at her door after ten at night? Through the glass she could see it was Noreen, bundled in a thick black sweatshirt with the hood up, hugging her arms tight to her chest. Mary felt like a dimwit for upsetting her earlier. She opened the door and invited Noreen in, hoping she'd have a chance to redeem herself.

"I need a quick word with you."

"Would you like a cup of tea?" Mary closed and relocked the door behind Noreen.

"Thanks, that would be great."

"What's up?" Mary asked as she led her toward the kitchen.

"I want to know what you saw the day Mabel was killed."

Mary stopped filling the kettle with water. She paused and

looked around at Noreen. Could something she saw prove or disprove Frank's innocence?

"What do you mean?"

"You said you saw my car on Plaza Street. What else did you see?"

Mary put the kettle on the stove and turned on the burner.

"You said it wasn't your car." Uncertain where this was going, she pulled two mugs out of the cupboard, then walked over to the pantry to get tea bags.

Noreen moved closer, intruding into Mary's space.

"Did you see me?"

"See you where?" Mary took a step back against the pantry door, trying to distance herself. "What are you talking about?"

"Don't play dumb. You think I killed Mabel."

"What? No! I don't." Mary, scared, inched farther to the right.

"I can't have you spreading stories about me," Noreen said, closing the gap between them again. "Things are bad enough already."

"What stories?"

"What have you told the police about me?"

"Nothing!"

Colleen had gone to bed. During dinner she'd filled Greg in on more of her adventures in Alaska. She told him about the school's biggest success: a student who'd not only received a full scholarship to college, but had stuck it out to become a registered nurse. He was currently training to become a nurse practitioner, with plans to practice in the village.

Greg, on an emotional roller coaster, realized all his years of self-punishment had been a negative kind of vanity. He felt his earlier resentment melting, replaced with respect for all his sister had accomplished.

Suddenly, Greg felt an overpowering need to share all this with Mary. He had to call her. If she wasn't already asleep, she'd probably think he was out of his mind. He entered her number in his cell phone anyway. Hearing her voice, getting her feedback, felt more important than anything else right now.

∼

Mary's cell phone rang. She and Noreen both looked at it lying on the kitchen counter. Mary grabbed it, saw it was Greg, and felt a rush of relief. She managed to push the answer button before Noreen tore it out of her hand.

"Give me that," Noreen said before she ended the call and threw the phone across the room.

Mary glanced toward the phone. "I should call back or he might start to worry." She didn't think Noreen had seen it was Detective Davidson.

Noreen didn't seem to hear her. She pulled a piece of rope out of her pocket.

∼

That was odd, Greg thought. That didn't sound like Mary's voice before he was abruptly cut off. He tried calling back, but there was no answer.

Suddenly he remembered what the forensic tech had told him yesterday afternoon about the long dark hairs found on Sofia's clothes and Mabel's porch. Hairs that didn't belong to either of them. Then he knew whose voice he'd just heard on Mary's phone.

He grabbed his car keys and ran out to his vehicle, calling the police dispatcher on the way.

~

Noreen turned her head toward the phone ringing on the floor. Mary shoved her as hard as she could against the kitchen table. Mary ran toward the front door, hoping to get outside and scream for help. She heard the table slide and crash against the wall. Then she heard footsteps coming down the hall behind her.

Mary unlocked the dead bolt and fumbled with the door latch, just before she was tackled from behind. She twisted her neck as she fell. The side of her head hit the metal door stop. A sharp pain was followed by swirls of blackness. Lily barked, but it sounded miles away. Noreen's face, misty and distant, wobbled in and out of her peripheral vision. Mary felt something wrap around her neck. She could hear Noreen grunting. There was a sensation of pressure. Then she couldn't breathe.

"Get off!"

Noreen's yell brought Mary back. She felt the pressure on her trachea ease. She sucked in some air before everything started to go black again.

Lily's growl brought Mary back once more. She tried to sit up, but was overwhelmed with dizziness. She forced her eyes open. Noreen stood above her, attempting to shake Lily off her leg. Mary grabbed at Noreen's loose sweatpants, trying to stop her from hurting the dog.

"Let go of me!" Noreen screamed, pulling her pants free of Mary's grasp. "Get this fucking dog off of me!" Noreen gave a violent kick, catapulting Lily against the back of a living room chair.

Mary heard a sharp yelp, followed by a whimper. She tried to push Noreen out of the way. She had to get to Lily. Noreen stooped down, wrapping the rope around Mary's neck again. Mary managed to scoot backwards a few feet. Her head fell back against the wall.

As Mary started to black out once more, she felt something warm and wet trickling down her neck. She was terrified Lily had been killed and realized, with a pang, that she was going to die as well. Instead of the relief she expected, freedom from her overwhelming grief over Enzo's death, she was immensely sorry.

Lily needed her; her little art students needed her. Greg needed her. Her last worry, before she blacked out again, was to wonder why she thought that.

19

G reg sped up Highway 101, anxiously monitoring the dispatch radio. The patrol officer who'd responded to his emergency call about Mary finally reported in. Dr. Bransen was injured, but alive. Greg called on his Bluetooth. The EMTs were taking her to the hospital. The officer told Greg he'd burst through the unlocked front door to find Noreen James bending over Mary.

"Bransen was on the floor, bleeding from a head wound. James had a rope wrapped around her neck. We pulled James away from her. Bransen started gasping for air immediately."

Greg let loose a huge sigh of relief, immediately followed by a wave of anxiety. If he hadn't called Mary against his better judgment and realized something was wrong, Noreen would have killed her. Mary's life had hung in the balance of that one decision. He thanked the officer profusely for his timely response to the call. After hearing that Noreen was being held at the station, Greg drove directly to the hospital.

Ángela met him at the door to Emergency. The ER doctor came out of Mary's cubicle to tell them that she was conscious, but had a head injury and needed a CAT scan immediately. Only Greg's desperate insistence convinced him to give them one minute to question her.

Greg pulled the curtain aside and took a deep breath. Mary's skin was chalk white, making the bruising on her throat stand out in stark contrast. Blood matted the hair above her right ear, ran in smeared tracks down her neck, and had seeped into her white blouse. But her eyes lit up and she managed a small smile when she saw him standing there.

"Are you okay?" Greg asked, moving closer to the bed, resisting the impulse to gather her in his arms.

Mary nodded her head slightly and winced.

Steeling himself against a desire to cry, Greg motioned to Ángela. "This is Officer Garcia. She'll be taking notes." Greg watched Mary turn her head toward Ángela with another wince. "I know it's difficult for you to speak and I won't keep you long, but I need to ask a few questions."

Mary's hand shot out from under the blanket. Her grip was firm as she pulled his arm toward her.

Greg bent down, wondering what she wanted to tell him. Beneath the coppery smell of blood he thought he could detect a faint whiff of vanilla.

"Lily . . ." Mary's grip loosened and her arm fell against her side.

"She's going to be fine. One of my officers drove her to the emergency vet right away." He didn't really know if Lily was going to make it or not. But he didn't want to tell Mary that now. She was traumatized enough as it was.

A tear ran down Mary's cheek. Still leaning over her, not wanting to move away, Greg gently wiped it with his finger. "Who did this to you?" Greg wanted to make sure the responding officer had interpreted the scene correctly.

"Noreen James."

Greg barely heard her. A piercing beep started in the adjoining cubicle. Footsteps and equipment rushed by. Greg had to concentrate hard to make out what Mary was saying.

"Car . . . I saw it . . ."

"What car?"

"Noreen's . . . license plate . . . Plaza Street . . ."

Greg was confused, but Mary's lids fluttered closed. The orderly pulled back the curtain and released the brakes on her gurney, preparing for the trip to imaging.

∼

Noreen looked anxiously at Greg and Blake as they walked into the interrogation room at the station Monday morning. Noreen's attorney wore a wrinkled pantsuit that looked a size too small. She shoved her cell phone into her bag and introduced herself with a frown.

Blake started the video recorder. "Monday, October twenty-seventh. 1100 hour. Present are Healdsburg Police Detective Davidson and Sergeant Maddox, Noreen James and her attorney, Greta Hofmann."

Noreen began speaking in her raspy voice before Greg could ask anything. "I killed them. Frank's innocent."

Greg took a deep breath. The sound of her voice brought back all the fury, relief, and concern of the night before, making it difficult to remain objective.

"Stop right there." Hofmann interrupted Noreen and turned to Greg. "We'd like you to contact the district attorney. My client would like to make a confession. She will agree to plead guilty if the DA will drop the death penalty in both the Molina and Garrity cases and drop the assault charges for the attack on Dr. Bransen."

Greg considered the request. It wasn't his call—it was the DA's decision. Two police officers had witnessed Noreen trying to strangle Mary firsthand. There would be a strong case for the murders of Sofia and Mabel if Noreen's DNA matched that of the hairs found on Sofia's clothes and Mabel's porch. But the odds of Noreen ever being executed by the state were slim, no matter what the sentence. "No possibility of parole?"

Hofmann nodded. She obviously thought Noreen was going to spend the rest of her life in prison, no matter how she pleaded. Hofmann was trying to get the best possible deal for her client.

Greg wanted the confession. He looked at Noreen. "Is this what you want, Ms. James?"

"Yes," she replied, firmly.

Greg called for a recess and left the room to contact Janet Flores. The DA listened to the proposal and told him to stop the interrogation until she arrived.

Greg knew a guilty plea would wrap up the case without a trial, saving the taxpayers a load of money. Execution in death penalty cases took decades, if it ever happened at all. This was a good bargain for everyone.

When Flores rushed into the station, Greg escorted her to the interrogation room where she discussed the deal with Hofmann and Noreen. Greg and Blake waited outside.

When Flores invited them back inside, Noreen kept her focus solely on Greg.

"We are prepared to accept the deal," Flores said.

Greg looked back at Noreen, who nodded.

"You're sure?" he asked.

"Yes."

Blake fetched the papers Janet Flores had requested her staff fax over and brought them back to the room. Once everyone had signed, Hofmann indicated that Noreen would like to proceed with her confession. Blake restarted the recording.

"Let's take this one step at a time," Greg began. "Who did you kill?"

"Sofia Molina and Mabel Garrity."

"Why did you kill Ms. Molina?"

"She was ruining everything." Noreen leaned forward

with an earnest, imploring expression on her face, as if willing him to understand.

Greg asked what she meant, hoping to appear empathetic.

"At first I thought it might be drugs," she said, shaking her head. "Frank hadn't been himself and wouldn't tell me what was going on. So I followed him from work to the hotel in Windsor. I saw her walk up to his truck and pass something through the window."

"Just for the record, who passed something through whose truck window?"

"Sofia Molina passed something to my husband, Frank James," Noreen replied, her voice rising and her eyes narrowing. "Then she went into the hotel. He followed her about ten minutes later. They stayed in there for a couple of hours. I decided to follow her to ask her what was going on."

Greg's excitement built as Noreen's version of events clearly corroborated those described by Frank. He hated to interrupt the flow of her confession, but there were key points here that had to be clarified. "When did this happen?"

"Friday—the tenth—the night I killed her."

Noreen's matter-of-fact tone was chilling. Greg thought he saw Hofmann's eyes widen for the briefest moment.

"Where did you follow her?" he asked.

"The market—can you believe it? The bitch screwed my husband and then she went grocery shopping, like it was no big deal. There weren't that many cars in the lot, but she parked way out back, which was convenient. After she went into the store, I pulled in next to her car and rolled down my window. When Sofia came out with her groceries I asked what was going on between her and Frank. She jumped about five feet when I spoke." Noreen smiled. "I guess she didn't notice me sitting there."

Greg struggled to keep a straight face. Remembering Mary's battered head and neck, he felt two consecutive life terms would be too lenient for this psychopath.

"What happened then?"

"Sofia said Frank was fucking her, just like that." Noreen pressed her hands against the tabletop and leaned forward. "I got out of my car and asked her if he was doing drugs. Sofia said not that she knew of. I didn't believe her, so I asked what she was handing him through the window of his truck. She said it was a room key. I was so angry, I . . ." Noreen paused, glancing slyly at her attorney. "She opened the back door of her car and bent over to put her groceries inside . . ."

"Let's take a break," Hofmann interrupted.

Reluctantly, Greg asked Blake to turn off the recording. The two of them stepped into the hallway with the DA.

"Damn," Blake said, slapping his notebook against his thigh. "She's a whack job. I never considered Noreen—even when we found the evidence at their house. I was so sure it was Frank . . ."

"Hey," Greg said. "None of us suspected Noreen. We all thought she was just another victim in this whole sorry mess." *And our shortsightedness almost got Mary killed,* Greg thought with a shudder. "But we've got her. And she's sparing us the trouble of a trial."

"Any chance of an insanity plea on her part?" Blake asked Flores.

"Too late now. And I don't think she'd get it anyway. She knew what she was doing."

They returned to the interrogation room. Hofmann looked satisfied. She had her plea bargain. And from Noreen's demeanor, Greg thought, it was a lot better deal than she would have received from a jury.

Blake restarted the recording. Noreen resumed, speaking directly to Greg. "I stepped up behind Sofia and slipped the rope around her neck. I just meant to scare her, but I guess I held on too long, because she went completely limp."

"Just to be clear," Greg said. "You were holding the rope when you got out of your car?"

"Well . . . yes . . . in my pocket."

Greg watched a little ripple of uncertainty pass across Noreen's face. Perhaps the full magnitude of what she had done was starting to sink in. But a look of defiant satisfaction seemed to take its place almost immediately.

"Where did you get the rope?" he asked.

"Frank kept a coil in his truck. I cut off a piece a couple of nights before I followed him."

"So you were planning to kill Ms. Molina two days before the tenth?"

"I wasn't planning to kill anyone."

"Then why did you take the rope with you?"

"It was the only weapon I could think of. I didn't know what I was going to find when I followed Frank. I had to eliminate any threats I might encounter."

"Threats?" Greg asked, confused.

"Threats to my kids—to their way of life. Something was wrong and I wanted to stop it before it destroyed our whole family," Noreen answered.

"Were you wearing gloves when you strangled Sofia?"

"Yes."

"Why?"

"I thought the rope might hurt my hands if I didn't wear some."

Greg glanced at Blake, wondering if Noreen had any idea how clearly these preparations showed premeditation. Hofmann obviously knew, but it didn't matter now. She remained silent, scribbling notes furiously. She had her deal. Noreen's confession couldn't change that.

"Were those the same gloves Sergeant Maddox collected in evidence from your home on Thursday, October twenty-third?"

"Yes."

Greg glanced down at Noreen's hands. They were large.

He and Blake assumed the gloves belonged to Frank, but they would have fit her as well.

"What did you do after Sofia died?"

"That was hard. She was heavy. I managed to shove her into the backseat of my car. Then I had to drive around, wondering what to do with her. I saw the entrance to that new office building on Healdsburg Avenue and thought that would be a good place to get rid of her."

Greg pictured the property, tucked well back from the street. Noreen spoke proudly, describing her problem-solving in the heat of the moment. Greg noticed Blake drag his eyes away from Noreen and back to his notepad, his mouth set in a grim line.

"I didn't have a lot of time to look for a better spot," Noreen said. "I had to get back by ten or Frank wouldn't believe I'd been at a PTA meeting. A few cars pulled out of the parking lot while I was considering it, so I drove past and waited in another driveway until everyone was gone. I turned off my headlights, pulled into the lot, and dragged her out of the car into the trees. It was the best I could do with such short notice."

"Why not just leave her at the market?"

"I panicked."

"Did anyone at the market see you with Sofia?"

"That witch, Mabel." Noreen's face constricted in a menacing frown, her eyes focused intently on Greg. "Saturday morning Frank seemed quiet, but also lighter, as if a burden had been lifted. I wasn't sure why he felt that way—there was no way he could know Sofia was already dead. But I knew she wouldn't be able to bother him anymore. Things could get back to normal. The kids would be okay. Then that bitch came over in the afternoon."

"You mean Mabel Garrity?"

"Who else?" Noreen shrugged.

"Let's take another break," Hofmann interrupted.

Noreen sat back in her seat with an angry huff, glaring at her attorney.

Greg felt the same way—they needed to get this done. But he, Blake, and Flores went out into the hall. Greg found Ángela and asked her to get a warrant for Noreen's SUV and all of her clothing.

"Are we doing okay in there?" Greg asked Flores, handing her a cup of coffee.

"You seem to be on a roll and she trusts you. Keep going," she answered with a smile.

Through the window, Greg could see Hofmann leaning toward Noreen, speaking and gesturing. Noreen shook her head vigorously, then started speaking herself. Soon she was crying. Hofmann watched her, looking impassive. Greg thought she might be telling Noreen to keep her answers short and to the point. Maybe Hofmann was in a hurry to get somewhere else. Noreen, on the other hand, obviously wanted to justify her actions. While Noreen was escorted to the bathroom, Hofmann came out into the hall.

Greg gave her a smile. Hofmann said she had to go outside to make some calls. They couldn't speak about the case outside of the interrogation room, but Hofmann looked pretty satisfied—probably relieved she wouldn't have to defend Noreen in a trial. Greg didn't sense a lot of empathy or concern for her client.

When they resumed the interrogation, Greg asked Noreen to tell them what happened when Ms. Garrity came over the afternoon of the eleventh.

"She said she was at the market the night before and just happened to look across the lot. She saw me standing next to my SUV, talking to a young woman. She went into the store at that point, but when the announcement about the unidentified body was made on the radio Saturday afternoon, she put two and two together." Noreen leaned closer toward Greg. "She tried to blackmail me."

Greg nodded—that sounded like Mabel. Her malicious personality had cost her her life.

"She said she'd give me until nine Sunday morning to bring a thousand dollars cash to her house, otherwise, she was going to the police. And she wanted the same amount every month for the rest of her life. There was no way I could give her that much money without Frank finding out." Noreen shook her head in apparent exasperation. "I considered calling her bluff. She didn't actually see me kill Sofia. But, in the end, I decided my only option was to shut her up before she told anyone."

"Mabel wasn't afraid of you?"

"She seemed to think she had the upper hand."

Mabel figured that wrong, Greg thought. "What did you do?"

"Sunday morning I dropped the kids off in Alexander Valley, like I told you guys. But then I drove back to our neighborhood. I parked one street over, on Plaza, and walked over to Mabel's house. I rang the doorbell and hid around the corner of the porch. When she came out to see who was there, I sneaked up behind her and slipped the rope over her head."

That's what Mary meant about seeing Noreen's car on Plaza Street, Greg thought. "What time was this?"

"It had just turned seven when I parked my car. I was driving back to the gym by seven fifteen."

"Were you wearing the same gloves you had on when you killed Sofia?"

"Yes. I still had them in my car."

"Why did you keep them?"

"I didn't have time to get rid of them—everything was happening so fast."

"Did Mabel struggle?"

"She tried to grab the rope and pull it away, but I already had it nice and tight."

The smirk on her face told Greg that Noreen had no more regrets about dispatching Mabel than she did about Sofia.

"She tried to throw me off, but I held on. She took a couple of steps forward, toward the front of the porch, then she slipped down as if she was sitting. Her feet dropped to the lower step. I just leaned her against the post and got out of there as quickly as possible."

"You didn't try to hide her body?"

"No, she was too heavy and I was too exposed. I had to get out of there before anyone saw me."

"Why didn't you take the rope with you?"

"It stuck to her neck a little and I was in a hurry."

"To get to your gym?" Greg asked, wondering how Noreen could murder someone in cold blood and then go work out.

"Like I do every morning." Noreen seemed particularly smug, in the way people who exercise on a regular basis can be.

Greg concentrated on keeping his voice even and emotionless.

"What did you do with the gloves?"

"After I got home from the club, I hid them in that storage cabinet in our garage." Noreen's mouth twisted. "I guess I should've looked for a dumpster where they wouldn't be found."

"No one saw you on Ms. Garrity's porch?"

"I don't think so."

Greg studied her for a few moments.

"Why did you let us arrest Frank for the murders?"

"I never expected that to happen. It was horrible for the kids. But I knew he'd be cleared —he was innocent."

You didn't mind letting him suffer in jail for a couple of days, though, Greg thought. *Poor stupid bastard.* It was time to bring the questioning around to the previous night. Greg tried to suppress the anger building again inside him.

"Why did you assault Mary?"

Noreen sat back, her expression wary, as if she sensed his conflict. "She told me she saw my car on Plaza Street the morning I killed Mabel. If she was stupid enough to tell me, I was sure she'd tell you. I didn't know what else to do."

Greg felt a surge of anxiety. What if Mary had died? A few more minutes and she would have. He couldn't bear to think about it. As it was, he still didn't know how severely she was injured. His hands balled into fists. If Mary had any brain damage he'd be tempted to kill Noreen himself. For the first time, he could almost empathize with Noreen's actions —almost.

Noreen's eyelids were drooping. Her face looked more haggard than it had when the interview began, but Greg wasn't about to cut her confession short. Not while she was talking. He was grateful Hofmann was hobbled by the deal they'd struck. Greg encouraged Noreen to continue.

"As soon as Frank went to bed, I cut a piece off my clothesline and grabbed my gardening gloves. I slipped out of the house and walked over to Mary's. She didn't answer her door right away. Part of me almost hoped she wouldn't. But when she did, I had no choice but to go through with it. The damn dog messed up everything. Then you guys came." Noreen sighed and her entire body seemed to relax. "I'm just glad it's over."

Greg could understand the tremendous strain Noreen must have been under. Even if she could justify the murders in her own mind, it was amazing she'd covered up as well and as long as she had. And they'd never suspected her for a moment.

Before they took Noreen back to her cell, she repeated she'd done it all to protect her children. "Sofia was messing with Frank. He wasn't himself. The kids need their father. My dad deserted us. I wasn't going to let anything like that happen to my kids."

20

Greg and Blake met with Frank and his attorney in the interview room when Noreen's interrogation was finished.

"What's happening? No one will tell me anything."

Frank's lawyer, Bracha Pacanowski, motioned for him to sit down.

Everyone took their seats. Greg rubbed his eyes and checked the time—1400. He'd only had a few hours sleep the night before and he still had a shit load to do today. He found it interesting that Frank brought his attorney with him this morning. How much had he known or suspected about Noreen's crimes?

Blake started the recording, giving the names of those present, the time and date.

"What do you need to know?" Greg asked, watching Frank closely.

Frank's fingertips gripped the edge of the table. "There were sirens, police, even an ambulance in the street in the middle of the night. I couldn't find Noreen anywhere. The kids were scared shitless. Then I was told Noreen had been arrested. What the fuck's going on?"

Pacanowski put a well-manicured hand on Frank's arm, urging him to calm down, and looked at Greg. "What can you tell us about Noreen's arrest?"

"Mary Bransen was assaulted in her home last night," Greg announced, watching Frank closely.

Frank slumped back in his seat, mouth open. "Assaulted?"

"Your wife was in Mary's house, trying to strangle her."

Pacanowski glanced up sharply at that piece of information. "What are you saying?"

Frank turned to look at Pacanowski, his eyes wide. "Noreen? What was she doing there?"

"You don't know?" Greg asked. *Obviously not.* Turning to his attorney for an explanation was almost a sure giveaway that Frank had been clueless all along.

"I don't understand. Noreen . . ." Frank stiffened and turned back toward Greg, his eyes rapidly narrowing with a dawning realization.

"Don't say another word," Pacanowski ordered.

Greg watched Frank slump back in his seat and cover his face with his hands. Greg couldn't help feeling sorry for Frank. It was starting to dawn on the poor guy that the mother of his kids was a murderer and his affair with Sofia had set the whole ugly tragedy into motion.

Greg called the neurologist who was treating Mary. She had a closed head injury from the blunt trauma and some damage to the cricoid cartilage and soft tissue in her throat. She was heavily sedated and couldn't talk. "We're keeping her at least one more night for observation, but I think she's going to make a full recovery," the doctor said.

Greg put the phone down on his desk and rested his face in his hands for a moment, letting his whole body relax in a grateful sigh.

Then he took another deep breath and placed a call to the Department of Justice investigator who'd been assigned to their case. She instructed him to continue wrapping up the investigation against Noreen. The investigator would be coming to Healdsburg to examine the evidence against Liam later in the week.

Greg handed out assignments. Warrants had been issued for Noreen's vehicle and her clothing. They would continue to use the media to seek witnesses who may have spotted Noreen's car at the Windsor Inn or the Healdsburg Market on October tenth. They had reexamined the CCTV footage from the market for the night of the tenth and confirmed that Mabel had entered and left the store with groceries not long after Sofia had shopped. They would question the health club to see if there was any way to verify the exact time Noreen arrived on the twelfth. But, with a full confession and plea bargain in the bag, these were minor technicalities. Greg felt a renewed surge of energy. The case was solved, it looked like Mary would be okay, and things had worked out amazingly well with his sister.

"What will happen to Noreen, do you think?" Sam asked.

"Hard to say," Greg said. "But that aspect of the case is out of our hands."

"What a waste," Blake said. "If she had just confronted Frank about the affair he would have told her it was over, said he was sorry, and none of this would have happened. 'Course, depending on his answer, maybe she would have killed Frank."

"She wouldn't have done that," Ángela said. "She needed Frank for her perfect family."

"What did you think about her confession?" Greg asked, curious to hear Ángela's take on Noreen's mental state.

"She sounds like a sociopath. She killed Sofia out of anger."

Ángela looked sad, Greg thought. Probably thinking about

her own abusive ex-husband. There were a lot of angry people out there.

"If Mary had just thought to mention Noreen's car when we first interviewed her, we might have solved this a lot sooner," Sam said.

"But it was such a tiny detail," Ángela said. "How could she know it was significant? If I had continued to watch the Healdsburg Market tape, I would have seen Mabel enter the store soon after Sofia left; it might have helped us connect the two murders."

How could anyone know what was important, Greg wondered. He hadn't known that throwing tennis balls at an old dog would completely change the course of his sister's life or that interrogating Liam about withholding critical information in their case would precipitate a devastating stroke. Frank couldn't have anticipated his affair with Sofia would drive his wife over the edge. Mary didn't know that sharing stories about her late husband would make Greg question his relationship with Julia.

Life was a crapshoot. And he was tired of facing all that randomness alone.

~

Greg sat on the side of his bed and yawned. He'd put it off for as long as he could, but he needed to call Julia before he went to sleep.

"I hope I didn't wake you again." Was that just two nights ago? It felt like weeks.

"No, I was reading. Is everything okay? I heard something on the radio about another assault in Healdsburg."

"It's over. We have the murderer in custody and a full confession." Greg had lost his earlier feeling of elation. He'd been dreading this conversation all day. Now that he had

Julia on the phone, he wasn't sure how to continue. "My sister's here."

"That's right—you were worried about her visit. How's it going?"

"She's not mad at me. She's happy. It's nice . . ."

"See? You were all worked up about nothing."

Greg let that slide. He didn't know how to do this. He probably should wait until he could see Julia in person.

There was a long, uncomfortable pause before Julia spoke again. "You're calling to break up with me, aren't you?"

How did she know? "I'm sorry, Julia."

"Is it because I won't live with you?"

"It's complicated."

"Not really."

"Look, Julia. I'm not sure why . . ." Although, to be honest, he had a pretty good idea. And she was lying in a hospital bed up in Healdsburg at the moment. "But I want more . . ."

"And I don't."

Greg plugged his phone into the charger after they ended the call. He felt sad. But he knew exactly what he wanted now.

He lay awake a long time, in spite of his fatigue. The phone rang at two-thirty in the morning, just a half hour after he'd finally drifted off. It was Karen Friedman's caller ID.

"Sorry to wake you, Greg. Liam passed away an hour ago."

Greg stepped back to allow a phlebotomist to steer a cart of test tubes out of Mary's room, then he knocked lightly on the door and walked in. The blinds were closed and it took Greg's eyes a minute to adjust to the dim light. A large dressing covered the right side of Mary's head. She looked so small in the hospital bed. Her eyes fluttered open. Greg reached down to take her hand. "I checked on Lily before I drove over. She has some cracked ribs, but she's doing great."

"I know," Mary whispered. "The nurse called the vet for me. Thanks for taking her in."

"All part of the service, ma'am." Greg tried to keep it light —didn't want to show Mary how worried he'd been. He'd just met her, had no idea where their relationship was going, but she'd come to embody his hopes for the future.

"Did Noreen kill them?" she asked.

"She confessed to both murders."

Mary turned her head toward the shuttered window for a moment, then slowly back to Greg. "I thought she was going to kill me. It made me realize how much I have to live for."

"I'm delighted to hear that." Greg thought he knew what she meant. He felt awful about Liam's death and disheartened about his relationship with his kids. But he had his sister back in his life, a new friend in Mary, and renewed faith in the possibilities ahead.

He didn't want to keep her talking any more than necessary. Mary's voice was still a hoarse whisper—it had to hurt. "I'm going to let you get some rest. But once you and Lily are fully recovered, would you like to go for another walk?"

Mary's smile lit up her eyes, sending warmth through Greg's body.

"We'd love to."

ACKNOWLEDGMENTS

It takes a village to write and publish a book. I could not have done it without the help and support of many people. I would like to thank:

Officer John Haviland of the Healdsburg Police Department and author T.B. Smith of Cop World Press, who is also a retired San Diego Police Department lieutenant. Both these experts enthusiastically answered all of my questions. To the extent that I have portrayed police procedures in general, and the Healdsburg Police Department accurately, all credit goes to them. Where I have made mistakes or purposely altered methodology, I take full responsibility.

Estéban Ismael Alvarado and the members of my San Diego Community College Writing Workshop who listened to my entire novel over the course of several years, providing thorough suggestions and encouragement.

The members of my Partners In Crime, San Diego Chapter of Sisters in Crime, read & critique workshop: Kristen Bentz, Cornelia Feye, Suzanne Haworth, Kim Keeline, Nicole Larson, Joan Mohr and Suzanne Shephard who offered invaluable advice.

My beta readers: Tamara Hampton, Sandra Kozero, John

Kozero, Donald Brooks and Gail Bettles who kindly read the full manuscript at various incarnations and provided feedback and support.

My editor, Lisa Wolff, who made meticulous corrections and recommendations.

Graphic designer Kim Keeline for her skillful cover design, map drawings, and author's portrait.

Publisher, Cornelia Feye of Konstellation Press, who encouraged me to publish this book in the first place, then expertly guided me through the entire process.

My life partner, Rick Fox, who read the manuscript from cover to cover and offered numerous ideas and praise.

And last, my beloved late husband, Larry Hansen, who never had a chance to read the book, but who never stopped believing in me.

Words cannot express my gratitude to you all. Thank you from the bottom of my heart.

ABOUT THE AUTHOR

Valerie Hansen is a retired Sonoma County optometrist who lived in Healdsburg for over thirty years. She now resides in San Diego. *Murder in the Wine Country* is her first novel. She is currently working on a futuristic science fantasy novel and a second book in the *Healdsburg Homicide* series. You may contact her at HealdsburgHomicideSeries@gmail.com.

Made in the USA
Middletown, DE
25 October 2020

22097077R00187